THE WIZARD'S STONE

Acknowledgments

Cover Design & Interior Formatting
www.helpingauthorseveryday.com

Beta Readers:
The Wonderful Mrs. Herman Hunter
and Daniel Shultz

Editing / Proofreading:
Krista Wagner

Ending Suggestions:
Gary Shipman
www.garyshipmanart.com

I've gone back and forth about this
DEDICATION, *vacillating. In the end, I decided
to dedicate this book to Almighty God, the source of
all Creation and He who has bestowed upon me the
many talents I have.*

*You sheltered me when the world was
collapsing around me.*

*You gave me hope when all my endeavors
seemed so pointless and vain.*

*You gave me a wife who encouraged me to
press on.*

*You refined me in the furnace of Life,
drawing away the dross.*

*I stand in awe, breathless to the beauty of
the world You have made.*

*Some live to their fullest, burning bright as the sun
but do so only once. Yet, You have given me a great
gift. The chance to burn brightly twice in one
lifetime.*

*So, it is only fitting that I give The Lord His due.
Thank You for so many things gifted to one so
unworthy to possess them.*

FOREWARD

There is a story to this story. It's neither exceptionally long nor complicated, but it does have its share of twists and turns. More or less, it is an illustration of my journey down the road I'm on. I probably should have done a foreword with *The Revenant and the Tomb*. Hindsight is always 20/20.

To my best recollection, I started writing about Odo sometime in the year 2020, or maybe it was 2019. Even now, I'm not sure of the exact date. The bones of the story were borne out of a frustration where the only thing I seemed to be able to write were novels attached to a series. Looking around at the fantasy genre landscape, it seemed like every author had their "series." I knew full-well that if I wanted to be published in the traditional space, my best bet was a standalone novel. This is that novel.

It was on a drive home from work when I first conceived of Odo's adventure (if my recollection is still true). Such things usually start with a concept, with my mind actively working to fill in the details. However, this time, it would be a story which would only span the length of a single novel. I picked a character from a series I was currently working on and decided on a backstory. With the bones of the book established, I set about the task of adding flesh, sinew, and skin.

Now, it was during this time I decided to query agents and publishers for my only completed novel. It was part of a book series I had been working on since the year 2000, or thereabouts, and one with which I formed a strong emotional attachment. It is a tale about a character named Frankie, a story I reworked from the original manuscript. The story was revised with my newly discovered voice and prose and sent out to be professionally edited. When that was done, I passed the work onto some beta readers (people who read and offer feedback on the work) to get their reaction. The response I got was strong, much to my surprise. They loved it.

While my beta readers loved the story, I knew deep down inside that the manuscript had no chance of being published. Still, I went about attempting the impossible, in the event I might have been wrong.

I wasn't.

So, it was during that long, fruitless quest of casting my fortune into the void when I set about writing the book you have now. I started it and then I stopped.

During the long, frustrating period of submissions to agents and publishers, it became evidently clear that the only way I was going to be published was if I did so at my own expense. I won't go into the details of how I came to this conclusion. I've made references to my reasons on my blog and in videos. Yet, despite my fears (which were many and well-founded), I eventually embraced the idea of self-publishing. So, to attract attention to my writing, I was going to give away one of my works as a marketing tool.

For several moments, I considered using this book towards that end. That lasted a whole five seconds.

I saw too much potential in Odo's journey to just give it away for free. I put this book aside, half completed, to start a novella I would offer in exchange for a subscription to my e-mail list. Thus, *The Revenant and the Tomb* was born.

The Revenant and the Tomb was, in my estimation, a mild success. As a promotion, it was a dismal failure. Virtually no one wanted to exchange an e-mail address for a novella from an unknown author. The irony of it all was that, in the end, giving the book away was far less effective than actually selling it to a potential audience.

As I approached the release date of *The Revenant and the Tomb*, I tried to spark flame once more to this story, the embers of it extinguished for nearly a year. Rekindling the passion and vision I had when I started was another lesson in frustration. The words and the ideas, that were so clear months before, flowed at a glacial pace. Yet, as I pushed myself, the obstructions cleared, though at a frustratingly slow rate.

What I have left out of the history of the book you now possess is how much quarantines, lockdowns, and actual sickness inhibited my progress. During the production of *The Revenant and the Tomb*, I contracted the dreaded COVID-19 virus. I spent seven days in a hospital and another month on supplemental oxygen. Along with other complications, I needed to have a tooth removed (which may have been partly to blame for my hospitalization). All of this happened during a period where I faced lingering doubts about my writing ability due to the constant rejections from agents and publishers. I feared self-publishing and the potential that my writing would wither away in a sea of obscurity. It was a fear that wheeled and glided above me like a carrion bird waiting for a beast to die. At least that's how it felt. At one point, I was ready to give it all up, throw in the towel, and quit. It was my wife who convinced me to keep pushing forward. So, if you liked *The Revenant and the Tomb*, as well as the book you now possess, you have her to thank for it.

But here we are now. The world is still not a certain place by any stretch of the imagination. The story of Odo, however, is now complete. Frankie will one day have his place in the sun. The readers I've garnered with *The Revenant and the Tomb* have led me to write more stories for Halsedric. Other ideas now drift through my consciousness, like spirits waiting for a life anew.

So many stories to write, and so little time to write them.

Concerning Halsedric and *The Revenant and the Tomb*, I always considered Halsedric to be a prototypical character. He was, to me, "one and done," meaning his journey might live on through characters of different names. Instead, by reader demand no less, I'm now scrambling to provide more for the man with the flaming sword. I have two more books planned, but writing, editing, and publishing books is a long and tedious business. Until then, you will have to be content with Odo.

Odo's story starts roughly four hundred years after the events of *The Revenant and the Tomb*. Like my other books in this literary world, it has ties into other stories I either intend to publish, have published, or am waiting to publish. Unlike *The Revenant and the Tomb*, it is not one long tense ride to the end. Odo's journey has an ebb and flow to it that is hard for me to describe. I liken it to a play in three Acts, with the excitement of Acts One and Three separated by what I call, "a deep draw of air before plunging beneath the waters."

Odo himself is not what one might call an overtly heroic character, though he has qualities which fall into that category. I've developed a penchant for writing about plain average folk as they are generally more interesting than the usual sword-slinging warriors, lost princes, or the politics of court. In the end, I find that when creating a character, attributes have only superficial significance. What matters most is what lies inside his heart, something of a reoccurring theme in my works.

While there are so many demands on my time, I do *love* writing these stories. I am working beneath the vision of writing a history of my world and its various conflicts through individual tales. Or, as I am fond of saying, I am building a world of fantasy one book at a time. It's an ambitious goal with returns that won't begin to show until I have three or four books in distribution. Doing this on my own, even with the aid of my family and friends, feels like I am moving at a snail's pace. I realize, however, that were I to go through traditional channels, things would move much slower.

The best I can do is write stories I would want to read, with the hope that others want to read them as well. I'd rather focus on providing a quality product whose sum total is much greater than any individual book. Or, to use a better analogy, making each book a piece of a puzzle that can be enjoyed both individually as well as collectively. At least, that's the plan.

And now you know probably more than you ever wanted to about my past, present, and future writings. To that end, I will cease my blathering on the subject and let you get on with the story.

I truly hope you enjoy *The Wizard's Stone*.

Herman P. Hunter

CHAPTER 1

Odo knew something odd was at hand the moment he saw the wizard set flame to the note. The wizard watched the flame grow on the folded parchment, kept aloft by his spindly finger and thumb. As edges blackened and curled, the flame spread, growing upward, greedily pushing into the interior. Gently, purposefully, the wizard moved the burning note to a nearby pewter bowl resting on a table next to his chair. As the parchment burned, the wizard poked his finger at the one corner still untouched by flame, which peeked out from the lip. The gesture a sure way to keep the fire contained.

"Come in, dear boy," the wizard softly commanded. "You and I must speak."

The chair in which Remfrey sat was his favorite, or at least that's the way it seemed to Odo. Narrow and curiously high-backed, the seat was carved from a single solid block of stained oak. Two spiral horns flanked the upright back, each coming to a point at the top. Between them, a convex curve spanned the horns, connecting them like the bald crown of some demonic thing. It was a strange throne for a strange man, as most wizards were. The dimensions of the chair were very much a reflection of Remfrey. Both were tall and thin, refined and mysterious, each imposing in their own way, lurking in the dark confines of his study.

Odo stood at the threshold for a time, mesmerized by the growing tongues of flame that consumed the note. His face did little to hide the wonder that filled his mind, puzzled as to the message that might be contained on the tan parchment. The many years Odo lived with Remfrey he had never witnessed the wizard discard of any correspondence in such a manner. He imagined some dark secret scribed in coded runes, especially the way the wizard disposed of it.

An otherwise fastidious and orderly man, the darkened hovel of Remfrey's study was filled with all sorts of things both mundane and macabre, devices and objects, the purpose of which only Remfrey knew. The interior of the space always smelled of spice and smoke.

What lay in the dark recesses of that room Odo could not say. He knew of instruments made of shiny brass that rested beneath a thin layer of dust. Misshapen skulls and the articulated skeletons of strange creatures gave the chamber a woeful aura. And while Remfrey called the place his study, it was a room where scrolls, rather than books, tended to be housed. Books were relegated to the library. They were too precious a resource for any other place.

Such a study might cause grown men to shiver in fright given the things contained within. At the very least, it might give pause to those who did not know the wizard and his ways. To Odo, however, it was familiar, even inviting. A storeroom of curiosities and hidden things. A place where he learned secrets both ordinary and arcane, under the tutelage of the lanky old man whose voice cracked and squeaked like the splintering of a dry limb.

The bony digits of the wizard beckoned Odo closer. "Come in and close the door behind you."

Taken from his trance, Odo pulled on the handle of the stout oaken door. The barrier creaked and ground on thick iron hinges before closing with a thud as wood met stone. A dull metallic click followed, signaling a latch falling into place.

"Pull up a stool and sit with me," Remfrey continued, motioning toward something in the shadows.

Odo's feet shuffled along, leathern soles rubbing stone as he maneuvered around a small table to the right of the wizard and into the darker recesses of the study. There a modest stool awaited, which Odo lifted from its place.

As wondrous as the mysteries of this room were to Odo, the whole of it stood in odd contrast to the master of the tower. The wizard was one who always reveled in the light. He delighted at the dancing flames in a stony hearth. On a cloudless spring day, he always smiled and sang to himself. Even at night, his eyes sought the skies, calling out by name each of the pinpricks in the veil of night above, as if he had met them during a long-forgotten age. In the moonlight, he often spoke to himself as if he were conversing with an old friend.

Yet, the dark was his cloak. The dark was the place he went to think and ponder—a place to meditate on those rare occasions when the world troubled him. Here in his chambers, with naught but three candles to light the interior and the low fire in the hearth, shadows lurked heavy and profound.

Wooden legs squeaked as they bumped and scraped against the slate floor where Odo placed the stool in front of the wizard. Rough and crude, the wood had been wrought by hand and fitted in a ham-handed way. When he climbed atop, and sat on the seat, the risers moaned beneath his weight. Folding his hands into his lap, he sat patiently as he waited for the wizard to speak.

Closing the lids of his bulging eyes momentarily, the wizard sniffed the air. "Hard at work, I see, pounding out the sulfurous ash." Then the bulges opened, revealing dark, probing eyes. Wild eyes, they seemed. Remfrey himself was gaunt and lanky. Thin strands of his ashen gray hair dangled down from an otherwise bald crown, bedraggled and disorderly. Long whiskers hung down from the knob of his chin, and only from his chin. The robe he wore was once a fine garment, though its glory had faded long ago from many years of use. Patched here and there, it was a favorite thing of his to wear day in and day out. An outfit both comfortable and reliable, like a second skin.

Perhaps it was all these features that most people found unnerving about Remfrey, though Odo knew better. His guise was that of a solitary madman in his bent tower of stone. Yet, beneath that persona was someone Odo knew to be kind and considerate, often gentle to a fault. A father figure of sorts. The only semblance of a patriarch in his life.

Odo lifted a sleeve to his nose and sniffed the ash-stained linen, smelling nothing. He had become so accustomed to the sour odor that he no longer noticed the lingering stench. "Apologies, Magus."

Remfrey's thin lips curled into a pleased smile, though only briefly. When it vanished, his face turned tired and old.

"No matter." Remfrey's voice was soft and slightly sad. The smile returned as he fell back into his chair and lifted his bony limbs to rest on the carved arms of his narrow throne. "I call you 'boy,' but that is something I have done for too long, I fear. Borne out of habit, I am afraid. I daresay what sits across from me is a young man."

Head tilting to one side, the wizard looked over the soot-smeared young man. Odo's skin was a ruddy tan. His earthen tinged irises were all but lost in a sea of white. A curly mop of black topped his crown. He sat straight on that stool as he had been taught so many years ago, never slouching and always attentive.

The wizard smiled again, though the curve of his mouth was not so striking. "A young man with a keen mind, filled with vigor. Why, were this the world outside, you might marry in a handful of years. Perhaps start a family?" He mused a question that needed no answer.

"My studies go well, Magus." Odo answered the wizard almost in an automatic manner, though inside he felt unsettled by what he was seeing and hearing from the old conjurer. It wasn't unusual for Remfrey to be quiet and contemplative, though always quick with a smile. Something, however, was different. The wizard was a man who lived in the now. He hardly ever waxed or waned nostalgic, even when telling stories of things that transpired long in the past.

"I have never known one so diligent as you," the wizard went on, "but that is not why I have called you here."

"Magus?"

"Sixteen years of age?" A long, slender eyebrow of the wizard arched, and then fell. "Why, you scarcely resemble that little child who found his way to my doorstep so many years past. I dare say, I would hardly recognize you now! Bright and strong!" He paused for a moment, as if contemplating his words. "Dutiful." He nodded as he spoke, his voice lowering.

"Thank you, Magus," Odo answered with a slow nod. The wizard rarely offered such quick praise, worrying him even more.

Remfrey looked him over again. "We have a visitor arriving soon. I suspect he will be here before nightfall if my thinking is correct. But, soon at the very least."

"Do you want me to have Hamilda prepare a room—"

"It is time for you to make your way in the world," interrupted Remfrey with a serious stare.

The words struck Odo hard and cold. "Magus?"

"You are all but a man, and it is time for you to leave this place. To wander out into the world outside of my walls."

Odo's eyes turned downward before moving side to side as he searched his thoughts and feelings. The tower was his home, perhaps the only home he ever knew. Since he arrived at Remfrey's doorstep, supposedly weak and near starving, his only memories were those of the Crooked Tower and the lonely moors that surrounded it like a sea of green beneath the summer sun.

Odo's brow furrowed at the wizard's last comment. "Have I not gone with you to the village?"

"Ambardell is not the whole of the world, I assure you. What I speak of is something, well, much larger."

A sick feeling started to well up within Odo. The prospect of leaving the tower without Remfrey terrified him, though he did not show it outwardly. He began to protest, but the wizard was too quick.

"I have an errand for you to attend. One of some importance as it turns out. One that I would only give to someone I trust. Someone I know who will do as I ask, in all circumstances. And to that end—"

Beneath the folds of his robe the wizard reached down and pulled out the charm. Bony fingers held aloft an item that Odo knew well but used only rarely. A many-faceted crystal, hooked to a chain of gold by a ring that grew from within. A talisman.

The only time Remfrey offered the talisman was when Odo needed to practice the spells, incantations, and rituals he was taught. It was a singular device that contained a speck of light encased by clear lattice all around. A seed of the wizard's power. A part of the wizard, but not the whole. It was a mystery Odo never truly understood, and a mystery the wizard was never willing to explain.

Odo's eyes widened as the wizard pulled it and the chain out in full, laying it atop the collar of his age-battered robe. "Come closer, Odo," beckoned Remfrey.

At first, Odo's eyes glanced at the parchment burning in the bowl, the flame dying as the fuel was all but spent. With hesitation, he rose from his seat, and with two reluctant strides, he stood before the wizard.

Remfrey's head bowed as he lifted the chain from around his neck and held it aloft. Presenting it to his assistant, the chain dangled and swayed as the wizard held it apart at the ends, waiting for Odo to bow his head. As Odo did, Remfrey placed the gift gently around his neck before his fingers pulled away.

Standing straight again, Odo touched the cool crystal of the stone, lifting it to his eyes. He gazed at the living light inside with the same sense of awe he felt when he first laid eyes upon it. The small golden orange dot of light that glowed within perplexed him. A simple thing containing the essence of the wizard. The source of powerful magicks dangling on a plain gold chain.

Odo's eyes sought out the wizard once more. The smile had faded from the weathered face of his guardian. The young man's mind was beset with doubt and concern, knowing what the gift meant. Never had the wizard offered him access to such power unsupervised and never for an indeterminant amount of time. This mission was dire indeed.

His hands were steady, but his limbs trembled inside. His lips moved to express something—doubt, gratitude, wonder, even he didn't know—but nothing came out.

The wizard's gaze fell, his tone sounding of shame. "I fear keeping you here was a small sort of vanity on my part. Though I must admit to a small measure of fear for your safety."

"Magus?"

"Your brown skin. Your dark hair. You are different than most of this region. Those that are different raise suspicions among others less…well…with those who are not worldly and well read," continued the wizard.

Odo felt confused. While he knew he was different from others, there had been no mention of his heritage through the years. He was simply Odo of the Crooked Tower.

"And the people of the village?" said Odo.

"Are fewer than the people of the world beyond," answered Remfrey quickly. "This you should know. There are those whose hearts are hard and whose memories of hurts, both real and imagined, are long and deeply held. Only time and trouble will change this, I fear."

"You speak of the Cathars," said Odo.

The wizard's eyes moved to the side, his head bobbing as he chewed on his thin bottom lip. It was a casual acknowledgement that told Odo more than the wizard wanted to say. And Odo knew the reason why.

The Cathars had cut a long and bloody track across history, their presence in the region reaching back before the Great War. A warlike people, they followed The Four, a bloody and blasphemous pantheon of gods. A constant threat to peace in the region, their aggression was only held in check by the combined might of the walled cities that dotted the open moors and coastlines. And by the efforts of the Oncathars—their estranged kin—who countered their threat by sea.

"Still, it is a fear of mine," said the wizard.

Odo's eyes went back to the stone once more, awe returning to his gaze. Remfrey saw this.

"You know what the stone holds," said the wizard in a low tone. "Power such as this is a dangerous thing to use openly. And I urge you to keep it secret. Use it wisely and—"

"Only at great need," answered Odo. "Yet, why give this to me?"

"Who else but you?" answered the wizard with a proud smile. "Perhaps this moment was always meant to be. Perhaps that is why you were brought here those many years ago." His brow furrowed as he went silent for a moment. "Remembering back, it seemed only fitting that I have done what I have done in instructing you in our ways. To teach mortals the secrets of our craft is simply not done."

To Odo, this revelation was new. "Not done?"

"Not forbidden," answered the wizard, "just simply not done."

Remfrey's finger went to his chin, his mind clearly reflecting on something deep. It wasn't uncommon for him to speak in riddles. And to ask the answer to a riddle was often to invite another riddle. Sometimes it was better not to ask.

"What is this task you bid me to do, Magus?"

Broken from the spell that took him, the wizard's attention returned to the moment. "Soon." Answered Remfrey. "Until then, finish your chores, and instruct Hamilda to prepare for the arrival of our guest. Find for yourself a staff among the stock of Hazelwood I keep near the stables. Gather what you may need for a long journey. Then—"

The wizard sniffed the air again, and gave a swift, toothy smile. "Wash. You stink of Sulphur! We cannot have our guest thinking you bathe in rotten eggs!"

CHAPTER 2

Early the next morning, after his things were packed, Odo rushed to the storage shed where the hazelwood was dried and stored. His destination was a low, hastily built shed with cedar shakes for a roof, barely able to keep out the wind and the rain. It didn't take him long to find a staff that suited him.

The appearance of the shed itself was not an unusual feature at the wizard's estate. Remfrey's compound had a dreary and ramshackle appearance at first glance, seeming more like a ruin than the residence of one so wise and powerful. It lay nestled in the hills of the Hadenglen, where the fog settled in when the conditions were favorable. Whether by consequence or design, the mists gave the compound an aura of mystery and dread. Because of this, few people ventured there save out of need. For Odo, it held none of the woe it inspired in others, but it was a lonely home. Beyond the labyrinthine hills and winding paths, a wide desolate moor lay, as foreboding as the hills themselves. Winters here were cold, and persistent damp seemed to linger the whole of the year. Yet, when the sun shone, spring grasses raged from the ground with a blaze of color that often left Odo amazed and awed.

But this was autumn. The only color was in the trees, those precious few that grew in the hills. The lively grasses were dying, and the evergreen scrub prepared for the onset of winter. The very stones of the Crooked Tower seemed suited to such a season, being brown and drab. The interior was not much better, with the rooms often oddly spaced and uneven. The dwelling places seemed more organic than constructed, much to the master's delight.

Odo never gave much thought to the oddities of his home until he saw how nearby villagers lived. The confines of the wizard's compound were not as much of a curiosity to him as they might have been to outsiders. Even now, making his way back to the tower, a dark Hazelwood staff in his hand, he gave little thought to the strangeness of the estate. Chickens scattered as he passed, bent-necked in their strides, clucking their protests. They dispersed in a flurry as Odo passed through them, preoccupied with his staff. Head down, Odo inspected the long straight stick he had selected for his task.

Hazelwood was a hard wood, dark and easily burnished once properly dried. A rare material to come by, it was only found in select mountain groves or deep in the remote forests of the world. Where Remfrey acquired his stock, Odo did not know, nor did he bother to ask. Wizards were strange in that way—knowing so much while revealing precious little.

Slung along Odo's chest and hanging down to his hip was a stained purse of sorts. It was a satchel given to him by the wizard that contained important things he was to deliver, along with a few components he might need for the spells he knew. The leather of the pouch was well used, the brown leather mottled and stained. Despite this, the exterior had a sheen to it along with a savory musk, indicating it had been well oiled and maintained despite visible evidence to the contrary. The wide strap pulled on his shoulder, the weight of the contents within bouncing and shifting with each step he made back to the tower.

The reception chamber of the tower was more like a cave than a formal place where visitors were received. With a room twenty feet or higher, the columns of twisted rock, the lack of windows, and the rough shape of the walls gave it a subterranean feel. Or perhaps it was the veins of red and orange that streamed through the dense brown stone that lent to the illusion that you were standing in the belly of some monstrous beast. Wax hung like stalactites from the bent black iron of lamp stands. They had held a thousand candles since Odo was taken under the wizard's wing and no doubt thousands more before then. As the light of their many flames flickered and smoked, a hundred shadows clung to niches and crevices in the stone. Even the long table within, where guests sometimes came to dine, had a wrought, twisted feel to it. Made of some dense wood both tan and gray, it sat in the middle of that space like a still, slumbering creature. There was no formality or refinement in the piece, its legs seemingly pulled from the mighty slab in a tangle and bent downward. While smooth as silk, the top was raw wood, unvarnished and unprotected. The chairs around it too had the same nature, as if hewed from the great slab, their features pulled like taffy into their final form.

"Come here, Odo!" Remfrey called out from the far end of the table, tapping the top of it just to his right. "Stand next to me while we receive our guest." The light and shadows of the candles made the features of the wizard rougher than they were in the sunlight. He looked older here, ancient even beyond the rumors Odo heard from the others. The hat he wore in the presence of strangers was leathery and tanned a mottled crimson. Conical in form and coming to a point at the top, the hat's embellishments spiraled around it like a coiling serpent, making its wearer woeful and intimidating.

For as long as he had known Remfrey, Odo always thought his behavior in the presence of visitors was out of place with who he knew the wizard to be. Soft spoken and temperate in nature, the wizard was always kind to him and the servants of the tower. Yet, when strangers came calling, he looked all the part of a distant, menacing figure; someone you approached with caution and measured speech. This hour, he donned such a mantle. A master of the arcane and strange, slayer of beasts and black sorcerers from a twilit past.

Odo did as the wizard instructed, standing next to him as Remfrey sat like a king upon his throne. Unloading the satchel he carried, Odo set it on the table.

"Did you pack everything you need?" Remfrey asked, his eyes fixed on the door.

"Yes, Magus."

"And Hamilda fed you?"

"Yes, Magus," replied Odo.

"Let me see the staff you chose," Remfrey commanded, lifting his hands to receive the long shaft of wood.

Dutiful, Odo handed the dark Hazelwood rod to Remfrey. The slender bony digits of the wizard held it gently as he inspected the length of it. Remfrey hummed as if puzzled.

"Magus?" Odo asked, a visible look of concern gracing his face. He feared Remfrey was displeased.

"As straight as a ramrod. Plain. A strange choice for someone who knows our ways and our needs."

Mouth slightly agape, Odo stared dumbly, afraid he had chosen poorly.

"What did I tell you about a wizard's staff?"

"It signifies the wizard."

Remfrey interrupted. "The staff and the wizard are one. It is as much a part of him as the hand that holds it. In a way, the staff is more than a means of focusing energy within. It also shows his path and his fate."

"I thought it more practical than the others," replied Odo, his voice sounding unsure. "For traveling."

Remfrey's answer was a single, dispassionate word. "Indeed."

Odo was silent as Remfrey handed back the staff, wondering what he may have said wrong. "Are you displeased, Magus?"

"You are soon to be a man," replied Remfrey. "This choice, like all others, is something that will stay with you until your time is done. That is the beauty of the Creator's design. Our choices make us. But they do not make us who we are."

Another cryptic answer, it did little to resolve the question forming in Odo's mind. Yet, hesitant, he spoke openly. "I am not a wizard, Magus."

"And what is a wizard?" Remfrey replied.

Before Odo could answer, the thin clang of a gong rang from outside the chamber. A signal that beckoned permission for strangers to enter. Remfrey raised his voice and commanded, "Enter!"

The first to come through the threshold was Jacks, who stopped at the entrance and stepped to the side. The caretaker of the grounds, he was a wiry man with slits for eyes and a profound nose. His thick hair was both brown and gray and his long face was marked with age, wrinkled and worn from the many years of his labors. In many ways, he was very much like the trousers and vest he wore. Old, rough, reliable, durable, and warm.

Looking back, Jacks motioned for someone else to enter. What followed was a tall, looming figure of a man who stepped into the chamber with an air of caution. Scanning the room after passing the threshold, he did so in a methodical manner as if wary of attack. Once assured nothing was amiss, he used those piercing, circumspect eyes to seek out the wizard on his throne of wood.

As he moved forward slowly, the hard leather soles of the stranger's boot scuffed and smacked the hard stone floor of the chamber. Standing straight, he stopped at the opposite end of the table where the wizard sat, as if presenting himself in full.

The light catching him in the gloom of that place, Odo got the first look of the man who was to escort him to his destination. His broad shoulders made his head appear disproportionally small. Over top of them, patched from long years of use and stained in countless places, a long dark cape shrouded the rest of his features. Beneath the cape, a dull gray shirt of mail could be seen covering the upper part of his torso. Though the day was dry, the thin, straight strands of his dark brown hair fell from his brow as if wet from the rain. A scar above his left eye made one lid droop, compounding the unnerving aura of the stranger.

Yet the thing that caught Odo's attention were the man's eyes. Some men have laughing eyes. Others have a gaze that burns with volcanic intensity. This stranger had pale eyes which gazed back at the wizard with cool composure. A long, dead stare that utterly lacked empathy and emotion.

"You Remfrey?" the stranger asked in a low, rumbling voice. He spoke the speech of the Valelanders well, though it was clear it wasn't his native tongue. If Remfrey's intent was to appear imposing or worthy of caution, it had no effect on this man. By all appearances, he was afraid of no one and nothing.

"Yes," answered the wizard with a nod.

"And he is the thing you want delivered?" The stranger flashed a brief glance at Odo and nodded. Even though the stranger's eyes were on him for an instant, the glance was enough to make Odo shiver.

"That *thing* has a name," Remfrey replied, the measured tones of his voice barely able to cover his sudden ire. "*He* is Odo. And yes, it is he whom you must escort to Horunass. Did you find the payment sufficient?"

The stranger nodded.

Odo leaned toward Remfrey. "Who is this?"

"His name is Inoch," Remfrey replied aloud. "And you need not be afraid of him. He is, after all, your protector."

Inoch's cold pale eyes now found their way to Odo. Odo wished he had held his tongue.

The wizard continued, "He and his compatriots are said to be the best at what they do, which is why I hired them for this task." He then turned slightly to Odo and said in a softer voice, "He is grim, I know. That is their way. Do not let it frighten you. You will journey with them for a long while. So, you should take some time to know them."

At once, the wizard's attention returned to the man standing at the end of the table. Remfrey's hand motioned to Odo. "Our friend here has another question he wishes to ask."

Once more, that cold dead stare made its way over to Odo. Flustered, Odo paused for a moment, trying to summon something appropriate to say. Remfrey encouraged him quietly. "Speak, Odo. I know what is on your mind. It is written on your face."

Eyes wide, Odo plucked up his courage. "What is it you do, good sir?" The words sounded weak and feeble in that room, but especially in the presence of that giant of a man who faced him.

"Kill, mostly," Inoch answered in his rumbling tone.

"For a price," added Remfrey.

"For a price," parroted Inoch.

"You will keep Odo, here, safe," Remfrey said in a calm yet forceful way.

"I will do my best," replied Inoch.

Odo was inwardly glad Inoch's attentions were being shifted back to the wizard.

"That was not a request," the wizard quickly followed. "He and all his things are to be delivered to the court of the King of Horunass, unmolested. That is why I have paid what I paid, yes?"

Inoch's gaze landed momentarily on Odo, then back to the wizard, repeating the cycle once more before answering. "As you wish."

"Yes." Remfrey confirmed. "It is as I wish. Odo, you see, is precious to me, and I would be rather upset if any harm should come to him."

"As you wish," answered Inoch coldly.

The wizard shifted in his chair, still sitting straight, and looking down his nose at his guest. Odo leaned his staff against the edge of the table and ran around the back to help pull the chair away as Remfrey stood. The wizard's hat shifted a bit as he moved, and he quietly cursed the thing as he straightened it on his head. Then, taking Odo's staff, he commanded, "Take up the satchel and be off. Horunass awaits and the day is not getting any younger."

Obedient, Odo put his head through the strap of the satchel and let it hang from his shoulder. The wizard waited to return him his staff and followed behind him as they walked around the table, stopping at the end. With a wide stare, Odo scanned Inoch up and down as those chilled pale eyes stared back. He may have been a head taller than Odo, if not a hand more. But to Odo, he looked like he was eight feet tall, and with all the tender kindness of a starving bear on the hunt for fresh meat.

"Come now, Odo," the wizard muttered as his arm draped itself around the shoulder of the young man. "The wild world awaits you. Let us not tarry here."

The day was leaden gray as they moved from the clutching dark of the wizard's tower and into the outside world. As grim as it was, the light still stung Odo's eyes, though both Remfrey and Inoch seemed unfazed. Once more, the wizard put his long, sinewy arm around the young man as they made their way down the path to the stables.

"Did you find a crystal for your staff that suits you?"

"No Magus," answered Odo, "I looked, but found nothing in your stores."

"No matter," Remfrey replied, "there is a man in the city of Collenshore that sells curiosities. Ask around for the merchant Vagmar, and you can look—"

"Collenshore?" Inoch stopped and turned to face the pair. His dead eyes were now suddenly aflame with a burning—if not angry—curiosity. "How do you know where we are going?"

Remfrey's head tilted back and the lids of those bulging eyes narrowed as he looked down his nose at his guest. "I am a wizard, after all."

It was clear that the answer was less than satisfying as Inoch had hoped, and for a moment the mercenary stood there puzzling. Then, the passion that once flickered in his gaze died suddenly. He turned slowly, holding his suspicious stare for a time before resuming his walk.

Remfrey continued his instruction to Odo. "As I said, ask after the merchant Vagmar. I have no doubt you will find something there."

"Magus?" Odo asked, head down. "What need have I of a staff and crystal?"

Remfrey sensed the question almost before it was asked. "I do not expect trouble on your journey, but if trouble does come, you should be prepared. That is why I have made sure you have all that you need." Motioning to Inoch, Remfrey continued, "Our friend here has gold enough and more to pay for anything you may require along the way. Mention my name to Vagmar. He will be more than helpful."

The conversation fell into silence. Small stones crunched beneath their feet as they traversed the path. Still, something troubled Odo, and it showed on his downturned face. "Magus?"

"Yes, Odo?"

"Why me?" Odo's gaze turned up to the weathered face of Remfrey. The wizard's long thready beard bounced and dangled with each step he took. In the reception chamber, the hat he wore looked obscure if not a bit frightful. In the light of day, however, Odo thought it looked garish, if not a tad bit silly. It was a small detail he had never noticed until now. Then again, Remfrey never wore it outside in the light.

At first, thin lips stretched across the lines and sags of Remfrey's face. Those bulging eyes looked back, something satisfied in their stare. His hand tapped Odo's shoulder lightly. "How long has it been since I found you there at my gate? Thirteen years? Fourteen? Time means nothing to one of my kind, but it is precious to a mortal such as yourself. As is purpose. Before either of us breathed the air here or laid eyes upon the glory of these lands, purpose was given to each of our paths. Mine was given to me from lands afar. Yours?" He paused. "Yours you must discover. In the joy and the terror that sometimes come, discovery is the greatest part of life. Don't you agree?"

"Magus?"

"Did I not say it is time that you must find your way in the world?" Remfrey's brows peaked, causing the bags beneath his eyes to vanish briefly.

"Yes, but...do I not have purpose here?"

"You do," answered Remfrey. "And you will. Or perhaps you will find something that neither you nor I intended. The Allfather does not reveal all, even to one such as me. Ah!" the wizard remarked. "We are here!"

Odo barely noticed the smell of wet hay that often came when in proximity to the stables. Like the rest of the compound, they appeared rundown, weathered wood resting atop a foundation of crude stone. Six narrow stalls that were more filled now than at any other time Odo had known. Two horses and a mule were usually quartered therein, the vacancies all but taken with the two horses Inoch had brought. Jacks was quick to mount the saddles and set the beasts with bit and bridle, bringing the horses from their stalls. Inoch was quick to take to his mount, saddlebags and sacks full and ready for their ride.

Remfrey withdrew his arm as Odo approached his horse, a chestnut gelding with a stripe of white along its snout. Just as he was about to mount, Remfrey halted him.

"Wait! One last thing," said the wizard as his bony hand poked into the recesses of his robe. In a second or two, out came a piece of parchment, neatly folded. Two thin digits held the paper firm as the wizard's hand extended to Odo. "You will need this after you are delivered to the court of the King of Horunass."

Taking the parchment, Odo inspected it carefully. Folded and creased, a disc of hard blue wax sealed the paper closed—the impression of a rune that was the first letter of Remfrey's name. This Odo slid into his satchel, tying the flap shut soon after.

"Yes, Magus," Odo said with a nod. Handing his staff to Jacks, he put one foot in the stirrup and a hand on the neck of the mount before vaulting himself into the saddle and throwing his leg around. Only after he was seated did his hand reach out for his staff.

"Fair travels, Odo," Jacks said with a wink, handing him the Hazelwood shaft. Odo nodded in reply.

Inoch led the way past the stable and to the gate that Jacks had opened before them in preparation. The gate was as weathered and weak as the wood of the stables, and for as long as Odo lived there, it always seemed in desperate need of repair. Yet, as he passed beyond, he secretly wished he could turn about and return to the sheltering arms of the wizard's estate. Excitement always followed him when he traveled with Remfrey to the village, yearning to know more of the world beyond. This excursion was different. Anxiety and dread passed with him through the stony arch, like hounds on the hunt following after his scent.

He heard the gate creak and clatter closed behind him and the bar shift quietly in place, wood upon wood. Odo stopped his horse and turned, looking back.

While he resided there, Odo's life at the Crooked Tower never felt like what he imagined a true home might be. He was the only child among the aged. A tawny-skinned boy among the pale. A lonely existence in many regards, endured in dutiful silence. No one his age to play with, no one to understand the persistent awkwardness of youth. It was a place that, in the still of the night, he wept bitter tears in the solitude of his bedchamber. Tears shed for unanswered prayers, petitioning the Allfather such that he might have the familial life of those children he saw in the nearby village.

Now, all that had changed in an instant. He knew little of the greater world save for what books and dusty old scrolls contained. Yet, this was no academic exercise, the sudden realization of that invoking a sickening fear. He traveled in the unfamiliar company of a stranger who was intimidating and cold. Quietly, as his eyes stared longingly back at the only home he ever knew, he yearned to remain in the shadow of the Crooked Tower once more. That he might again find sanctuary behind the rough crumbling walls that enclosed the wizard's compound. Somehow that felt safer from peril than this. Though the gate had closed and only vague forms moved in the gaps between the planks, Odo's eyes sought the wizard. As if seeing him one more time might offer some sense of comfort and reassurance.

"Keep up, boy!" Inoch scolded as he stopped and turned.

The harsh voice of the mercenary set Odo on edge. The young man suddenly felt numb inside, uncomfortable in his own skin.

CHAPTER 3

It was scarcely past noon when Inoch brought the trek to a sudden halt. The wind picked up across the chilled heath, the gray skies above them mottled both dark and light. Bringing his horse about, he drew close to Odo and those cold pale eyes stared hard.

"We're far enough away," Inoch said, as the wind came to a sudden lull, "so now is the time we have words."

They were ominous words spoken in an ominous place. The moor was as familiar to Odo as Remfrey, Hamilda, or wily old Jacks. But out here, far from the Crooked Tower and the watchful eye of the wizard, it was a terrible, unsympathetic place. The wind that blew across the heathers and the sparse juniper was cold, whispery, and mournful. The gray sky above dreary at best, threatening at its worst. Each step forward by the horses, and each minute further from home made the queer chaos of the wizard's compound seem cheerful by comparison. And now the man with the grim, lifeless eyes of a killer wanted to have "words."

Odo's eyes went wide as one hand clutched the satchel and the other his staff and reins. "Sir?"

"Captain," Inoch corrected Odo before commanding, "Off the horse."

At first, Odo seemed confused as he looked nervously at Inoch. Letting go of the reigns, he threw his leg around, and jumped from the horse. Stalks of dried heather and meadegrass crunched beneath his feet and cushioned his landing. Wading through a sea of vegetation, Odo came around to the horse's muzzle, taking hold of the reins once more. Inoch turned on his mount and came about, stopping only a few feet from where Odo stood, staff in hand.

With a withering gaze, Inoch asked, "You know the first rule of a freelancer, boy?"

Odo looked up innocent and nervous, his dark pupils like holes in a sea of white that grew wider as the captain spoke. Clutching tight his staff, Odo shook his head.

"Live long enough to spend your gold," answered Inoch. "I've done this for too long to know when something is too good to be true."

"Sir?"

"Captain!" snapped Inoch before adding with a growl, "Remember that!" As stunning as Inoch's rapid change in temperament was, it was grimly refreshing to see something more than a cadaverous presence from the man escorting him.

"Captain?" Odo's voice was unsteady and uncertain. More than a few times he thought about the talisman and maybe Remfrey's warning being more than just a coincidence.

"No one pays what your master paid for so simple a service," Inoch said. "So, what is it that I risk my life and that of my men? It's not for some dusky-skinned boy, that I know."

At first, Odo started to direct his attention to his satchel and the contents within, mindlessly. He stopped soon enough, making the movement seem only a twitch. Yet his silence didn't satisfy Inoch in the least. It only made him angrier.

A sword sang as it was drawn from its sheath. Holding out the blade for Odo to see, the mercenary captain edged his horse closer. "Best speak, boy. Play games with me, and I leave with the gold while you remain here."

Inoch was an imposing figure, and on that horse with sword displayed he looked like Death incarnate. Again, Odo's mind went to the talisman as the words of Remfrey echoed in his scattered thoughts.

Use it sparingly. Use it wisely.

Head down, eyes darting this way and that as he debated what to do, Inoch nudged his horse closer. Odo backed away, let go of the reins and paused reluctantly. Then, cradling his staff in the hollow of his shoulder, he untied the thong of the satchel, pulled back the flap, reached in, and pulled out the package. At first, he merely held it close to him in the palm of his hand, but after a few moments, he lifted it high for the captain to see.

No bigger than a large potato, and very much of the same form, a lump of something rested in Odo's palm. Covered over in thick parchment, a series of runes covered the surface of the wrappings. At the seams, crude disks of blue wax held the paper in place, sealing the object within and hiding it from prying eyes.

Inoch's face showed an uncharacteristic curiosity as he scanned Odo's burden, furrowing his brow for a moment. With a sudden graceful motion he dismounted, his heels thudding hard against the soil of the moors. Sword in hand, dead, desiccated vegetation hissed as it scraped against his pants and cloak as he moved closer to look at the object. Odo hazarded a look at Inoch.

Hands reached out to grab the paper-bound package, only for Odo to pull away. "No!" he exclaimed. "No, sir!"

"Captain!" Inoch growled, those dead eyes narrowing in anger as he pulled his hand away.

"Apologies! Captain!" Odo replied, looking scared.

For a moment, the mercenary captain analyzed the thing up close, noticing the markings on the paper, and paying special attention to the wax seals. "What is it?"

"I...I don't know," replied Odo, trepidation and concern dripping from his words. "A rock, I think."

The wind picked up slightly, and the grasses sighed in response. A horse snorted as the grim soldier's eyes stared once more at the package. "Open it."

"No," Odo said softly, with a shake of his head.

"Then I will—"

"The runes," replied Odo in a nervous rush.

"The markings?" Inoch asked as his finger danced over the wax seals.

"Yes," Odo answered with a nod.

"What are they?"

"Protective wards, I think," said the young man as his brow creased with concern and confusion. He started to sway a bit in the wind, more nerves than anything else. "The wizard has shown me a few, but—"

"But what?"

"These I do not know. There are three of them," explained Odo. "One, I think, keeps others from knowing what is contained within."

That remark got the captain's attention. "Others?"

Odo didn't hear the question and continued agitated. "The runes, I think, are protective."

"Didn't you hear me boy?" pressed Inoch forcefully. Pointing to the rock, he said, "Who wants this?"

"I do not know," Odo replied, swiftly, fearfully. "The Magus said nothing. Only that it was important that I deliver it to the king. That is all I know."

"You know runes. You must be a wizard then," said Inoch, his voice less commanding.

"No sir...captain!" Odo replied, suddenly remembering.

"What are you then, if not a wizard?"

Odo began to relax, and he withdrew the stone, pulling it closer to him. "Mortals cannot be wizards."

"Is that the only secret you bring with you?" Inoch asked, his head nodding at the stone.

Odo paused before he answered, wondering what to say next. "Yes, captain."

Those pale, dead eyes then fixed on Odo with a stare so hard, Odo could barely stand its glare. He began to perspire, even though the wind was gusting cool.

"Hear me, boy." Inoch spoke with a voice that had the growl of a wolf defending its kill. "I have known all sorts of thieves and liars in my time. I know a lie when I smell one, and you stink of it! One more lie from you, and I take the wizard's gold and leave you here, alone. To make your own way back."

Closing his eyes, the young man let out a frustrated sigh. Opening the flap of the satchel with one hand, the other laid the wrapped bundle within. Leaving the flap to close on its own, Odo then dug beneath his cloak and the lapels of his robe to produce the talisman. With one hand, he pulled the chain taut and let the stone dangle a bit from his fingers.

For the first time, Odo saw Inoch's eyes burn with an intense curiosity. The captain's lids narrowed as his head drew closer, the pale orange dot of light at the center catching his attention. The fingers of his left hand slowly went up for the stone, looking to touch it. Odo was quick to wrap his own around it and pull it away.

"No!" exclaimed the young man. "It will burn you!"

Pulling back, the mercenary looked furious at first, but this faded quickly as he withdrew his hand. "What is it?"

"A talisman."

"You think me a fool, boy?" snarled the captain. "What was that in the center?"

"A part of the wizard," explained Odo. "Something he has given me to use. Mortals cannot use magic. Only wizards. The power is granted to them by the Maker." He paused for a moment and tucked the stone beneath his robes. "It is only meant for me. It will burn others who try to take it for their own."

Sniffing at the explanation, Inoch looked amused—if being amused was a trait he possessed.

"What?" asked Odo, but the captain didn't reply. Instead, he answered one question with another.

"Any other secrets you carry?"

"No," Odo replied, before following with, "Captain."

Once more, pale eyes scanned him over, and Inoch's face fell slightly. Curiosity showed itself clearly now as the freelancer pondered his next move. A moment or two passed and then a quiet nasal sigh.

"No more secrets, boy," Inoch said softly, but with a serious stare. "Gold may buy my sword, but my word is law. I command. You do. Understand?"

It took a moment for Odo to parse that in his brain, his eyes looking one way, then the other. Finally, they gazed off into an unseen horizon, Odo understanding the meaning behind Inoch's remarks. That if magic was required, he would need to supply it.

Inoch grew impatient. "You understand, boy?"

Odo replied meekly. "The power the Magus has given to me isn't—"

"My skin has more value than your conscience," interrupted Inoch. "You understand, boy?"

It sickened Odo inside, the very thought of the choice he had to make. Remfrey was a father to him—as much of a father as he had ever known. As reluctant as he was to use the talisman, he was doubly more hesitant now. But there was the satchel, the stone within, and last words Remfrey spoke to him. Closing his eyes, the nod he offered Inoch was barely above a twitch.

"What was that?" Inoch pressed, not satisfied with a wordless reply.

"Yes, captain." The words sounded forlorn and filled with shame. Odo didn't want to look at the mercenary, so his eyes gazed downward.

Inoch stood up straight and scanned his young charge once more before turning his head and spitting. With a lazy wave of his hands, he mumbled as he turned away, "Mount up boy. It's a ways to Collenshore and the daylight is burning."

Somewhere in the wind, Odo thought he heard a whisper. But it was just a cold breeze over the heather. The moor did not get friendlier from that day forward.

CHAPTER 4

Inoch peered through the spyglass with a singular intensity. Hidden beneath sleeping heather and the desiccated stalks of grass, he lay on his belly atop a grassy rise. The sun just slightly behind him, there was nothing to give away his position, save the wind. With a spyglass that jutted out imperceptibly from the brush, he tracked several forms cresting the top of a small knoll far in the distance.

The wind spoke in whispers as it blew through wintered vegetation. Odo waited in silence just down the hill, tending to the horses as they grazed. One minute passed, then two, then three, each one of them feeling like an eternity. Something was wrong, he could feel it. It wasn't the silence from the mercenary captain; Inoch seemed always grim and quiet. Yet, there was a tension that crackled around him. His still seriousness spoke volumes. Or did it? Odo needed to know.

"Is something wrong?"

Odo's answer was more silence. He asked again.

"Quiet!" shouted the captain in reply. That was the last time Odo asked.

Not long after that, Inoch returned from his perch, sliding on his belly and crawling down the hillside like a snake for some distance. Then, assured the hilltop concealed him, he stood and collapsed his spyglass in a single movement. From there, he strode down the hill, swift but confident, gravity playing a part. Slowing his pace as he approached his horse, he fiddled with one of the saddlebags with the spyglass tucked beneath his arm.

"Captain?"

Once the flap flew open, Inoch laid the stub of his spyglass inside. "Eight of them."

"Bandits?"

"Most like. Too far to say," replied the captain in that cold, rumbling voice of his. He spoke the Valelander tongue well, but there was always a hint of clumsiness in each of his words. "What is sure is that they are following our trail."

"How, Captain?"

"I had hoped that two alone on a trail would not raise suspicion," Inoch said as he secured his precious device. Tying close the flap on the saddlebag, he turned to face Odo. With short strides he approached the young man, a menacing figure who loomed over Odo as he neared. "You said you can cast spells. Can you cast a spell that hides our passing?"

Odo's fingers reached beneath his cloak, his hand pressed to his breast. The flesh of his palm pushed on the sharp corners of the talisman concealed beneath his clothes. His body froze in place for a moment while a million thoughts whirled in his head as he searched for an answer. "I can cast one that allows us to go unseen for a time—"

"One that can cover our tracks?"

Odo's wide, questioning eyes met Inoch's steely stare. "Captain?"

Inoch pointed to the hillside behind them and Odo spun about. Brown and gray stalks were framed by a sky peppered both gray and blue. Odo wondered at first what it was the captain was referencing.

"Our wake," said Inoch. "In the grass. Can you cover that?"

Odo turned back again as he puzzled the question. "No, sir." He stopped speaking at once, realizing his mistake. "I mean, Captain. I know of no spell that—"

Inoch turned his back to the wizard's apprentice, staring off in the distance to the west. A hand went to his hip as his head fell. He was like this for a time, stock still and silent.

Odo waited nervously, his burning curiosity tempered with a tiny bit of fear. His desire to know all that was transpiring was restrained by sober reason. He knew full well that too many questions with this man were something you did at your own peril.

Then, a thought occurred to him. "I could lay a ward." It was a half-hearted offer, but the only thing that came to mind. It was enough to cause Inoch to turn.

"What say you, boy?" A flicker of life showed in that icy stare of his.

"A ward. A rune in the ground," explained Odo, the whites of his eyes all but glimmering against the sea of reddish-brown skin.

"To do what?"

Odo's head dipped as he summoned the words to answer, his hand falling from his chest. "Many kinds. One to jolt, one to make a man retch, one to—"

"To kill?" asked the captain. That flicker in his eyes burned hot now.

Not liking the question in the least, Odo was slow to answer. Unsteady as he met the captain's glare, he replied, "The wizard forbids the use of such devices."

Inoch took one step forward, the narrow space between the two making the young apprentice uncomfortable. His stare bore down on a nervous Odo with a merciless sort of energy. "I care less than a damn what the wizard instructs you, boy! I carry quite a sum in our bags. Gold I intend to keep. And I have laid my mark on a bond to deliver you to Horunass." Curling his hand into a ball and sticking out his thumb, Inoch pointed behind him. "If they catch us, I dare say they will take the gold and kill us both as it pleases them. So, when I ask you the question, I do not want feeble words."

Hands on his hips again, Inoch pivoted about looking to the west before turning back. Odo stood there shamefaced, staff in his hand, his fingers gripping tightly the dense wood in confusion and angst. Inoch spoke. "I will ask you one more time—can you draw a rune to kill?"

Odo reluctantly nodded, and Inoch's hands fell from his hips. Then the mercenary started to pace in a wide circle inspecting the ground. Several yards away he stopped, and with his boot cleared away some of the grass. "Boy!"

"Yes, Captain?"

"Can something be put on top of the mark?"

"Captain?" Odo was confused.

"Bait," answered Inoch. "For a trap. Can you lay a rune, put something atop it to attract attention?"

The captain was laying a trap, and Odo discerned his intent straight away. "Yes, Captain."

"Get what you need!" exclaimed Inoch as he pointed at the barren patch of ground he had made. "Put it here."

Lifting the satchel from around his shoulder, Odo removed his cloak and stuffed it beneath his arm as he approached the spot.

Inoch fumbled with something in his saddlebags. It took some time, but when Inoch was done, he let the flap of his saddlebag fall and returned with a small cloth pouch no bigger than the size of a dinner roll. "Use this," he said.

Exchanging the cloak for the purse, Odo kept his staff in one hand, palming the pouch in the other. It felt heavy for such a small thing, and the characteristic clink and grind of metal discs made the contents within obvious. Coins.

"Put down your rune and lay that on top," instructed the captain, referring to the pouch. His voice rose just above the hiss of the breeze and the rustling of the grasses. "If you can, lay some grass on top. No need to make the snare too easy to see."

Eyes on the pouch, Odo listened intently as Inoch added, "Understand?"

"Sir?"

"Captain!" grumbled Inoch.

"Captain, yes...apologies," replied Odo, his face turning hot with his obvious mistake. There was a pause afterwards.

"Spit it out, boy," commanded Inoch.

"A rune to kill?"

Inoch's eyes studied Odo for a time. "If it bothers you so, then no. Leastwhiles, not now," Inoch replied before adding, "but I want a trap that is loud. Sudden. Enough to make them think twice on continuing further."

Odo looked around, seemingly confused.

"What, boy?"

"Take the horses away, captain, if you would." Pointing with the staff to the west where they were originally heading, Odo added, "Over there."

"Why?"

"They may stumble into my work," said Odo.

Nodding, the captain flipped Odo's cloak over his shoulder and moved leisurely to gather the horses.

Taking up the satchel, Odo wandered over to the spot Inoch prepared for him and knelt. He watched intently as the mounts were led away, the autumn air now colder without his cloak. Assured they were at a safe distance, he laid his staff and satchel to one side along with the pouch. Bending over the bare patch, he cleaned away the stray shafts of grass, ripping out more by the root if they threatened to impede his work. Patting the ground solid and flat, he raised one hand to his chest, pressing the talisman to the flesh of his breast. He spoke softly the words the wizard instructed him to say so many years ago, his finger tracing lines in the dirt. Purposely, patiently, he chanted the canter over and over as the flesh of his finger retraced the symbol on the ground. He stood with one hand still pressed against the talisman, the tips of the stone digging painfully into his chest like the points of daggers. With his free hand he took up the pouch. Setting runes was a skill he was well accustomed to, the momentary discomfort of the wizard's stone having little effect as he went about his task. Somewhere in a distant memory, he heard the wizard speaking to him from years past, one of the first lessons he ever learned there in that twisted tower of stone.

All power comes with a price, for good or for ill. The question you must always ask yourself is: was the gain worth the price you paid?

Repeating the words of power in a cycle, he laid the gilded bait on the center of the rune. Continuing his chant he laid stray leaves, bent stems, and soil-encrusted roots over top, covering the trap as best he could. Ceasing his chant, he stood and cautiously backed away from where he had laid the rune, lifting the hand from his breast. Once again, he took up his staff and satchel as his fingers probed deep beneath the rude cloth of his robe, massaging the painful indentations left behind by the talisman. Circling around his magic snare, he gave the trap a wide berth, as if what lay there was like a coiled viper. He rejoined Inoch many yards away.

"It is done?" said the captain as he handed him his cloak. Odo waded knee-deep through the low tide of vegetation.

"Yes, Captain." Clumsily cradling the staff in the hollow of his arm, Odo threw his cloak around his shoulders, grateful to be protected once more from the chill of the breeze that rushed over the moors. The air smelled of rain despite the patches of blue that peeked through the gray canopy of clouds above them.

As Odo struggled with his things, Inoch reached in and took Odo's staff, a strange gesture of aid.

Looking away to the west, Inoch sniffed the air as Odo worked on the clasp of the robe. "There is a place near here where we can water the horses. Then we continue until nightfall." His stare went in the opposite direction, as he added, "Their numbers are greater, but they move slow. They still have leagues to go in order to ford the river we crossed earlier. That is fortunate for us."

A question came to Odo's mind as he pulled the fringes of the drab brown cloak around him. His hand went out for his staff as he asked, "Captain?"

"What?"

"If they are moving so slow, why then the ward?"

"A little fear is as good as a stumbling block," Inoch replied as cold as a winter's stream. "They will follow. They will see that we stopped, and they will search. Dead bandit or no, they will think twice before they continue."

"But now they know we have gold."

"They already know," answered Inoch as he turned to go.

"Captain?" asked Odo, his head up now and looking at the back of Inoch as the freelancer started to move away.

Inoch stopped and turned about, looking down at Odo with a flinty stare.

"What, boy?"

"Will you ask me to do more such things? Setting wards and runes?"

"You can weave spells," Inoch replied. "A handy thing to have in such matters."

"I...I...if I am to do such things," Odo stuttered and stammered, loathing to speak, but knowing he must.

"Spit it out, boy!"

"I will need to acquire a crystal," Odo said, raising his staff up slightly. "From the merchant in the city. As the Magus said."

"Done," answered the captain. "If we get there. Many miles lay between. We are upwind and there are killers at our backs. Now, on your horse. We ride until nightfall."

CHAPTER 5

A puck of blue-gray stone scraped along the edge of pointed steel as Inoch tended to the edge of his sword. A small campfire popped and hissed, defying the night's chill, painting the trees that encircled them with light. Inoch's silence was grim and unsettling. His intense focus on his sword troubled the young man. Exchanging an anxious night for an anxious day, Odo was unable to sleep despite the exhaustion from constant travel. In a contest between weariness and fear, it was unclear which would prevail before the arrival of dawn. At present, his nerves had the upper hand.

It wasn't just Inoch and his sword that troubled Odo. The events of that day still weighed heavily on the young man's mind. Their trek brought them to a forest where they halted, Inoch demanding that Odo lay another one of his wards. This time, a ward that could kill. Odo protested at first, concerned that an innocent might unwittingly run across it. When he did, Inoch scowled. "Rather an innocent find your mark in the dirt than bandits find us unawares. Lay the mark boy or remain here."

And it was clear, by the determined expression on the mercenary's face, he would be true to his word.

But now, Odo sat contemplatively by the fire in the strangeness of the wilds, pondering the consequence of his actions. Just beyond the fire's glow reigned the harsh dark of the night. Wrapped in his cloak, he grasped the hem of the garment, pulling it taut across his frame in an attempt to stay warm. The soft hoot of an owl sounded in the distance, a subtle reminder they were not alone in the forest. Tall trunks surrounded them like the legs of giants, a great host closing in and yet remaining still as if keeping watch.

One more quiet scream rang from the steel of his sword as Inoch took another pass with the sharpening stone. A sound, Odo feared, that might call some unwitting traveler from afar. One that might cause them to stumble over the deadly trap he laid earlier. It was an irrational fear, given the distance that lay between the pair and the forest fringe. Still, he fretted over the power the wizard entrusted to him and the ends to which it had been employed. Uses contrary to everything Odo had been taught. That fact alone troubled the young man the most.

"Tell me, boy, how well do you know the wizard?" Inoch flicked his thumb over one edge of his blade, testing the result of his labor.

Odo's wide eyes looked up from the flames, pearls amongst shadow and flame. Fear seeped into his expression as the question was asked. His gut filled with an acute unease as Inoch honed his blade, asking questions that reeked of suspicion and hidden malice.

"Captain?"

"You heard me, boy," answered Inoch, flipping his blade around and preparing to work on the other edge. Those passionless eyes scanned the bright steel as he once more took up the puck of stone and ground it along the edge.

"The Magus is...is a godly man. That I know," answered Odo, reluctantly. Words came off feeble and uncertain from his tongue as fear began to clutch at his heart.

"Let me tell you what I know of godly men," interjected Inoch, rotating the puck slightly in his palm. He pushed it along the length of the steel in another pass. The stone growled and hissed as it tore away at the metal. The weapon may have been a typical blade for a man of his profession. But as Inoch sat there near the fire, his back against the trunk of a tree, the sword he held looked like it was seven feet long. Orange and yellow flashed and danced in the bright steel, giving it the illusion of life. A long, terrible blade made for splitting the links of mail. A wickedly sharp tip for finding the tender gaps in a well-armored foe. Inoch tended it well.

"I was there in the war of the Five Princes, in the service of this King Merrith—another 'godly man.' The man whom you are to be delivered." Inoch's voice was calm and absent emotion, even as his words mocked the phrase Odo had used. He rotated the puck again and did another screaming pass along the length of his sword. "I was there at the village of Forning at the Grun. We took it without a fight and placed the villagers in a pen while we ransacked and looted the homes and stables. And when we were done, your 'godly man' ordered the whole of it to be razed. Everything to be slain. Man. Woman. Child. Ewe and goat, dog, bullock, ox, horse. Old women and suckling babes were put to the sword, their bodies burned with the whole of the village. And when we were done?"

The puck screeched and screamed once more, Inoch's hand pushing the sharpening stone spitefully across the steel. "He ordered what remained ground into dust. We set to pounding the bones with hammer and stone, mixing them with salt and casting them to the ground. When we were done, naught remained but ash, dust, and salt. As if Forning were a ghost."

Inoch stopped to inspect the blade once more, thumbing the keen edge as he worked the other side. Silence reigned as his attention turned towards the sword, leading Odo to wonder if he was preparing it for him.

"I know naught of King Merrith."

"The gold of godly men weighs the same as the wicked," Inoch explained, his eyes never lifting from his blade. "And I care little whether a man worships one God or many. Blood is blood and gold is gold, and I aim to keep both of mine. Answer the question, boy." Now that dead, emotionless stare was focused on Odo, seeking him across the dancing flames and glowing whispering coals.

Odo swallowed hard, his throat suddenly parched and with a strong desire for a mouthful of water. His words initially came out in a croak. "All the years I have known Master Remfrey, he has always been kind to me." He reached for the bladder of water next to him, unstopped it in preparation to take a swallow.

"It is a long ride to water, boy," warned the captain as his attention returned to his sword again. "Drink sparingly."

Ignoring the warning, Odo filled his mouth and held it while he stopped the skin. Setting the water aside, he let a trickle of the mouthful dribble down his throat. The question, the naked blade, the keen edge of the steel, and those distant, pitiless eyes of the mercenary made his heart race. Odo's large bright eyes turned bloodshot as his cheeks turned hot. He feared the end of his days were drawing near, no matter what came from his lips.

Odo's words stumbled from his mouth, his attempt at a reply failing at first. The gears of his mind turned, thinking. "I know him well enough. He is true," Odo finally jumbled together. His hand drew closer to his chest. In the back of his head, he secretly wondered where he had set his staff, fearing the approach of a fight.

Then a question came to mind, and in his haste he blurted it out. "Why would the Magus send others to kill us? When the deed is yet incomplete?"

"To rid himself of a burden?" replied Inoch. "Stranger things I have seen in my time."

"Burden?"

"You," said Inoch coldly.

"Then why not just pay you?"

Inoch stopped what he was doing as he lifted his head, pondering the question. Odo continued his thinking. "I was but a babe when the Magus took me in and raised me." He paused for a moment before adding, "Why would he teach me all I know—"

"What I know is that I spoke to no one where I was going and for what purpose." Inoch's rich accent tinged his words. "None followed me into those hills. Yet now, I find strangers at my back."

"If it is one thing that I am certain," Odo answered quickly, "they go not at the bidding of Remfrey. That is not his way."

"We shall soon see."

Odo relaxed, a warm rush of relief washing over him as Inoch spoke. The word 'we,' said far more than the sword that lay across the captain's lap. A plural word instead of the singular. It meant more than one would continue the journey come the morning's light.

"Captain?"

"On first light, we will go around and double back," explained Inoch, his eyes resting on Odo. "We shall see if that snare you have laid has been sprung. And by what."

The captain paused for a time before he took up his blade and the sheath that lay nearby, depositing one into the other. A scabbard well used, it looked stained and battered, the blade making a hiss before the tang met the brass rim, ending with a muted metallic click. Setting the weapon next to him, he looked to one side and then the other before his eyes found the blanket folded at his side.

"I need rest," proclaimed the captain with a sigh. "Tend the fire and keep watch. Wake me when you can keep watch no longer."

Odo, too, let out a relieved sigh as his hand fell from his chest. Gazing at the ground around him, he located his staff and drew it close to him. Settling in, Odo let his mind wander for a bit, deep thoughts churning as he stared at the dancing flames of the meager fire.

As the captain took hold of the blanket and drew it to him, Odo asked, "What do you believe?"

"What say you?"

"What god do you pray to?"

"None" answered Inoch bluntly.

"None?" parroted Odo, the brow of his head creased in confusion.

"Whether there be one god or many," Inoch replied, "I have seen none."

"Not even the God of the West?" asked Odo, serious now in his bewilderment. "It was He that sent us wizards."

"I have taken the lives of many men," Inoch said as he unfolded the blanket to cover his torso. "I am sure many prayed that death be turned aside upon my approach. Never once has an unseen hand stayed my blow." Arranging the blanket to cover him, the captain continued, "There is nothing in the sky above to hear your prayers. Nothing but earth below us. Nothing lay beyond the mists of the western seas save but—"

Inoch's voice stalled for a moment as his mind set to consider the words he wanted to say. "Nothing save more water. Pray to your creator god if that is your desire. I will not waste my breath."

With heavy lids, Inoch reclined his head against the trunk of the tree.

"Captain?"

"What is it now?" Inoch growled as his lids closed.

"What is it that you believe, if not the God of the West?" Odo's curiosity was truly getting the better of him. Remfrey always spoke of the Creator God as if such a thing was certain and assured. Odo could not believe that someone—anyone—thought of Him as fanciful fantasy.

"I've seen many things boy," answered the captain, his accent bleeding through his words as fatigue started to set in. "I have seen fish-men rise from the waters in the south and horned devils descend from the mountainsides. Two-headed giants that feasted on men and hook-nosed quill-back Morgurs whose stench could make a man retch their very vitals. I have seen brother killing brother for land, or gold, or a woman, or all three. And in all these things, I saw no hand of a just or loving god in their making."

Pulling tight the blanket around him once more, the captain added, "If there is anything I believe in, boy, it's this: blood and gold. Blood and gold and keeping both for as long as I can. Now, let me sleep, boy. Or I can fix that waggling tongue you have."

Odo threw a nearby stick on the fire, a popping and crackling following after. Inoch's eyes closed as the silence of the night still played upon his nerves. He should have been tired after a long day of riding, but an uncanny restlessness gnawed at him. Whether it was the fear of what lay behind them or the man who rested against that tree, Odo was troubled. His hand reflexively went to the talisman, pulling it out from his clothes. For a moment, he stared at the gem, pondering the mystery of the light contained within, a piece of the life force of the wizard. His eyes stared intently while his mind raced, knowing the importance of the thing he held. Beset by trouble and worry, Odo stood and pulled his satchel closer.

As Odo moved, Inoch's one eye peeked open. "What are you doing, boy?" asked the captain.

Saying nothing, Odo withdrew several items from the bag, clutching them in his hand before throwing the flap closed again.

"Boy?" Inoch said, anger flickering in his tone.

"I...I need to do something," replied Odo, pivoting around to face his protector and guide after he stood. Using his head to nod and point he added, "Out there."

"Out there?" Inoch sounded deeply suspicious.

"Prayers. Petitions." Odo's voice wavered, his words hasty and uncertain.

Both eyes were open now, Inoch clearly suspicious. "That is quite a handful for prayers."

"The wizard's instruction," answered Odo, holding out his clutched hand. "The sage is incense, and it helps focus. The emberbalm is—"

"If this is a wizard's trick, rest assured I'll kill you before you are done," warned Inoch in a growl.

"No! No, good sir...uh...*Captain*!" protested Odo. "It is simply to calm the mind and help focus!"

His gaze alternating between the bundle in Odo's hands and his wide bloodshot eyes, Inoch pondered silently. Eyes closed, and beneath the blanket that covered him, Inoch crossed his arms over his chest. "Stay close. Return soon. There may be more than bandits in these woods. I will leave you for them if you are daft enough to get lost."

"Yes, Captain."

Odo was quick to take up his staff as one of the horses snorted. Making his way into the woods, he pushed past bent brambles that tugged at his cloak and clothes. Tree roots reached up and threatened to trip him, and loamy soil seemed to give way beneath his weight.

Looking back constantly, he kept a clean line of sight to the fire until an open patch of bare ground presented itself. Feet crunching on the leaves, he cleared away the debris with his foot until the ground was bare. Using the staff to mark a circle in the dirt, he knelt in the center. The items he held were distributed along the circumference, Odo trying his best to recall the wizard's instructions. At times he paused, muttering to himself trying to clear away the confusion that plagued him. When he wasn't doing that, he was looking over his shoulder, worried the mercenary was approaching while he was distracted. He remembered what the wizard said to him before he departed.

This choice, like all others, is something that will stay with you until your time is done. That is the beauty of the Creator's design. Our choices make us. But they do not make us who we are.

It seemed so strange when the wizard taught him the specifics of the ritual. Odo was made to repeat the instructions until memorized in full. A lesson learned that was never to be used. A ritual whose completion had consequences. Consequences mentioned, but whose details were never expressly enumerated. When questioned as to the reason he needed to learn such a thing, Remfrey's response was, per usual, cryptic.

You never know what you need until you need it.

Setting the satchel outside the circle, Odo looked down at the assemblage, checking and double-checking, mouthing the words to confirm each detail. Digging beneath his robe, he retrieved the talisman, removing it from around his neck. Holding it in his fingertips, he closed his eyes as he mumbled the incantation. Over and over he did it, eyes clenched tight, concentrating, the quiet words droning in his ears. As if in reply, the light in the stone grew brighter. Sweat poured from his brow as the sage, emberbalm, and the dried tomfrout root smoldered from the hidden arcane power being released. Before long, the light penetrated the flesh of his fingertips. The bones of his fingers revealed themselves as dim silhouettes suspended in a casing of red. Over and over he repeated the words, reverent and quiet, perspiration dripping from his brow, Odo utterly lost in the sound of his own voice.

Weak from his labors, Odo stumbled back to the campsite like a drunkard. Exhausted, heavy-lidded eyes spied a dying fire, pale tongues of flame reaching up from red-hot coals. He collapsed to his knees with a huff as his staff tumbled from his hand, falling clumsily to the ground. He paused for a moment as he gazed at the fire, panting, knowing he had to tend it, and loathing his watch. His hand trembled as he took tinder and cast it over the coals, coaxing the flames to rise higher.

Setting a dead hunk of branch over top, his mind repeated the warnings of the wizard concerning power. Rarely did a cross or scornful word ever pass the lips of Remfrey. A flame licked up at the dead wood of the pine bough as he added another, a bead of sweat running down from his brow and settling into his right eye. The sting of salt made his eyes blink rapidly. As the infant fire grew, Odo searched his heart, recalling once more the events of the day. In a hostile world, and in an uncertain time, had he done the right thing? Or would the wizard curse his foolishness for what he had just done?

Lobbing one more twig, Odo pulled back, fearing he might fall forward. As the light returned to the hasty camp once more, a long stare set into his eyes as he pondered the choices he made. One of the horses grumbled in the dark as if knowing what it was that weighed so heavily on his soul.

CHAPTER 6

Covering his nose and mouth with his sleeve, Odo approached the dead corpse. The smell was atrocious—acrid, foul, and sickly sweet. It reminded him of the time when the wizard sent him off hunting with old Jacks. They felled a modest buck, dressing the game in the field. Odo vomited twice from the stench and the feel of the slick vitals in his hands. The words of Remfrey came back to him quick and clear as the memory of the event rolled through his head.

Sometimes life is unpleasant. Better to learn this early than to be fully grown and facing its realities for the first time.

This was no downed stag they stumbled across on the moor. They were the remains of a man. His chest and belly were burned away, a gaping hole yawned down the front of his torso. Slick and charred, the flesh there was black, ash mingled with the mass of innards, wet with crimson blood.

It was Inoch who discovered the site of the ward and followed the drag marks where the heels of the dead man marred the ground. The victim had tripped the trap and his fellows dragged him off into the bushes, leaving him there to unceremoniously rot. Odo saw first-hand the deadly effectiveness of his art, and that alone made him physically ill. He ran from the site, and in a gastric fit vomited the contents of his stomach onto the fringe of the moor. Something about taking the life of a man sickened him more than the stench of death that hung thick in the air.

There was no mistake or error here. He had killed a man.

His head jutting out, hands on his knees, Odo let his satchel hang down and his staff was cast into the weeds. He held that stance, bent over, spitting twice to get the foul taste from his mouth. The heaving never seemed to cease, partly instigated by the smell that wafted up from the ground and partly from a surge of sorrow and guilt. The realization of his act crashed through his heart and mind like the ravaging waves of a storm-swept ocean. Over and over he retched, unable to halt the convulsions of his body and secretly unwilling to try.

As the waves of nausea waned, Odo did his best to stand. Threads of thick saliva hung down from his lips, his eyes wide and bloodshot. A glassy look set into his gaze as he momentarily disconnected from the world. Righting himself at last, he stumbled around discombobulated. Somewhere in the chaos of Odo's brain it occurred to him to wipe his mouth. Lifting his sleeve, he suddenly halted, realizing he may need to use his sleeve to block the stench of the man he killed. Instead, he dropped his hand and grabbed the fringe of his cloak, spitting in the vain attempt to remove the bile from his mouth.

As Odo stumbled and staggered, Inoch crouched next to the victim, dagger out. Gently he used the tip of his blade to lift the charred flaps of what clothes remained. The body was stripped clean of its effects, and the dead man's companions left little behind save for the ruined clothes he wore and the thin linen undergarments beneath them. Dark and lifeless eyes stared up at an overcast sky. Black curly hair splayed out, twisted and tangled in the scrub. His face expressed the last moments of his life—mouth open and eyes wide in terror.

In his inspection, the mercenary captain delayed for a time on a spot. Using the tip of his dagger, he lifted a piece of burnt black leather that was once a doublet. There on the pale skin of his shoulder was the black ink of a mark—or what remained of it. Something that vaguely resembled two circles intertwined, most of the tattoo having burned away with the man's flesh. Above that, the remains of a diamond, resembling a crude representation of an eye centered between the symbols below.

His attention focused on the markings for an uncomfortably long time. When he was done, Inoch withdrew his blade, letting the flap of the ruined cloth drop. Rising slowly, he took the fringe of his cloak to wipe his dagger clean. As he did this, he spat angrily at the corpse as if it somehow insulted him.

Looking back for a moment, then turning away, Odo continued to clean himself up. It wasn't the bracing chill of the morning that made his hands tremble. Over and over in his head, he heard the voice of the wizard speak to him, a splinter of time lodged in his memory now tormenting him each time his mind recalled it.

Every life is precious to the Allfather. 'Tis a shame it holds no value for many He had made.

Forcefully stuffing his dagger into the sheath on his belt, Inoch turned about. He started to make his way back to where Odo stood, then stopped, observing Odo in his state of distress. Eyes down, Inoch sighed dismissively, shaking his head in disbelief and disgust.

"Your first kill?" Inoch said as his form cut the grass and foliage that surrounded the site.

Instead of turning about, Odo continued to spit and wipe his mouth with the fringe of his cloak. His lips and chin had been long clean of whatever offal might have remained. He continued in this way, not knowing what else to do. The last thing he wanted was to turn around and see what he had wrought.

"I'm talking to you," growled Inoch as he came alongside Odo.

Odo, for his part, was shocked as he looked up at the captain. The normally placid expression of Inoch and the virulent disinterest of his pale blue eyes were replaced by the vague semblance of emotion. Subtle and hard to discern, it didn't seem to be fear or pity. Odo guessed it to be more like anger.

Odo started to back away. He didn't get far. Inoch's hand reached up and grabbed him by the shoulder. The mercenary shook Odo as one might shake an apple tree, forcing the fruit to drop. "Get ahold of yourself. This is no way for a man to act."

No way for a man to act. The phrase stilled the wizard's voice in Odo's head. Somewhere between the tremulous hands and the fog in his brain, Inoch's forceful shaking rattled things into place. He was no longer a boy. He was a man now. Remfrey even said so.

As the mercenary withdrew his hand, Odo stopped his staggering. Standing still now, he let his head fall as if in shame. There were no tears. What remained was remorse and regret.

His disdain for the young man seemed to fade, the expression on Inoch's face changing to one of annoyed exasperation. He breathed deeply before asking again, "Your first kill?"

"Yes, captain," replied Odo in a muted sort of shame.

Looking to the horizon as if collecting his thoughts, Inoch was slow to continue. "The first? Never easy," he said in a sort of a grumble. Gazing at the ground, he shifted left and right before looking upwards. "They passed here not long ago. The blood is still wet and none of the carrion birds have found him. We are still well ahead of them." Looking back over his shoulder he added, "They will follow our tracks, return here and know for certain we know they follow. It will buy us time."

"What now, captain?" asked Odo sniffing as he lifted his sleeve to rub his nose.

"We follow the forest fringe and ride day and night," answered Inoch as he casually trod through the trampled brush. "Come!"

Odo was reluctant to follow at first but traced the path of Inoch through the tall vegetation of the moor.

Stopping where the horses were tied to the trunk of a tree, the captain produced a bladder of water and unstopped it before holding it out. Odo reached for the skin before Inoch pulled it away. "Cup your hands, boy!" Inoch rebuked. "I'll not have a mouth full of bile on the lip of my skin!"

Doing as Inoch instructed, Odo watched as water filled the bowl of his hands. "Rinse and spit," commanded the captain.

Twice they performed this routine as Inoch commented, "Always clean your mouth when you purge. Saves the teeth."

Odo tried to remember anything the wizard told him about having to rinse after vomiting. Oddly enough, he couldn't recall a time when he did, or at least not immediately. It was then he realized that Inoch was speaking to him in a manner that seemed almost...friendly.

As Inoch stoppered his supply of water, he instructed, "Take a drink from your skin, but only one. And take a crust of bread. I need you able for the ride. It will be long and hard."

Odo moved to his horse and started to search for his supply of water as Inoch continued speaking. "You may not think it now, but that ward you set may have saved our skins."

Unstopping the skin, Odo took a mouthful of water and swallowed, saying nothing as he did.

Keenly aware of the silence, Inoch continued, "Killing a man is not like killing a beast, much less the man-beasts of the south. Thank that God of yours that you had cause."

Odo was reluctant to speak at first, digging through the provisions packed for him in his saddlebags. "Master Remfrey says that murder is the bane of our kind."

Inoch came around the front of his horse, taking the reins. He stopped several paces from the young man, wrapping the leather straps around his fingers. "Easy to say for a wizard who hides in his tower. Out here, those who do not kill themselves oft pay the likes of me to do so in their name. That is the world." He paused for a moment and looked away. "I was not much younger than you when I slew my first man. He was the son of a magistrate. A pig of a man. He tormented my mother and our brothers, taking from us what he will."

The lifeless chill returned to Inoch's gaze as he continued, "One day he comes alone. He wanted more than a piglet or a lamb. I was chopping wood when I heard the screams. Axe in my hand, I went to the house. My brothers, they tried to stop me."

Inoch fell silent, prompting Odo to ask, "What then, Captain?"

"I wedged the axe so deep in his skull, it took two to pull it free. I fled. Now, I live the life of a freelancer."

His gaze focused briefly on where the dead man lay, then the captain's head turned back to Odo. "The man you killed? A pretty little boy like you? He would have done worse and more. Remember that before you continue to wring hands over words of a wizard who knows nothing of the world."

The shame Odo felt was brief as it swept through him, soon to be mingled by the revulsion he felt for what he had wrought. Whatever emotions swirled in his heart were kept in check by the sober understanding of the gravity of the situation. That, and the intimidating presence of a mercenary who, no doubt, did not suffer open anguish and shed tears. Odo's head went down as the captain spoke, then up again. "Who was he? The...the man I slew."

"Remember how I spoke of the War of the Five Princes?"

Odo nodded.

"He was a Watcher."

The big eyes of Odo narrowed as his lids closed slightly and his brows turned downward. "Watcher?"

"They mark themselves thus," Inoch replied, using his left hand to tap on Odo's right shoulder. "Your King Merrith? Been at war with them for years. Fanatics who work with shadows and secrets. Led by blind priests, they are everywhere...nowhere. Now they follow us. Many I have killed in my time as I took the gold of Horunass, fighting their wars."

"Evil men?"

"'Evil' is but a word, boy," replied Inoch. He looked away for a moment, reconsidering his words. "But, if such evil exists, they are not far from it. If they catch us, we will die and not so quick." He turned and looked at Odo with a hard stare. "You remember the code of one such as me, yes?"

"Yes, Captain," answered Odo with a nod. "Blood and gold and keeping both."

At that, Inoch let slip a shy smile, as brief as it was. The bright eyes of Odo went wide with surprise; he was inwardly shocked at the uncharacteristic show of emotion. "Bright boy," remarked Inoch. "Now, mount up."

A greater sense of urgency hung over them now as they moved hard and fast along the fringe of the lonely forest. Travel was easier on the moor, despite the undulating land. The wind picked up, cold, moving east at first, then finally south. In time, they continued once more into the sparse trees along the fences of much thicker woodlands, the pair pushing into stands of pines that reached high to the gray sky above. Tall, pointed spires of evergreens petitioning sunlight from beyond the veil of clouds. The gnarled limbs of oaks spread out from thick trunks like the many arms of sleeping giants, frozen still in their near-winter sleep. Along with them sprouted the erect bodies of hibernating maples and aspens, their skin silver and white. Leaves and needles crunched and cracked beneath the hooves of the horses as they galloped towards their goal.

The sun was beginning to set by the time they reached the banks of the river. Odo was sore from the near-constant travel. His back ached, the insides of his legs chaffed. His cheeks burned from the cold that buffeted his face as they rode. He tried his best to not walk bow-legged in front of the captain as they watered their horses at the stony edge. By now the clouds had started to clear and the western sunset was bright. A world of brown and drab green was painted orange and gold by the rays of the dying sun. The beasts that bore them all this way drank greedily from the water's edge, desperate from a hard ride over long miles without nary a drop to drink.

Odo, himself hungered, pulled off a small hunk of bread to eat. The loaf itself had gone stale and hard, though it was still in the range of edible.

"Save some of that," the captain warned. "We may yet need it for the beasts."

Odo rooted around in his satchel and produced half a loaf yet uneaten, holding it up for the captain to see. He dared not speak, his mouth full of hard bread whose consistency was reaching that of leather. Chewing it took effort.

"Good enough," the captain muttered low. His stare went to the rise where they had just come from. His spyglass in his hand, he paused to think. "Stay with the horses," he commanded without taking his eyes away from the nearby hilltop. Odo seated himself on a large stone, tore off another chunk from his crust, and went about the effort of chewing it.

Inoch crested the hill and stood erect this time. Extending the eyeglass, he put it to his eye and slowly scanned the northern horizon for the longest time. When he was done, he collapsed the device, turned, and made his way back. Halting many paces from Odo, he scanned the sky, noting the position of the sun.

"Unbridle the horses, and let them graze," said Inoch. "I will keep watch on the hill.

"Captain?"

"We will not make the city this night. I see nothing on horizon. We are far ahead. I rather feed the horses than ride them starving."

"Where shall we shelter?" Odo dared inquire.

Inoch gave him a hard stare for a moment, then relented. "I know of shelter. Now, be quick about it!"

Chapter 7

Inoch cursed the darkness as they fumbled their way forward, blind, unable to distinguish wilderness from open field. Odo offered to use magic to provide at least a light to find their way. Cryptically, the captain refused. "It will wait."

Making camp was out of the question, Inoch never offering a reason why. "Keep moving," he said in a grunt. "Not in the open." Odo thought once, maybe twice, to demand an answer. Still, there were bandits at their back and Inoch was intimidating at best. Pestering questions seemed futile, if not without a measure of peril.

The wet-sweet vinegar tang of rotting apples wafted to Odo's nose as they trudged their way into a grotto of trees. Loose leaves, recently fallen, sighed at their passing. In the dark, all the trees looked the same. Thin, dark fingers persisting in the dense black of night, their digits gnarled and twisted. Tall or small, their size was the only distinguishing difference. The odor grew stronger as they moved deeper in. They were at a farm or a homestead. Something with an orchard, but one left to go wild, as evidenced by the roll and squish of fallen fruit beneath their feet. When the tree line gave way to open pasture, Odo heard something he hadn't heard before—something that sounded like joy coming from the captain's lips.

"There you are!" The rumble of the words said slow and silent made Odo look up. Not far in the distance, wreathed in the night's inky embrace, he detected the dim outline of a large building. A barn, perhaps.

Hastily they made their way around the perimeter of the structure. Being closer now, Odo could see vague features, feel the rough grain of the slats with his fingers. The timber was old and weathered, boards bent and gaps growing between. The young apprentice and his horse stumbled over pieces of siding that had fallen away into the tall grasses, left unattended over the years. The captain whispered to himself something in a foreign tongue—one that Odo didn't recognize. When they came to the very end of one side, they halted. "Give me that light, boy."

Odo let loose the reins of his horse. Cradling his staff, he crouched and felt around the thick, unruly grass for a stick. Laying hold of a shard of rotting timber, still wet on the underside, he reached beneath his clothes and pulled out the wizard's talisman and removed it from around his neck. Wrapping the chain around the fingers of his left hand, he palmed the stone, burying it in a fist. The timber slat he held in the other hand, holding it at arm's length away. As he muttered the incantation in a whisper, the end of the stick popped and sparkled once, then twice, but never lit. Odo sighed hard, vocal in his frustration. This time, with his eyes closed, he repeated the words. After a pop and sparkle, a brilliant white light erupted at the end of the stick.

The horses snorted and nickered, shuffling back in fear. Inoch withdrew and shielded his eyes with his hands at first before adjusting his gaze to the light. "Keep it down, boy!" he grumbled.

"I cannot dim it," Odo weakly protested.

"No, hold it down! Out of my eyes!"

Immediately Odo lowered the light, placing it at his side. Only then did the captain slowly lower his hand, rubbing his eyes as he did.

Blinking afterwards, Inoch began his investigations. The gaps of the boards showed the first traces of how dilapidated the structure was. Just how broken-down the building was remained unclear. Split and shattered timbers lay everywhere, barring a good portion of the doorway. These Inoch quickly cleared away, leaving a gap wide enough for both man and horse to enter.

"In," Inoch ordered, pointing to the interior of the barn.

"This barn is old. The roof might give way at any moment," protested Odo, half cringing as he did, fearing the freelancer's wrath.

Forcefully, Inoch pointed at the entrance once more, barking at Odo. "In!"

Brow furrowed in frustration, Odo's heart thumped faster as he stepped through the doorway and into the blackness beyond, the captain following quickly behind. White light filled the expanse, highlighting every crack, crevice, and groove within the structure with light or shadow. Odo stopped just inside the entrance, his eyes scanning the ruined construction above. In its prime, it might have looked impressive—a fine place where many animals were housed. It was larger than any out-building Odo had seen in the village near the Crooked Tower. Now, however, it was a ruined relic, forgotten, emptied, and abandoned. Mighty timbers which once held up the roof had long given way at the far end, the roof all but sunk into the ground. Slats and shingles were missing here and there, dark gaps in an otherwise regular orderly arrangement of cut timber and shaved wood. A pigeon or two fluttered about, their nightly nesting disturbed by unforeseen daylight. Otherwise, the place was empty. A fact made evidently clear as they pressed further into the expanse within.

Debris had fallen from above, forming a winding passage through the wrecked remains of the barn. Odo could see fragments of wood among the structure and debris, the whitewash not yet worn off by time and the elements. The floor was naught but dirt and moss and pieces of shattered, rotten wood. A stray stagnant puddle formed here and there, the ruined roof no longer a shield against the rains. Vines and creepers invaded along the edges, some dead and wooden, others still living, though barely so. Stubborn plants, their invasive nature was unwilling to yield to a shaded interior. Some pushed back through the missing gaps in the wood siding, others reached out or coiled on the fruitless ground. The hay once stored here had been transformed into moldering compost. Only miniscule fragments remained as evidence of what the mounds once were. All these things Odo noticed, along with the dank smell of dying wood and decomposed vegetation. Inoch, however, seemed to observe their surroundings in a uniquely different manner.

"Good!" the captain exclaimed with a nod. "This will do."

Inoch moved quickly, commanding Odo to follow. As they reached the midpoint of the interior, he ordered Odo to wait. Exiting to the outside, Inoch brought the horses in one by one, putting them in the back behind another pile of debris.

"Make a fire," said Inoch, calling out from where the horses were kept. Odo could barely see him past the tangle of fallen beams, shingles, and dead vines.

"Where?"

"Where you stand, and no further."

"I will need to douse the light," explained Odo.

"Do it! And be quick!"

Making a fire wasn't difficult. While water penetrated from gaps in the roof, some places remained dry. Odo fumbled a bit, having only one hand to work with. Setting aside his staff, he cleared away a bare patch of ground with his hands and feet before filling it with fragments of broken wood.

Inoch returned as Odo finished tenting together several small pieces of wood. In one hand, the captain gripped a long wooden stock affixed with pieces of iron. In the other he held an elongated slender iron bow, a thick bow string attached to the ends. Clumsily weaved between his fingers were three wooden quarrels with hooked heads that looked small but vicious.

"The light is going out," Odo warned.

"Do it," said the captain, his forward strides coming to a sudden halt.

Casting aside the light, Odo knelt next to the arrayed sticks. Once more gripping the amulet as his makeshift light started to dim into nothingness, he laid his free hand over the tented wood. *"Arros el saidu inflama."* He spoke the words weakly, vainly commanding the forces of the arcane.

Nothing happened.

"Arros el saidu inflama!" he exclaimed, and this time louder. There was an orange spark as a small yellow flame leapt and quickly died.

"We have no time for this, boy," Inoch grumbled, clearly impatient. "Can you make fire or not?"

"A moment!" snapped Odo, frustrated and annoyed by his own failings. "This is not as easy as a ward!"

The captain went mute.

This time, Odo collected himself, inhaling deeply and summoning his wits. Eyes closed, he wrapped his fingers tightly around the talisman.

"*Arros el saidu inflama!*" His voice squeaked, boldly trumpeting the words. This time, fire sparked along the lengthwise side of the arranged wood, the whole of it immediately catching flame. Feeling the heat, he withdrew his outstretched hand quickly, rubbing his fingers together as if they were burned.

"Good!" Inoch drew near, pushing the tips of the quarrels into the ground before assembling the pieces of his crossbow. The darts stuck up like fletched straws as the captain set about affixing the metal bow to the front of the stock.

"Will you need more magic?" Odo asked. Inoch was preoccupied with assembling his weapon. One hand on the stock, the other fiddled with a tool shaped like a coin. This he used to secure the bow onto the stock of the weapon.

"No," Inoch replied, barely looking up from his work. When the pieces were assembled to his satisfaction, he put the bow end on the ground, slid his foot in a slot, and used both hands to pull back the bow string and hook it into an iron latch.

"You read books, yes?" Inoch said, grunting. "Ever read of a Nightarie?"

"No." Odo had read many things in the wizard's library, but nothing called a *Nightarie*.

"Troublesome thing from the last war," Inoch continued as he held up his newly assembled crossbow. "If there be a wizard among our hunters, they will send one."

Hesitating, Odo dared ask the question that formed in his mind. "What are they like?"

"Head like an egg," answered Inoch, checking his weapon. "Eyes like fish. Spikes for teeth. They only come in the night." Taking a moment, he looked around at the interior of the space before adding, "This place is good. One way in. One way out. If one comes, it will come through there," he said using the crossbow to point at the entrance.

"So, what must I do?" Odo's concern was plain on his face.

Inoch lowered his weapon, his gaze cast towards the fire. "Stay here. Feed the fire."

"Are you saying to me that I am bait?"

Inoch lifted the crossbow. "Can you aim this? And reload?"

Brows creased, Odo stammered back, "I...I...no."

"Then you are bait." Rethinking what he had said, Inoch's head tilted slightly to the left. "Less bait. More...*distraction*."

Standing erect, the captain then bent over and withdrew the quarrels, plucking them out of the earth one by one. "Stay here. Feed the fire. The horses will know when it is close. They will tell you." His instructions given, the mercenary captain made his way through the debris, heading to the partially collapsed portal. Peering out and around, he checked the sides and the sky before slipping into the darkness somewhere, leaving Odo alone in that wretched place.

Feeding the fire was no great task, Odo having lots of fuel to choose from. He returned the talisman to his neck, took a seat on the ground, laid his staff by his side, and waited. Minutes passed, and in time he fell into reflection.

He shivered as the images of the dead Watcher came back to haunt him. The smell of burnt flesh and sour vitals. The blackened flesh and the gore. Buried deep in his heart was the knowledge he had killed a man. And not just that he killed a man, but that he had used the power entrusted to him to do the deed. The guilt leaked from his heart, welling up in his gut like a sickness in his bowels.

There was no reason to doubt Inoch as to the nefarious nature of the man he slew. A part of him tried to rationalize away his direct participation in the act. He was, after all, ordered to lay the ward, was he not?

Still, a part of him worried desperately as to what Remfrey might think. What the Allfather might think. Was the fear he felt justification enough to have done what he did? Should he have protested harder?

A horse snorted, but only one. There was silence afterwards. Throwing another chunk of wood on the fire, he fixed his eyes on the hypnotic dance of the flames, leading him deeper into thought and despair. From the moment he left the wizard's holdfast, he felt evermore lost and alone. This wasn't the passive sort that lingered within him in the company of the wizard. It was an itchy sort of discomfort, like ill-fitting clothes or dining with strangers. He longed to return home again, where everything made more sense. His chores, his routine. Morning porridge and the taste of fresh noontime bread from the kitchen. Searching the meadows for important herbs and...

Another snort of a horse, followed by one more. Hooves pounded dirt and dead grass. A throaty grumble. Somewhere in the distance, past the decayed wood of the barn, a deep fluttering sound was heard. It was barely audible above the crackle and hiss of the fire, further obscured by the noise from the mounts. It came and it went, but the reaction of the horses remained unchanged. From the cold ground he scrambled to his feet, his eyes towards the holes in the roof above. Straining, his ears opened themselves wide to the sounds of the night, his eyes closed, and his mind focused on the senses that remained. The low whoosh of something large passed overhead, emanating from one of the missing roof slats above. His head turned in reaction to the sound, seeking its source as his eyes opened. Again, the ruffling of wings in the air, and then quiet. The anxiety of the horses grew fevered, moving from snorts to grumbles, nickering, and shallow cries. Hooves pounded the earth as the creatures paced nervously.

Odo reached down and grabbed his staff. Standing quickly, he pulled the talisman from his clothes and clumsily pulled it over his head. The loop of the chain caught beneath his nose, painfully rolling off as he pulled harder. Wrapping the chain around his hand and setting the stone within, he clutched tightly the dense brown wood of his staff with both hands. Setting his feet apart, he held his Hazelwood staff almost perpendicular to his frame, as if ready to spar. There was a rush and rumble, another, and then something thumped hard at the far end of the barn. Debris fell from the rafters and a fragment of a cracked shingle fell to the ground below.

One of the horses thumped a supporting beam of the wall, causing the structure to groan. Odo barely noticed. He no longer concerned himself with the horses or the hazards of the crumbling structure. His attentions were directed exclusively to whatever had landed on the roof. The pop and sizzle of the fire was replaced by the ever-frantic sound of his beating heart. It almost made it hard to hear as he listened to the thing moving about over his head. Click, clack! Click, click, clack. Back and forth it went along the shattered spine of the main timber. Each time it did, something fell—wood, dust, bits of dried moss. A telltale trail of falling debris that tracked the movements of an unseen predator. Odo watched with a singular anxious intensity, his body pivoting with the sound. Each pass the unseen thing made along the roof, it drew closer and closer to the opening. By now, the horses had broken free of whatever crude corral Inoch had fashioned for them, retreating away from what they sensed above.

It was near the entrance, the supports at the one end of the barn creaking and groaning beneath the sudden weight of what perched above. His feet slid apart, Odo taking a defensive stance. His fingers gripped his staff with a white-knuckle intensity and a sickening feeling festered within as if his innards were melting. Pulling his staff closer, his breathing became labored, pushed, and pulled from between clenched teeth. Odo's eyes fixed their gaze on that black gaping hole that was the only entrance and exit. He knew it was coming. Time seemed to stand still. The world around him vanished, replaced by the abyss beyond those rotting timbers and a wickedly brittle silence. The stone pressed hard into the flesh of his palm, the pain all but unnoticed in the building panic. It was coming now. At any moment.

He heard the fragile shingles snap and give way as the creature launched itself from its perch outside. He saw it move in a flash from the darkness past the doorway. It swooped in, sinister talons gripping the wooden debris with a crunch. Landing on a nearby pile some ten feet away, the very presence of it made Odo's brain snap. He froze like a rabbit beneath the glare of a stalking wolf. Panicked. A primal instinct surged, something long forgotten but making itself known in a most inconvenient way.

From its talons to the top of its egg-shaped head, it was all of five feet high. Though to Odo in that moment, it looked as if it were fifty, the young man stunned and wide-eyed with fear. An oblong head on a goose neck, the creature had big bulging eyes that put those of Remfrey to shame. Set wide apart, they turned and moved independently of one another, as cold and mindless as a fish in a net. Flat-faced, it had slits for nostrils and a great gaping maw filled with needle-like teeth, long and wickedly sharp. Yet, as horrible as the thing was to behold, it was adorned with shimmering plumage of blue, red and yellow, like the colors of some bright tapestry. Colors that continued their way into the slick flesh of its head.

Glorious and terrifying all at once, Odo stood there transfixed and awed despite sensing it was far too close for comfort. One eye looked at him, then the other. As if announcing its murderous intent, it splayed its mighty wings in a grand display, puffing up the monstrosity, making it look far larger than it was. It moved its head up and out, and that fiendish hole below the nostrils opened and let out a cry Odo would forever hear in his nightmares.

A second's silence ensued. The world turned on its end as Odo stood frozen. His ears heard the whisper of a whistle, then a sickening thump. The creature croaked, its head flung back and twisted around as it flapped its wings reactively. One wing fell, but the other stretched and twitched. Swaying, it did a strange little dance on its unsteady perch, trying to remain righted. Awkward and noisily screeching, it turned to face the blackness behind it. As it did, Odo noticed something caught below the joint of its left wing, preventing it from functioning—a fletched bolt from Inoch's crossbow. As it struggled, there was the sound of another thud as the mercenary launched another missile at the Nightarie. The creature lurched forward, overcompensated, and fell back letting loose another croak from that frightening maw. This time, the sound was agonizing and long. Wood snapped and tumbled as the thing rolled to the ground, got up, and jumped up on the pile once more.

By now, Odo had come to his senses, breaking out of his daze. As the Nightarie's head extended up from its body, exposing the back, he aimed the end of his staff for the bright plumage of the beast in front of him.

"YEN-GIRIN-MAR!" Odo screamed, the words spilling from his lips like a curse. The tip of his staff glowed an electric violet, and from it a bolt of light and energy flew like a bullet. The violaceous missile hit its mark dead square on the back of the creature's head. There was a sound like the cracking of a whip as the smell of bitter smoke and burnt feathers expelled into the air. The Nightarie spun about, wavered, stumbled over, and fell with a screech, disappearing from his view behind a pile of debris, momentarily hidden, save for an outstretched wing whose tip reached up heavenward.

Seconds passed. Inoch appeared in the doorway, looking first at Odo, then to the winged monstrosity. Laying aside his crossbow, he let the last unused bolt fall to the ground. Pulling a dagger from his belt, Inoch approached the beast warily as it flapped and twitched. With one hand out, he shuffled forward a pace, then waited. Moving as the creature moved, the wary mercenary waited until the conditions were right before he fell upon the abomination. Holding down the creature with one hand, he stabbed it repeatedly, grunting with each thrust of the blade. Over and over he did this, each savage strike succeeded by a vile sound of steel slicing flesh, heralding the monster's demise. Odo watched as the outstretched wing twitched rapidly, relaxing after the final thrust.

Inoch rose slowly, his eyes never leaving that feathered monstrosity. With a sniff, he used his sleeve to rub his nose. Then, those pale eyes turned to Odo, the pair exchanging glances. This time, Inoch's eyes were not absent emotion, but burned with a failing cold flame—the dwindling rush from conflict and battle. Without blinking, Inoch gave Odo a shallow, respectful nod, wordlessly signaling the appreciation that would never come from his lips.

Soon after, Inoch turned away, leaving the scene of the carnage to collect his things. Whatever was said in that brief and silent exchange, Odo sensed it heralded a fundamental change between the two.

CHAPTER 8

Odo barely had time to inspect the beast they slew the night before. The sun hid just below the horizon, its light all but a rumor as he scanned the carcass. Earlier that night, Inoch had dragged the thing out of the barn, pulling it around the side, mostly to calm the horses. Even now, it still had that wretched charred stench, the haphazard result of Odo's magical bolt.

Odo plucked a bright red plume to be preserved as a macabre souvenir. Holding it up to catch whatever light the sky afforded, he marveled at his prize. Despite its origins, it was beautiful. Rippled red and orange, there was a pearlescent glint that made it shimmer even in the darkened gray morn. And unlike the dead man they left charred and ruined by the side of the trail, there was no sense of guilt this time. No shame in taking a life. Odo pondered the mystery of this as he observed his little prize, eventually tucking the token into the confines of his satchel. The dying grass hissed its protest as he tramped his way back to where the mercenary stood.

Inoch was preparing the horses for their journey, pulling taut the straps on the saddle of Odo's horse, laboring some distance from the ruined barn. The very scent of the creature made the beasts nervous, deceased or not.

"I do now recall something of these beasts," he said to a distinctly disinterested Inoch. "Though in the scroll, they were not called Nightarie."

Inoch grunted, less of a confirmation of what Odo said and more of an indication of his struggle with the saddle.

"They are not some recent creation." Odo paused for a moment, recalling the details of what he read. "The scroll did not mention the eyes, but did note the colors of the feathers and the shape of the head."

"Dead is dead," remarked Inoch as he walked around the other side of the gelding.

"How did you know that they could only be slain from behind?"

Inoch tested the saddle to make sure it held firm to the horse. Afterwards, he went about lashing heavy bags to the wooden braces of their pack horse. The creature snorted and swerved as the weight was applied, the best protest it could muster under the circumstances.

"Three dead men," replied Inoch as he adjusted the bags, making sure the weight was distributed equally on the horse's back.

"What I am saying is," Odo went on, "this is not some new creation of these Watchers. It is something far older. I believe they were used as messengers in the time of the Great War. The thick hide along the breast was used to protect against Elanni arrows."

Inoch returned to Odo's horse. There, he stopped and turned. Laying a hand on the hindquarters of the mount, his dispassionate stare said it all. "We have no time for this. Our hunters may have moved in the night. We need to be off. Now. So, if you do not mind." He motioned to the saddle.

Odo approached, handing him his staff. This time, Inoch was quick to help, holding the staff, and giving him a lift from behind. Doing so allowed Odo to slide his foot more easily into the stirrup. After Odo was situated in the saddle, Inoch handed him his Hazelwood stick before departing to his own beast. It was a simple courtesy. Something never offered before, though it was done with a mood that was far from cheerful.

Prodding his horse, he used heel and reins to guide his mount over to where those of Inoch waited. Watching the mercenary ascend the saddle, Odo dared to speak. "You knew this place was here. And you knew that thing might come for us. How?"

Inoch took the reins of his horse, barely taking note of the question. "First rule of war," he replied. "Know your enemy. Know the land." He prodded his horse forward.

Their pace was not as frantic as it was the day before, and it was a matter of a couple of hours before the presence of civilization made itself known. Split-timber fencing partitioned pastures where lumbering cows grazed lazily in the chilled morning air. Long tilled parcels were left bare. Orchards of trees waited to be tended and pruned for the next year's yield. The heralding crow of a lone, unseen cockerel echoed through the flat open lands. Of those that occupied these settlements, some watched briefly while some stared and gawked for an uncomfortable time.

Inoch was keen to the reaction of residents and travelers along the road, their shocked and fearful expressions and the hard sudden stares at Odo. As they drew nearer to their destination, Odo could almost feel the anxiety building in his protector. Passing a way station, the pair paused to water their horses, eating what was left of their loaves, the bread now tough and thoroughly stale.

Approaching Odo, the captain reached out and raised Odo's hood, pulling it as far over his head as he could. Odo resisted at first, surprised by the move. Inoch, however, was unyielding in his insistence, the young man relenting after a second attempt.

"Keep yourself covered, and your gloves on," Inoch said as he chewed on the hard bread, a crust in his other hand.

"Captain?"

"Your skin."

"My skin?" Odo sounded insulted.

Inoch's fingers reached into the space of the hood, his knuckle brushing against his chin. Odo pulled away, the touch unwarranted. It was a reminder of his tanned skin, the one undeniable feature that distinguished Odo from every other person he had ever known or seen. Something about the realization or Inoch's recognition of this fact made him bristle inside.

"They may think you a Cathar," said Inoch.

His chewing slowed, Odo looked up at the mercenary with wide and angry eyes. A mute protest for the sudden change in tone.

Inoch looked both ways on the road, making sure they were alone. Bending down, he looked at the young man in the shadows the hood provided.

"Cathars are hated in these lands."

Grumbling in his protest, Odo defended himself, "But I am not a Cathar."

"Dark skin, dark hair," Inoch replied coldly. "To them, you are all the same. Maybe if you lived among them, it might be different. Strangers are strangers. They see what they see. And they will see Cathar. Hood up. Head down. Best they wonder who you are."

Lifting himself straight again, Inoch pulled off a chunk of his stale bread and consumed it.

The remains of the loaf he divided in half and offered to the horses.

The mounts consuming the bread, Inoch clapped his hands together to rid them of the crumbs. "We will be on the ship soon. Safe. Get you out of sight. Then you walk about naked for all I care. But in the city, I want no trouble. Understand?"

Odo grunted his answer, the bread suddenly turning bitter in his mouth. He spat out what remained onto the ground. The stare of those they passed along the road unnerved him at first. Knowing the reason why struck him at his heart. Whether it was his youth, or the presumptions made by strangers as to who he was, their revulsion of him was like a thorn burrowed beneath his skin. One he could not easily remove.

"Understand?" Inoch made it less of a question and more of a command.

"Yes, Captain," replied Odo, his words as bitter as the bits of bread that still stuck to his teeth.

"Good."

A tense silence lingered between them for a time, Odo stewing beneath his hood.

"If you are done, give the bread to the horse," said Inoch.

Odo thought about this, scanning the bread, his stomach no longer desiring food. At once, he offered the loaf to his mount. The horse was quick to accept.

Inoch stared at Odo for a time, gauging his mood. "Do not hate them," the captain said quietly. A strange and oddly compassionate thing for him to say given his nature. "I have killed many in my time. If I wore a brand of a murderer, they would hate me just as much, even as I fight to protect their walls. A grudge dies hard. Old hatreds live long. It is the way of the world. The only justice is what gold brings. Remember that, Odo, and the world will not trouble you."

The pair remained on the road, following it up a rise. As they crested a hill, Odo dared to lift his head and catch the only glance of the city proper. Built upon the rise of a rocky shore, sheer walls the color of well-tanned skin rose from the scattered buildings of the outer city, some fifty feet high. Rectangular towers pointed skyward like the tines of a crown, appearing along the wall in regular intervals. Each was topped with a low sloping roof on which a banner was raised. The cry of gulls sounded in the distance, their white forms dotting the sky both near and far away as they wheeled about overhead. The sun did little to warm the air. Many streams of gray smoke reached skyward, issuing from chimneys and outside ovens from the many homes and constructions in and around the walled city. Threads that lazily reached skyward, bending and swirling as the breezes caught them. Beyond this was a dark blue sea riddled with caps of white from the waves that crested and fell against unseen shores. A long breakwall stuck out from the shore, jutting out into the waters, resisting the crash of the waves. Within the encircling arm of stone, still waters reigned as ships of many sizes came and went. Large vessels anchored in the deeper, rougher waters. Smaller skiffs moved slowly, bobbing over the cresting waves. The nets of fishermen that piloted these vessels searched for the bounty that lay hidden beneath the undulating blue.

Structured, smoky, and bustling, the city was a stark contrast from the holdfast of the wizard. The solitude and emptiness of the open moor was a far cry from the masses that milled about the buildings and in the streets. A population of staggering proportions to Odo, who was more accustomed to a village of a few hundred, at best. From their distance on that rise, the scene struck Odo as being chaotic, majestic, and troubling all at the same time.

As they breached the outskirts, the distant majesty gave way to an unsavory reality. Mud roads and stagnant puddles formed where recent rains collected. The eyes of the residents gazed on in suspicion as the duo passed, Odo feeling the stares through his clothes. He could see them pause and gawk, Odo daring to peek just beyond the hem of his hood. Smoke hung thick in the air, giving the world around him a sort of indistinct fog, the color washed out of everything he saw. Then there was the smell. Acrid. Musty. The sour smell of fish long past their due. Barkers calling out for people to buy their wares, the hammering of wood, and the neighing of horses. Gulls baying from above, ravens croaking their displeasure on the rooftops. The shrill screech of a woman chastising her husband while others laughed. The hooves of their horses as they thumped and squished against dense dirt and mud.

This was all a shock to Odo. His world was the tower, the hills, and the village where they sometimes traded. Tall meadow grasses as far as the eye could see, foxes and hares, a lonely stag on a hilltop. The distant howl of wolves roaming the open spaces in the dead of night. This place, however, was alien to him. Dirty. Smelly. Noisy. Hard faces and hollow eyes. With his head bowed, it only allowed him enough space to see the rear of Inoch's pack horse. This he followed as close as he could, fear and frustration hounding him. The hooves of their mounts clobbered and sloshed through the main street in a slow, thoughtful pace to the main gate.

Even the clothes the people wore looked worn, drab, and dirty. Those few residents Odo could see with his downcast eyes seemed haggard and old, tired and worn down by the world. Odo dared not look long for fear of the captain's warning. Still, their faces looked as sour as the smell of rotting fish as they shambled about with backs bent. It was as if the burden of the city had been borne on their backs for years unnumbered, leaving them broken and weak.

Waiting at the main city gate, Odo took a chance to inspect the construction of the fortifications. The main passage through the walls resembled a tall arched portal bored through a smooth tan exterior. He spied a coat of sun-aged plaster that covered whatever lay beneath, mottled and sometimes uneven. His mind harkened back to something he read about the construction of fortifications and the use of things like plaster to protect them. Whoever tended to the city's defenses was careful to keep the exterior well maintained, with lighter areas providing evidence of recent repairs.

Gold exchanged hands between Inoch and a guard, the bribe for passage being acceptable. Not long after, Inoch turned and barked, "Odo. We go."

The interior of the city was not much better than what lay beyond the walls. Paved and cobbled streets made for swift passage, most lanes littered with garbage and filth. Shallow ditches were filled with brown water, Odo caring not to guess to what purpose they served. Narrow alleys broke off from a main throughfare, avenues crisscrossing the city like a chaotic web of stone-covered paths. It was the tendrils of this web they traveled, moving lane to lane, eventually turning into a curved, cramped alley. Then through another.

People were everywhere. They passed a street bazaar where a hundred merchants and vendors hawked their wares. Covered tents made from colorful cloth were erected along the side of the lanes, tables positioned without and within.

Goods were stocked atop for trade, each merchant keeping vigilant watch for potential thieves.

Children mobbed the pair as they passed—street urchins, roaming in packs, abandoned by their parents. They crowded around, hands up, begging, a few nimble fingers reaching for their bags.

Inoch saw the thieving hands and with a harsh, threatening voice cried out, "Get back, lest I take your fingers!"

Yet, it wasn't Inoch who frightened them the most. One of the children managed a glance at Odo beneath his hood. Quickly after, the multitude of grasping hands withdrew, and the whispers began. Fearful, the mass of children backed away as if being too close was to invite death itself. A Cathar was among them. Something feared worse than deprivation, starvation, and the plague. At first, this ground at Odo, angry that the color of his skin was viewed with fear and loathing. Then the words of the wizard came to him.

Remember, Odo, not all bad things are bad, and not all good things are good. Sometimes you need to look for the blessings in disguise.

One thing was for sure, they were left unmolested from that point on. Passing by the street vendors, Odo caught glimpses of the goods in the stalls. Colored beads, dyed and patterned cloth, wine in bottles and kegs. One sold dried fruits in open bushels, arrayed like shrunken and shriveled nuggets in all the colors of the rainbow.

The stink of the fish mongers wafted to Odo's nostrils a recent catch brought in from the docks. Dead, gutted fish looked up at him as he passed, mouths agape and glassy-eyed, laid out like stacked lumber on beds of salt. An ooze of red-tinged water dripped from the tables, the smell making him retch. The stink reminded Odo of the man he slew. He, too, sported the same look in death. An image Odo wished he could forget.

Thankfully, their trek through the open bazaar was brief. Before long they were lost again among the alleyways and side-passages. Taking one alley after another, the pair eventually came to a halt. Above the rumble of the street and the distant shouts of strangers, Inoch cursed low and loud.

CHAPTER 9

"Rojo! Rojo! Maddie. Pretty Boy. Snickers. Curse you, come out!" Inoch bellowed like an angry bear. Odo and his protector waited in the shaded narrow lane stationed outside a three-story tenement. When no response came, Inoch repeated the shout, this time with the names in a jumble. "Get out here, you dogs!"

This is where their long trek from the Crooked Tower took them. An urban building whose plaster fascia was tanned and cracked by the elements. Brown brick and gray mortar lay exposed where some of the plaster cracked and fell away. It was one building among many of its type, hastily built with no plan or blueprint other than the design that existed in the builder's head. Plain on the outside, such dwellings made for strange habitations due to the many quirks of their construction. Around the corner, a tall set of doors on the second story exited out to a crude balcony made of bare logs and bent branches. The additional supports that supported the platform seemed dodgy at best.

The door rattled as Inoch laid his fist to it, barred from within. The wood of the door was old, weathered, thick enough to be an impediment, but too thin to withstand someone determined. The doorway itself seemed like an afterthought cut out of the existing wall, a plaster coating making it uniform and smooth around the edges. Above it and to the right, a window was cut out of the wall. Crooked and splintered shutters flanked it, in desperate need of replacement. Cobbles lined the alley, which wound down and around in a curve and disappeared from view. Many such habitations were along this path, though the lane itself was lonely. Perhaps that was the reason Inoch chose this very location.

A shrill whistle passed Inoch's lips, followed by silence. Another was issued, unanswered.

From above there came a commotion. A voice rang out, muffled by thick walls and distance, "Yes, Captain." Several seconds passed, and the shuffle of wood on wood was heard as the bar was removed from the door. Soon after, the door creaked open, coming to rest as it banged against the stone of the interior hall.

"Who is on guard?" Inoch inquired with a scathing tone. "Who left their post?"

Odo kept his hood up and his head down as he sat there perched upon his horse. A voice answered the captain, as low as the bottom of a dry well. "You were gone—"

"Be glad time is short," Inoch replied in a menacing growl, "lest I flog you and the fool who left."

Another set of feet were heard to scuff along the stone pavers, and a form passed Odo. "Who is this?" This voice was feminine in nature, but the tone of it sounded as keen and cutting as a newly sharpened blade.

"Never you mind," Inoch replied to the woman. "Get the bags inside." Inoch's attention shifted to Odo. "Dismount and come with me."

Throwing his leg over one side, he all but fell from the horse, his feet feeling the hard stone beneath the leather of his soles. Following along the line of horses, head down, he stopped when he saw the legs and feet of the captain. Suddenly, the hood came back as Inoch pulled it away. "Won't need that for now."

Anxiously, Inoch scanned the streets and the buildings surrounding them, wondering if hidden eyes noted their arrival. "Follow me," he said, stepping up from the street. Past the doorway he plunged, Odo following after.

Someone else filed in behind Odo, the wizard's apprentice taking little interest to discover who it was. Just past the door, they stepped into a small, windowless entry chamber. Thick beams, roughly cut, ran at regular intervals along the ceiling, the marks of the adze that formed them clearly visible along their length. To the left of them, a stone stair ascended upwards to a landing, shifting left and disappearing from there. Each step was stained nearly black from years and years of use, countless feet treading over their surfaces. Before them lay a hallway where shadows gathered, the hint of a door at the end. The light that shone down from above gave evidence of a room beyond. It was here Inoch turned to Odo and asked, "Did anyone see beneath your hood?"

"The children, I think." Odo could hear the person following behind huffing and puffing beneath the weight of the load she carried.

The cacophony of many feet sounded out as a train of forms ascended to the second floor. The harsh voice of the woman behind Odo cut through the noise they made. "Street rats," she said with a tone that was hard and strained. "They won't say nothin'."

It was another two steps amidst panting and grunting that the woman groaned, "What's in these?"

"Soon," Inoch replied.

As they reached the landing, a sour musk assaulted Odo's nose. It was a pungent stink of many men corralled in a small space with little water available for proper washing. Far different than the musk of those that ventured in the wilderness, Odo observed, which was tempered by the smell of smoke, ash, and diminished by cold. No, this was heavy and hard, with each step upward a blow to the senses. Odo coughed before he reached the top stair, the reek of it hitting him hard.

At the top was a claustrophobic foyer that led to a much larger room on Odo's right. Here, the smell was most profound, despite open windows to air out the place. The strength of the odor made it abundantly clear that those quartered within hadn't bathed in some time. A small window and a set of double doors were opened for the free flow of air. There was no breeze to carry it away. Stray particles of disrupted dust revealed themselves in the golden rays of the sun.

Several crude cots with mattresses supported by rope netting were laid out against the orange walls, in a room barely big enough to contain them all. Like the exterior, the plaster that covered the brick beneath had chipped and broken from years of neglect. Greasy smoke stains marred the walls from countless nights where lamps burnt, along with brown stains where oily hands errantly scraped across them. A shallow balcony jutted out to the alley where they came to stop, the wooden double doors cracked and weathered, having collapsed against the sides.

In one cot, with his legs over the side, sat a man of middling height, rubbing the sleep from his eyes. His dark hair rose over the top of his crown, the sides of his head shaved to a stubble. With his boots on, he had remained fully clothed while he slumbered.

"Get up and help Maddie with the bags," Inoch commanded, looking directly at the man.

"Yes, Captain," the man said as he rose, drowsily passing Odo as he made his way to exit the room.

Inoch pointed to the bed where the man lay. "Odo, sit there."

Odo did as commanded, sitting on the uncomfortable stave that framed the cot. Raising a hand to his mouth, he stifled a cough. Sliding back a bit, he ended slipping into the dip in the center of the mattress, resting his back against the wall as his legs flew upward in response. Even through his cloak and his robe he could still feel the warmth of the man who lay resting there only moments before.

Piles of gear were deposited around the room, some beneath cots, others arranged haphazardly on the floor and in the corners. "Where is Pretty Boy?" growled Inoch, looking around the room.

Maddie went to the opposite end of the chamber and let the bags fall from her shoulders. "He *was* supposed to be keeping guard," she said in a huff before unfolding to her true height. She was nearly all of six feet tall, her curly blonde locks cut short at the top of her head, the remainder of her hair trimmed neat along the sides. A stained blue tunic covered a shirt of mail, her arms bare. Lean and muscular, almost to the point of being lanky, she was every bit of a man as were the others, save for the bulges high on her chest. Neither homely nor pretty, she was none the less imposing. And her voice was as hard and sinuous as her arms.

Maddie exhaled her relief as she straightened her tunic. "It was his hour for the watch."

Inoch replied in a grunt. Then another soldier entered, this one having skin the color of molasses. He was tall, broad chested, and had thick arms commensurate with his stature and strength. As the heavy bag slipped from his shoulder, landing with a thud, the dark man stood upright, nowhere near as winded as his female compatriot. Half-a-hand taller than Maddie, he was intimidating despite having a face that bordered on kind. Long black hair was knotted into a sheath of braids that ran the length of his back.

"I go find him," the dark man said in a deep, rolling tongue. His speech was uncouth and short. Like Inoch, the words he spoke were clearly not his native tongue, his vowels smooth but pronounced. Odo remembered the names the captain called out, and through a process of elimination, determined that the dark man was Rojo, a name common to the Cathar, or so Odo once read.

"Who this?" Rojo asked, motioning to Odo.

"The mission," Inoch answered. "Where is Pretty Boy?"

"On guard," Rojo replied.

Inoch turned in place, cursing quietly. "We have a ship?"

"They wait. They complain. Do not like to wait."

"Make them ready," Inoch said, pointing at Rojo's chest. "We move to the ship before sundown."

"Why not now?"

"I want some sleep," replied Inoch, "and a few words with Pretty Boy."

Inoch scouted the interior of the room, sniffing as he moved towards the double doors. His head looking up and out, one hand shading the sun, he peered around the sides both left and right. Pacing silently as Maddie took a seat on a cot near the rear of the room, he looked restless.

Maddie eyed Odo up and down with hard choleric eyes. On her right wrist dangled a bracelet that looked to be made from fragments of ivory, though Odo was reluctant to look too long on the tall woman. A hump on her nose revealed it had been broken some time in her past. Her upper left canine was absent, leaving a gap in those amber-tinged teeth of hers. As she scanned Odo up and down, she quickly became distracted when another member of Inoch's crew appeared at the top of the stairs. His huffing and puffing as well as the sigh of his steps announced his arrival before he appeared at the topmost landing. And when he entered the room proper, one arm stuck out as he tried to balance a huge load slung over the other shoulder. Passing Odo, a wave of unwashed smell followed in his wake, eventually unloading his burden at the back of the room with a groan. Promptly, he fell into the cot next to the bags, the ropes that held aloft the dingy, stained mattress letting loose a groan beneath his weight.

Kneeling where the baggage was piled, Inoch set about untying one of the flaps of a bag and flipping it backwards, leather slapping against leather. From within, he retrieved a small sack of burlap stuffed to the full, a leather strap tied at the top. With it nestled into the flesh of his palm, his long fingers wrapped tightly around the contents like a precious mug of ale to one deep in his cups.

There was heft to it as well. Maddie stood puzzled as Inoch handed her a bag. Nearly dropping the sack at first, the weight of it took her unawares. As her second hand came swiftly to support her first, her hard blue eyes filled with a strange sort of wonder. Her fingers turned pink then red as she gripped the bundle, the contents within having a distinct sound of metallic objects grinding together. The weight, the sound, and Maddie's odd reaction said as much to Odo as if he had looked inside the pouch itself. It was either silver or gold, a large cache of coins stuffed snugly into a rough burlap sack whose fibers were barely strong enough to contain them.

"Snickers," Inoch muttered as he retrieved another stuffed sack. Passing by Odo, Inoch unceremoniously dropped the bundle on the man lying on the cot next to him.

With a huff and a grunt, Snickers swiftly removed the weight that pressed hard against his stomach. After coughing, he sat up and examined his newfound prize, stunned and scratching his head.

Inoch returned to the saddlebags. He rose with a third bundle in his hand and strode over to where Rojo stood, roughly pressing the sack of coins against the broad chest of the Cathar. The precious metal within rumbled and creaked as Rojo's hands rose swiftly to take hold of what the captain delivered.

"What's this?" Maddie said, clearly befuddled. Her voice clanged like that of an iron pan hitting the ground.

"Gold."

"Captain?" mumbled Snickers, his eyes slits.

Odo watched as Snickers and Maddie looked to one another, the same wordless question passing between them. In unison, their lips stretched and turned upward slowly into a smile, brimming with avarice and joy.

"That's half," added the captain.

"Half?" Maddie's mouth fell open. "What's the mission?"

Inoch turned and cast his gaze at Odo. He paused for a moment, his eyes scanning Odo up and down before answering. "Him. We deliver him to Horunass. More awaits us there."

"Why so much?" Snickers said holding out his golden parcel. "This is near a king's ransom."

"Don't matter," answered Inoch before turning back to Rojo.

To Rojo, Inoch spoke in low tones. "Watchers on our trail."

"Watchers?" piped up Maddie. Motioning towards Odo with the hand that grasped her fee, she added, "For him? He's a boy."

Inoch's head craned around, his voice somewhere between a bark and growl. He chided Maddie. "Don't matter. But that's why when I say to post a guard, you don't leave your post. Barely been a year since we've seen action, and the lot of you have gone soft."

Turning back to Rojo, Inoch softened his tone. He started to speak but suddenly went silent. The soft scratching of footsteps was heard from the doorway, the sound of leather soles against stone. Inoch's attention was focused past Rojo, waiting to see what appeared at the top of the stair.

Confused at first, Rojo turned to look upon whatever his captain was eyeing. Soon after, a man appeared in the doorway. He was of middling height and young in contrast to the others. Pale skin and fresh-faced, he had dark curly locks cut short at the sides, the remnants pulled back into a thin ponytail that hung down in the back. Wearing a woolen vest over a linen shirt and an oddly matched pair of linen trousers, he was not as imposing as the others. Lively eyes complimented a kind demeanor. When he saw the captain, his face lit up and his lips curled up into an attractive boyish smile. It was clear to Odo why they called him Pretty Boy.

"Aye, Captain!" he said with a voice that had a hint of a laugh beneath the words.

Inoch said nothing, the whole of the room going silent. Like a still picture in a frame, reality paused for an instant, a moment in time hung upon a wall for the dispassionate observer to view. This did not last long.

In a rush, Inoch stomped over to the doorway, a terrifying scowl on his face. The smile so cunningly sported on Pretty Boy's lips fell, the young man confused for a critical moment, yielding space as his commander approached, but not nearly enough.

Grabbing Pretty Boy by the hair, Inoch pulled his subordinate from the doorway. In response, the young man yelped as Odo watched in frightened fascination. With practiced skill, Inoch dragged the young man across the room, Pretty Boy's legs struggling to keep up.

Inoch pulled Pretty Boy around him, sending him skidding against the wall next to the double doors of the balcony. The younger of the two slammed hard into the plaster and stone. Having lost his footing, Pretty Boy crumpled to the ground with a grunt. The captain spared no time in letting this set. Reaching down and grabbing his soldier by the arms, he lifted him to his feet. Inoch was more than a match for Pretty Boy, being roughly a hand taller and better built. Inoch's long fingers clutched at Pretty Boy's throat, pressing him back against the wall with a force the younger of the two could not counter. Desperate hands gripped at Inoch's forearm as Pretty Boy struggled, his face turning red, his breath hoarse from constriction.

As Rojo moved in to support his captain, Inoch spoke in a malevolent snarl. "Why did you abandon your post?"

"Captain!" Odo stood up sharply, the satchel pulling at his shoulder. Earlier shocked into silence, he did his best to protest.

Inoch's reply was swift and hot. His enraged eyes cast a glowering stare at Odo. "Quiet you! Sit down."

Rojo also turned. Looking an exasperated Odo up and down with a disdainful stare, he merely said in a clumsy tongue, "You sit as captain tell you."

The Cathar and Inoch worked as a pair as the mercenary captain continued his interrogation. Inoch barked his questions, Rojo supporting him with his intimidating presence. "Where were you? Speak quick!"

Pretty Boy struggled to speak as his face twisted in pain. What few words passed his lips were naught but hissing and squawks, his captain's fingers squelching the flow of air through his throat. As his hand fruitlessly wrung at Inoch's fingers, he eventually squeezed out a few words. "I...I was...ladies."

"Ladies?" Inoch answered as he leaned in. "Are pretty girls worth the lash? You forget what happens to men who leave their post?"

"No...no...Captain."

Maddie and the other soldiers stared intently at the scene, Maddie eventually sporting a satisfied smirk. Finally done with his questioning, Inoch pulled Pretty Boy forward only to slam him hard against the wall. Pieces of plaster came loose, falling as Pretty boy slunk to the ground, some of those pieces landing in his hair. Inoch spun about to face the others.

"Look here, all of you," Inoch snapped, his voice filled with steel and stone. He pointed at the sack Rojo cradled in his hands, his head turning one way then the other as he continued his beratement of the others. "That be more gold than I have seen in ten years of blood. And another sum awaits us in Horunass when we deliver Odo alive. I intend to collect. So, remember your discipline."

Looking directly at Maddie, Inoch commanded, "Maddie, take guard." Looking around at the others he added, "The rest of you, get the gear to the ship and meet back here."

Turning to face Rojo, he approached closely and spoke softer. "Sell the horses. Don't set a firm price. Get what you can. Don't attract attention."

"Yes, Captain," Rojo said with a nod.

Hand balled up in a fist, his thumb sticking out, Inoch pointed behind him to Pretty Boy. "Get him out of my sight."

"Yes, Captain."

At once, Rojo started barking his commands. "You heard Captain. To your feet! Grab bags. Go. Now!"

At once, the others started to move, Rojo heading towards the slumped form of Pretty Boy. Still rubbing his neck and clearing his throat, he interrupted his activity to angrily slap away Rojo's hand extended in aid.

Rojo shrugged before turning towards the stair, eventually departing the room. Pretty Boy placed his hands on the wall behind him and lifted himself from the ground. Making noises in his throat, he shot Inoch a hot but pained glance before he shuffled a path to the doorway. Maddie followed close behind, one of the heavy sets of bags draped over her shoulder. Inoch stood, supervising. One by one, the others came back, grabbing their gear, then departing. Inoch took special note of Pretty Boy, staring him down as he came and went. Pretty Boy, for his part, did his best to ignore his leader, keeping his head down and avoiding Inoch's gaze.

When the room emptied, Inoch moved toward a nearby cot and started to lie down.

"Captain?" Odo piped up.

Turning his attention to Odo, Inoch locked eyes on the wizard's apprentice. The leader's glowering stare made Odo feel all of three inches tall. "You are the mission. You do not tell me what to do. Or tell my men what to do. Understood?"

"Yes, Captain," Odo answered, his head bowing in fear and shame. At that moment, Odo rather preferred the cold dead stare than the searing rage Inoch sometimes showed. Odo mumbled, "What shall you have me do?"

"Nothing." Inoch turned, pacing a bit, looking around the room. His rage seemingly abated, he slid into a cot, pulling his feet up and over, not bothering to remove his boots. "You remain with me while I get some rest. When I wake, I take you to this Vagmar whom the wizard spoke."

"Yes, Captain."

A moment of silence passed. As Inoch prepared to close his eyes, his head lifted suddenly and tilted towards Odo. "And stay away from the windows," he grumbled before letting his head fall back.

"Yes, Captain," answered Odo in a furtive whisper.

CHAPTER 10

In the amber glow of candlelight, Odo scanned the crystals as Vagmar laid them out one-by-one on a crimson cloth. They were tinier than he imagined, the largest of them roughly half the length of his index finger and no thicker than a pea pod straight from the vine. Hexagonal in form, their tips formed hard points as sharp as a pin, the pale violet color of the rough gems tainted by orange-yellow candlelight. Of those laid out for display, one was straight and plain while another bent slightly, the formation of one segment having merged with the other. Several visible fractures formed deep within the matrix, making it unsuitable. One was flawless, uniform in color with no dark inclusions. Yet, the one that caught Odo's eye was mottled with clouds of pale blue within like a dim fog trapped forever within the stone.

"That one," Odo said, pointing to the mottled crystal.

"Are you sure?" A balding portly man with a scraggly beard, Vagmar had thinning hair, as much gray as it was brown, the ends of it curling inwards. Dressed like a dandy, his gaudy shirt of red, green, and yellow had a sheen to it, the light of the candles reflecting off its surface. It was clear he was fond of his wealth, wearing it with a lurid sort of relish. On both wrists he sported bands of wrought gold. Rings with cut stones adorned his fingers and a gold tooth glinted in the light whenever he spoke.

Odo nodded in reply to Vagmar's question.

Odo didn't know what to expect when he stepped into the dim hovel of the trader's niche. Located on some nameless alleyway in the city, the establishment was tucked away, unmarked, and anonymous. Only Inoch followed Odo inside. The others were ordered to wait outside and stand guard as the late afternoon sun started its descent.

It smelled musty and dusty in that place, the light of the candles doing little to push back the dense shadows. Bolts of cloth sat atop nameless boxes stuffed with goods. Clay jars filled with wine littered one side of the wall along with fat pots that held oil. Near the back, a crude counter was erected surrounded by nameless things covered with sheets and blankets.

Vagmar bent down slightly, his meaty finger tapping one of the flawless crystals. "For an adornment like no other, this one is among the best you can find. No voids. No occlusions. No faults in the stone. And the color? No heating required, if cost is an issue."

"No, good sir," Odo replied, pointing once again to the mottled crystal. "That is the one I require."

Inoch shuffled around impatiently as Vagmar straightened. The merchant's head bent to one side and the fold of flesh beneath his chin quivered. "Are you sure?"

"Yes," Odo replied with a nod.

"Is that staff Hazelwood?"

Odo pulled his staff closer to him, wrapping his arms around it. "Why do you ask?"

"That's something a wizard might pick," Vagmar answered.

"You ask too many questions," Inoch muttered menacingly, the merchant's sudden interest troubling him.

"I assure you, if there is one thing that my profession values above all, it is discretion." Vagmar offered an unsatisfying smile, his golden tooth flashing in the dance of the candle flame. "Your business is your business, especially for a friend of a wizard. I have made many a transaction with their kind over the years, acquiring some rather obscure items. Though, I must say, I have yet to meet any so...young."

"How much?" Inoch grumbled, his cold displeased stare fixed on the husky merchant.

"Fifteen."

"Fifteen?" Odo replied, sounding shocked.

"Discretion has its price," answered Vagmar as slick as lamp oil.

Inoch's withering stare lingered on Vagmar for a time, causing the smile on Vagmar's face to fade. The merchant's hands came up and his fingers began to fidget and play with one another in the tense, lingering silence.

"Perhaps a jar of wine to sweeten the deal? Eh?" Vagmar's voice had a nervous uncertainty to it. His stare jumped rapidly between Odo's bright eyes and the hard stare of the mercenary captain.

Inoch's drooping lid enhanced the unsettling nature of his gaze. Odo was already accustomed to the tense, threatening quiet of the mercenary captain, though he did not like to lock eyes on Inoch for over long. Now Vagmar was getting his fill.

Vagmar's voice quavered a bit. "A fine vintage, straight from the hills of—"

"Two jars," Inoch countered.

"Two?"

"You deaf?"

The merchant considered the deal for a moment. "Done."

Slowly, Inoch went for the purse cinched to his belt, hidden beneath the coat he wore. As he brought it out into view, Vagmar's eyes enlarged as he saw the size of it. Gold rumbled and ground as Inoch pulled out a handful of coins, letting them drop one-by-one on the table. As he did, Odo picked up the gem he wanted and stuffed it into a pouch on his belt.

Near breathless and with a broad smile, Vagmar laid his hand over the small pile of coins. "A pleasure doing business with you." His golden tooth blinked once more, catching the candlelight as he moved, the coins rumbling as he slid them off the table.

Throwing up his hood, Inoch took one of the jars in one hand before cradling it in his arm. Odo followed suit. Positioning the earthenware jar on one shoulder, he clumsily balanced his staff in the other. The jars were long and slender, the exterior of the container that held the wine was rough, pulling against the coarse weave of his cloak and robe. As the liquid contained within sloshed back and forth, Odo struggled to hold it firm.

The late afternoon sun blazed as Inoch opened the door to the outside. Odo's eyes stung in the bright light, and for a moment he was blinded. He kept his head down so that the cloth of the hood better hid his face. His eyes blinked rapidly as they adjusted to the dying sun. As he stepped over the threshold and entered the street, his ears detected the cries of gulls as the door behind him closed with a thud.

There was a certain art to following Inoch as they made their way to the docks. Odo remained mostly stooped for the purposes of obscuring his identity. From time to time, he looked up and saw a familiar face. Maddie one time, Pretty Boy at another. The mercenaries were both ahead and behind them, just on the periphery. They too had their hoods up, their faces obscured by cloth masking their nose and mouth. Keen-eyed, they maintained a moving vigil for any that might cross Inoch and Odo's path.

Odo's arm began to hurt. His hand cramped under the weight of the wine jug as they neared the docks. His ears detected the creaking of wood and the splash of water against stone. The cries of the sea birds rang out, mingled with the shouts and rough voices of men who plied the seas. Daring to look, he spotted the tall lean form of Maddie shadowing his left, the thick muscular body of Rojo just ahead of her.

Their steps made a hollow sound as they thumped over the wooden boards of the docks. Thick planks groaned beneath the weight of many feet, reverberating into charred timber posts whose exterior was covered by pitch. Below them, moving rhythmically back and forth was the water of the sea.

Odo had always wondered after the waters of the western oceans and the Great Inland Sea. The books he read described them in many forms, from dark and brooding, stormy and treacherous to the emerald colors of the southern coasts— waters that were said to glow in the presence of moonlight and stars. Yet, such romantic descriptions did not apply here. The water below him seemed sickly, bordering on diseased. The color was a nauseating greenish brown specked with refuse. A dead fish floated atop the water just beyond the edge of the dock as well as a half-eaten fruit. With them, bobbing on the ripples was something brown whose origin Odo dare not guess. And it smelled horribly, the entire location having a distinctly fishy and unwholesome reek. There was nothing romantic, clean, or intoxicating about it.

Maddie grunted her displeasure. "I hate being dockside."

They turned this way and that before they stopped, a deep voice hailing them as they came to a halt. By now, Odo's arm and hand were screaming for relief. Much to his surprise, dark fingers reached out and grabbed the handle of the jar he was carrying, pulling it away with a single swift motion. The sudden change in weight put him off-balance and he nearly fell backward. A hand reached out and clumsily pulled back his hood.

Standing before Odo were three tall men whose skin was far darker than his own. Two were clean shaven and bald while the third was clearly older, sporting a balding crown bordered by tight curls of hair peppered both black and white. All three were imposing figures, each one standing six feet tall or taller and as thickly muscled as Rojo beneath their woolen jackets and linen shirts. Only an inch or two smaller than the others, the older of the three had hard eyes, perhaps harder than those of Inoch. A great beard sprouted across his jaw, wooly, thick, neat across his jowls, coming to a point past his chin. Beneath it was a face marked with scars of a long-healed pox, his brow lined with creases. Stouter than his comrades, he had a slight belly, his hands visibly chapped and scarred.

The other mercenaries crowded around tightly, screening Odo from spying eyes. The older man pointed to Odo in curiosity. "This?"

Rojo moved around Inoch. In his hands he held two bags, each the size of a grapefruit. Odo could hear the muffled clink of coins as Rojo handed one bag to the man with the beard and the other to one of his companions. The sheer weight of the coins and the size of the bags astonished those that held them. Confusion yielded to silent exasperation as the sable-skinned men looked to one another in wonder. A dark hand bobbed as if weighing the contents within.

"If this be a trick, I warn you, I'll leave you to the sea." The man with the beard growled. Pointing to Odo, he added, "Him first."

"It's all there, and more," Inoch replied, his face turning hard. Motioning to Odo, he continued, "Count it on the ship if you like. But get us off this blasted dock. Him first."

The dark men parted as Odo was led to a wooden ladder. Halting at the edge, the young man peered down and spied a boat waiting below. There, two other men sat in a dinghy, their skin as dark as the others on the dock. These wore rags on their scalps and were dressed in breeches and vests of wool, their arms exposed and their feet bare against the water that had seeped into the bottom of the boat. He deduced quickly that they were part of the same crew, and a quick glimpse to his left made it clear now where they were going.

The gathering of sailors and soldiers stood at the end of a dock. In the distance, inside an encircling breakwater, three ships lay anchored, merchant ships by the look of them. They appeared as Odo imagined them, having read the descriptions of such vessels in books. Tall on the water, raised decks covered both aft and bow. A pair of them were two-masted vessels, the larger one having three, their sails rolled and lashed to the yardarms, each of them anchored and resting peaceably in the still waters of the harbor.

As Odo swung around to mount the ladder, he felt two strong hands aid him in his descent. The rough splintered wood of the rungs was dry at the top but promised to be slick at the bottom. Low tide extended his travel to the dinghy below, much to his general loathing. While the rungs looked clean, the darker wood belied a coating of muck and slime that once clung to the fibers, fostered by the water. The knowledge of this, in conjunction with the odor wafting up from the water, made him cringe as he lowered himself to the awaiting skiff.

His descent was not easy. The stone inside his satchel bumped on the rungs. The fringe of his cloak was constantly catching on the crags of the weathered wood. His staff was an encumbrance. Due to the stress of the situation, his hands began to sweat inside his gloves. Yet, if there was ever a time he most desired his bare hands covered, it was here and now given what once clung to the rungs of the ladder.

Near the end, two hands grasped at his waist, holding him firm as he clumsily transitioned into the boat. The dinghy began to shutter and sway, the sickening water around it lapping the sides and splashing his boots. Warily, he found a place to sit in the back, stepping over the bench where the oarsmen sat. Maddie followed soon after, though she was far more deft with the ladder, making clear she had done this numerous times before.

One of the oarsmen turned to look back at Odo as she passed. With a smile on his face he asked, "Your momma?"

Maddie scowled as both oarsmen began to laugh. With a swift and angry pull, she brandished the dagger from her belt—a long silvery thing as vicious as the hand that wielded it. Her intent was clear. No one was going to talk to *her* like that.

"Maddie!" Inoch barked from above.

Odo watched as she stood there glaring at the mocking faces of the oarsmen whose smiles had not diminished in the least. Slowly, she returned the dagger back to its sheath, though the scowl remained. Her anger raging, she thumped Odo on the arm with the back of her hand.

"Move over," she grumbled.

The oarsmen laughed as Odo slid to the far side of the dinghy, away from the dock. Maddie sat, her rear hitting hard against the wood of the bench as the boat rocked back and forth. Pretty Boy followed, taking a seat near the bow.

The human cargo secured, the boat shuddered as the oarsmen pulled in the lines that held them to the dock, coiling them inside the bottom of the boat. Maddie eyed the sailors with scorn, the smile on their lips still broad and beaming.

Odo cringed at the very notion of having to grab anything that had been soaking in that water.

Pulling out their oars from their pivots the sailors used them to push away from the dock before settling into their places on the center bench.

"I ain't your momma, boy," Maddie growled beneath her breath, just loud enough for Odo to hear.

The dinghy pulled away from the dock as the oars dipped into the water and pushed. Only then did Odo look up at the dock, inspecting the timber pillars that held up the walkway. Barnacles and a sickly green sludge clung to the blackened wood, encasing them nearly the whole length. It was a curiosity to him, the life that clung to those posts, causing a tingle to rush up his arms. It was something alien to him, slimy and mottled, something slick and clutching beneath those conical shells. The books he read mentioned nothing of them, nor of the messy details of what lingered beneath the waves. A part of him was glad to be gone from the dock. Another part of him dreaded the voyage to come. And as the dock grew smaller in the distance, Odo longed to have cold hard earth beneath his feet once more.

CHAPTER 11

It was clear by their accommodations the Sarajwebo was not a ship commissioned for comfort or pleasure. A two-masted vessel, the mighty oak of its decking and hull was cunningly crafted and sturdy, its berth well suited for hauling cargo. However, the room in the forecastle provided for the group was musty and cramped. There was only a brass porthole for a window and hammocks made of rope strung across the walls for beds. A crude table was nailed to the floor. Odo placed his things at the foot of the table, near where the others unloaded their saddles, tack, and gear. Two buckets were placed near the door that had a faint but rancid smell. He dared not consider what they might be used for.

A dagger in his hand, Odo knelt on the floor carving a void in the top of his staff. This was to receive the crystal he purchased from Vagmar. Hazelwood was a struggle to fashion, the wood being dense, hard, and known for dulling an edge of even the finest steel.

"What are you doing?" Pretty Boy said as he lounged in a top hammock. He strung a length of woven leather between his fingers as he passed the time. The rope netting that held him aloft twisted and bent as he rolled onto his side.

In the dim light, Odo struggled with his task, pulling out one sliver after another and cutting them off with the tip of his dagger. He was careful to keep as many of the fragments as he could, laying them atop his satchel next to him.

Odo didn't bother to look up as Pretty Boy made his inquiry. His gaze fixed on the void he was trying to make. "I need to put a crystal in the top."

"What for?"

"For focus. And control." Odo pried another sliver free and gingerly set it atop the small mounds he was collecting. He took a moment to stand, wandering over to the porthole, using the light that streamed inside to inspect his work. Sunlight was dying with the approach of night. Returning to where his satchel lay, he knelt again and resumed his work.

"Do all wizards do that?"

"I am not a wizard," Odo replied. Pausing his work, he rethought his words. "But yes."

"Then why make a wizard's staff if you're not a wizard?"

Odo stopped again and sighed. The steady stream of questions from Pretty Boy had become an annoyance, disrupting his concentration.

"Might I have a candle? It is growing dark," said Odo.

"Right," Pretty Boy said before calling out loudly to Maddie, who stood guard just on the other side of the door. "Oy! Maddie! The wizard needs a candle."

"I ain't his momma," Maddie replied, her hard voice muffled by the wood of the ship's walls. "He can get it himself."

"Oy, Maddie. He's doing wizard things. Get the boy a candle."

There was silence from beyond the walls and then a hard thud that rattled the wood of the door as she shuffled off. Whether she kicked it or hammered it with her fist before storming away, Odo wasn't sure.

Halting his activity, Odo let out a despairing sigh.

As if sensing the inner turmoil of the wizard's apprentice, Pretty Boy piped up. "Aw, now, don't let Maddie get to you."

"She hates me."

"Naw, that ain't it at all. She's just got her knickers in a twist. If she was mad at you, you'd know it."

Pretty Boy's eyes widened as he continued. "Hey, did the captain tell you 'bout Maddie? 'Bout how she came to be with a bunch of ruffians like us?"

"No," said Odo as he returned to his work.

"You seen the bracelet around her wrist?"

"No," said Odo softly.

"Them's teeth."

That got Odo's attention. With the tip of his dagger wedged into the wood, he looked up at Pretty Boy, a question in his eyes.

"Seems Maddie was married once," Pretty Boy went on. "To a man, if you can believe that." His characteristic smile flashed, a reminder of why he was so popular with the ladies as he often bragged. Handsome to an extent, there was little use in denying that his roguish charm was disarming. But it was those friendly eyes spiced with the hint of a wink and a gleam that grabbed the attention of anyone he so desired.

Pretty Boy continued his tale. "A nasty sort of drunk he was, or so she said. He used to come home stinking of ale and wine. And you've seen Maddie. As far as women come, she ain't no prize. He used to beat her, hard."

"Why?"

"'Cuz she was ugly and long. Too tall. Feet too big. Teeth like a river beaver. As much of a man as any if you've ever seen her fight. He hated her bein' so ugly, bein' so tall. So he'd come home and beat her bloody, then in the morning demand she make him breakfast, if you can believe that.

Then one night, he staggered home as drunk as ever. She was toastin' bread in a pan or so she tells it. Well, he boxed her hard 'cross the chin, bein' drunk and all. Somethin' snapped in Maddie.

She came around with that pan, and whack! Hit him so hard, she cracked his skull and sent his teeth flyin' out of his mouth. Not knowin' what else to do, she picked his teeth up off the floor and tried to rouse him, but nothin'. With one blow to his skull, she killed him dead. Right on the spot!

"Killin' your man?" Pretty Boy said with a shake of his head. "They'd hang her for sure. So, she left. Her husband's teeth still in her hand, she stole a horse and fled. I don't know how long it was before she found the captain, but she joined up with him and been a fightin' woman ever since."

The netting of the hammock moaned as Pretty Boy leaned over the edge a little more, his voice lowering, the words coming out just barely above a whisper. "Every man she kills, she goes back after the battle and pries out a tooth for her collection. Then she bores holes in them and strings them through her bracelet. She must have thirty or forty of them on there, wrappin' it around her wrist."

Odo looked up, dumbfounded. His tongue unconsciously grazed the flats of his molars inside his mouth, instinctively checking for any that might be missing.

"If she wanted to kill you, you'd be dead already," Pretty Boy added. "But Captain won't let that happen. And Maddie? She knows how to follow orders."

At some point, Odo returned to his work, only to have Maddie throw open the door with a bang. Wood smacked wood, causing the buckets to jump. Odo looked up quickly, shocked at the interruption.

Maddie stood tall in that narrow doorway, candle in hand. She stared down imposingly at Odo, her dark blue eyes stewing with malice and spite. In her anger she was even more menacing, especially with the hump on her nose. Pretty Boy had described her as ugly, though Odo had a hard time seeing that, even as he glanced at her long face. While time and fortune had not been kind to her and battle had marred her nose, at best she looked plain. Yet the dour expression she showed Odo, frown and all, could easily make a man her size think twice about meddling with her.

Candle in hand, she thumped against the timbers of the floor as if she were purposely trying to make the wood feel pain in her passing. Striding over to the table in the room, she set candle and holder on top. Bowing to stare Odo directly in the eyes, she spoke words with as much venom as any viper. "Anything else, your highness?"

Odo mumbled something that sounded like "no," and that was good enough for her.

Unfolding and spinning about on her heel, Maddie marched out the same way she came in. Grabbing the handle of the door as she exited the cabin, she pulled it closed behind her. Another explosive bang resounded in the room, her fury finding a means to make itself known. The floor shuddered.

Odo paused for a moment, looking at the doorway, trying to process what had just happened.

"Oy," Pretty Boy exclaimed. "I think she likes you good enough."

Odo could almost hear the sarcastic smile that graced Pretty Boy's face as he picked up the stray Hazelwood fragments that were scattered by Maddie's return. One by one, he returned them to the top of his satchel.

The candlelight was a great help in carving out the hole. Odo continued his work, slowly at first, stopping only to glance at the door from time to time. "Why do you call her Mad Maddie, anyways?"

"If you've ever seen her in a fight, you'd know why," Pretty Boy said. "Why, the last scrap we were in, you could hear her laughin' and a-cursin' as if it were all sport. That's how she gets in a fight. Wild-eyed. Smilin' like a madman. Rojo thinks it's 'cause it gives a fright to the enemy. But I think she likes a good scrap."

The wood of the door shuddered, the latch barely holding it shut as it trembled against Maddie's blow. The message was clear, at least to Odo. Stop talking about her. Now.

Pretty Boy just laughed.

"And what about you?" said Odo, quickly changing the subject. "What's your story?"

"Me?" Pretty Boy leaned back into his hammock. His bed of woven ropes began to sway on iron hooks. "I found the captain a few years ago in the war with them Watchers. I think you see why they call me Pretty Boy," he said with a chuckle as his hand passed beneath his chin.

"What about before?"

"Well, I spent a year in the service of the guard of Anon Lethor. I was one of the few who survived the battle of Rosen Fields, early in the war, before the Horunasians invaded to take back the Regency. I was fleein' west when they found me.

Before that, I was a farm boy in a remote village doin', you know, farm boy things."

"Sounds peaceful," Odo said as he rechecked the slot he was forming.

Pretty Boy snorted. "Peaceful? Ever been on a farm? Ever lived in a remote village? Geldin' sheep. Geldin' goats. Separatin' hogs, cleanin' the coop. Six days to till the fields, three days to sow. Then five days with a scythe in the hot sun, reaping the barley and wheat. Porridge in the morning, root stew at night."

He held his hands up from his hammock. "See these hands? Wasn't holdin' a sword that made them hard. 'Twas years of toil and dirt and skin rubbin' against wood.

And the women? If another farmer had a daughter, that was the best you could expect for a bride someday."

The hammock groaned again as Pretty Boy shifted to his right and peered over the edge at Odo once more. Sticking his thumb out towards the doorway, he added in a harsh whisper, "Make Maddie look like a true beauty, they did."

Odo quickly looked to the door, waiting to see Maddie's response. There was nothing. He breathed a sigh of relief.

"I left that nonsense," Pretty Boy said, speaking normal now. "Took what bread I could and headed west. Maybe adventure. Maybe sail on a ship. Didn't care. All I knew is I wanted to be away from there. And there was plenty of folk lookin' for a strong lad for this and that, if you take my meanin'. Sailed a ship smaller than this one, the open top kind. Found some work protectin' a merchant somewheres in the city of Yeussel before the Anon conscripted me for the war."

Pretty Boy fell back into his hammock and began to hum a tune as Odo continued his task. It wasn't long before the channel bored into his staff was complete. He put the knife away and set the staff down onto the floor as he carefully dug through his satchel. From it, he withdrew two small bags and a tiny pouch about the size of his thumb. From the smallest pouch, he emptied the crystal he bought from Vagmar into his palm. Setting the pouch aside, he laid the crystal into the channel, a perfect fit. Odo smiled, satisfied.

Next, he took the other two bags, opened them, and withdrew a pinch of the contents with each. One looked like yellow sand, the other like coarse salt. These he mixed with the wooden splinters before packing the material around and atop the crystal.

Pretty Boy shifted again in his hammock, watching intently as Odo carefully set his staff on the floor. From beneath the folds of his clothes, he withdrew the talisman Remfrey gave him, pulling the chain that held it around his neck and head. Laying the stone of the talisman in the center of his palm, his fingers closed around it tightly. The chain he wrapped around his closed fist, pinching it tight between his middle and index finger.

"Oy, what's that?" asked Pretty Boy.

"Nothing."

"Don't look like nothin'."

"Something the wizard gave me," Odo replied, annoyed. Carefully, he pressed the palm of his free hand against the slot in the staff, covering the shavings and all.

"What's it do?"

Discontent rumbled up from Odo's throat. "It lets me do magic," he said in a low voice. Try as he might, Pretty Boy's questions began to annoy him. He did his best to remain polite and calm.

"Oy, really?" Pretty Boy said excitedly. "Would I be able to use it? You know, to make magic?"

"No," Odo replied in a grunt. Odo's irritation grew, especially now that the talisman became the focus of his inquisitor's probing. Odo didn't like that at all.

"Oy. You sure? Let me have a go." Pretty Boy stuck out his hand and shook it with expectation.

Head down, peering up from beneath his brows, Odo said with a slight snarl, "No, you cannot. It will burn you if you try. Now see here! I need quiet to do this. So, if you do not mind?"

"All right, all right," Pretty Boy said with a vanishing smile. "Do your deed. Act like I'm not here."

There was a part of Odo that wanted to say something nasty in reply. Something along the lines of Pretty Boy being somewhere else. But he cautiously checked his tongue.

Odo's focus returned to the staff. Eyes closed, he pushed down on the wood, one hand gripping the wizard's talisman tightly as he uttered the chant over and over.

"Azurharatha, amaddeyugermana. Aeol, eloiami. Aeol, eloiami."

Three times he repeated, with a fourth strain to follow. Steam began to rise from the hand pressed against the staff. Five times, then a sixth chant as the steam increased. By the eighth time, he stopped, soon after pulling away his hand from the staff. Steam rose in thick curls from the head of the Hazelwood branch. Loosening his grip on the talisman, he unfurled the chain before quickly returning it to hang around his neck. Odo shot a sidelong look at Pretty Boy, his eyes filled with suspicion and concern. Stuffed beneath his robe, the wizard's gift was secure, out of sight from wondering eyes.

Lifting the head of the staff near the candlelight, he blew away the steam and smoke to reveal his work. Anxious eyes scanned the wood looking for even the smallest flaw. He found none. The wood was uniform and the grain restored once again. Only a minute depression remained near the middle of where the gem was encased.

"That will do," Odo said to himself under his breath.

"Lemme see," Pretty Boy said with a smirk and an eager gaze.

Odo rose before shuffling over near Pretty Boy. Lifting-the still steaming wood of the staff, he presented the tip a few inches away from the young mercenary's face.

Pretty Boy's eyes grew wide as a finger reached to trace the wood of the staff. No sooner did the tip of his finger touch the wood did his hand recoil with a snap, the wood still very hot. "Ah!" he exclaimed, following with a slight hiss.

As he flapped his finger in the air, Pretty Boy remarked, "Amazin'!"

As Odo pulled back the staff, Pretty Boy asked, "Oy, can you conjure up some of that good brandy them Valelanders make?"

CHAPTER 12

Odo clung tight to the bucket as the room tossed this way and that. The sour smell of his previous meal, expunged into the bucket, rose to invade his nostrils. He wedged himself against the table and the wall of their cabin, trying to keep the bucket from spilling all over the floor, and him with it. Water dripped slowly from the porthole above, a small leak having formed over the years the ship had been at sea. A cold drop every now and again hit his hair, oozing its way down onto his scalp, eventually forming a channel to his brow. It wasn't much to bear. Still, it made him all the more miserable as he sat there, stomach churning as the boat swayed. Up and down, left and right, sometimes soft, and sometimes abrupt.

The sickness started their first day at sea and only worsened when a storm hit on the second. Now and again, he could hear a thunderclap and rumble as the ship jarred and shuddered. It wasn't even that bad of a storm, as one of the mercenaries put it, but bad enough for Odo to feel like the world was coming to an end.

The others swayed in their hammocks relaxing and chatting. Maddie brayed like a mule every time Odo retched, a rebuke from Inoch following swiftly after. Despite his pitiful state, Odo had a delicate balancing act to perform as the world turned and tumbled around him. The strap of the satchel pulling on his shoulder one moment, the stone within pressing against his chest the next. His leg wedged the staff against the legs of the table while he struggled with the bucket and the rank contents therein. Part of him longed for sleep. Something he knew was utterly impossible.

Nothing he read and nothing he learned from the wizard prepared him for this. Yes, he had knowledge about the sickness of the waves, but knowing and experiencing it were two separate things indeed. Whatever he ate came up shortly after. With each bout of retching there came relief, then nausea once more. Over and over the cycle repeated with maddening consistency, made all the worse by cold and inclement weather.

He now hated the sea and everything in it.

The humiliation of it all was the worst part. As he sat there clutching that stinking bucket in his arms, the world spun. The mercenaries took their pleasure in making it all the more worse. Whether it was Maddie's brash equine laughter or Pretty Boy's constant mentions of frying bacon and boiled eggs, each mocking sound or word felt like pinpricks on his skin. He was the outsider. A weak link in their indomitable chain of fighting and fellowship. Each jab they threw at him was merely a reminder of that fact. Even in his addled state, he could feel the condescension rolling off them in waves. And it never let up, even after one of Inoch's rebukes. It was worse than the city and worse than the fear he felt on the trail. Remfrey never treated him that way, nor any of the others back at the Crooked Tower. How he longed to be home again.

During that time of trial, only Rojo showed some empathy. When the bucket became too full, Rojo was the one to replace it. When Odo needed water, Rojo retrieved some from the ship's stores. It was something unexpected from the Cathar, given his large menacing frame and disposition. Still, whatever kindness he offered, friendly or not, Odo welcomed.

Three days the sickness took him. On the fourth, his tender wave-tossed stomach abated. Ship's biscuit and broth gave him nourishment and desperately needed fluids. With bowl and spoon, he ate on the top deck where the air was cleaner, colder. He made his place there, nestled into a crevice in the bridge of the ship's forecastle. Cradling the steaming bowl in his hands, he sipped slowly at the meal, foregoing a spoon, taking in the salty broth with a relieved sort of relish. The wind was cold as it spilled over the railing, mingled with a hint of sea spray. Sometimes the sun broke through the clouds above, painting the upper deck with warmth and light. Those moments he cherished, for they were too few for his liking.

As he huddled there in his corner, his satchel slung across his chest and his staff wedged between him and the railing, he had the occasion to witness a conversation between the captains. Sipping on his meager meal, he monitored the unlikely pair with a newfound interest. There was something about the two that made for a strange combination. Inoch was tall and lean with his cold, expressionless stare. The ship's captain was a burly brute of a man with commanding eyes. His stern and menacing nature along with his bellowing voice were a counterpoint to his overall appearance. The ship's captain dressed in tidy clothes. His beard was trimmed and manicured, such that it came to a dagger point on his chin.

Inoch, however, was garbed in the same road-worn clothes he wore when he first boarded the ship. His face was thick with stubble, having not been shaved in many days. The two captains were like opposing sides of the same imperial coin, each as strong and unyielding as the other, and both worthy of respect from those who followed them.

The conversation they had was not long, though the ship's captain looked irritated by whatever Inoch was telling him. Yet, at one point in the conversation, the two seemed to come to an agreement of sorts, the ship's captain smiling before long. They clasped arms soon after, a signal that an arrangement had been struck. It was then Inoch turned away, heading back to their quarters.

The ship's captain turned to enter the cabins in the aft deck as Inoch briefly glanced over at Odo. Inoch made a path to the young man, suddenly stopping midway.

All who were on deck heard the cry from above—a lookout minding the waves of the rough seas. Inoch, at once, ran to the nearest mast, embracing the stout wood. The shouts of other sailors followed as men rushed chaotically along the decks, seeking something to hold on to. Moments after, the ship swayed hard, a large wave slamming into its side. Odo grabbed his things while, alternatively, grasping a handhold of...something. His fingers clutched a coil of rope as he started to slide from his little niche, his hot soup sent flying. The deck beneath rumbled, and sea water spit and sprayed as the wave ruined itself against the stout oak of the hull. Those things not tied down and secured slid along the decking as the ship tilted, men crying out in alarm. Icy saline droplets spattered his face while the warm sensation of spilt soup penetrated the cloth of his robe, trousers, and cloak. Wide eyed, he looked past the railing, his heart pounding in his chest as the dark and deadly waters of the sea inched their way closer to him, the ship lumbering to one side. For a moment in time, he stopped breathing, the end of his life rising before him all black and frothing.

The ship righted itself, bobbing from side to side until the natural sway of the sea was reestablished. His heart thumping in his ears, Odo breathed heavily. The sudden relief he felt was tempered by an anxiety-fueled chill, one that was charged by the pull of gravity and the fatal black depths of the sea as they rose to greet him. Even as his life flashed before his eyes, he could not help but notice that his bowl of soup, whose contents were emptied onto the upper deck, had inexplicably escaped from the very same fate he thought had been destined for him.

Inoch loosened his grip on the mast. He looked up the length of the vertical timber to the rigging and the sky, but only for a moment. When that moment passed, he continued his trek to where Odo sat. Seeing the bowl nearby, Inoch bent down and plucked it from the glistening deck. As Odo tried to reorient himself back to where he had been sitting, Inoch inspected the object in his hand before speaking.

"Sea sickness has passed?" If there was any concern for Odo's wellbeing, it was well hidden deep beneath that emotionless stare.

"Some," Odo muttered. The young man did his best to avoid looking as flustered as he felt. Even now, his heart still pounded in his ears.

"I want you back in the cabin. I do not want you washed out to sea, and the rest of our payment with you."

"Yes, Captain," Odo said the words, but they tasted bitter on his tongue. He had no love of that pungent closet they called a cabin.

Inoch looked up and around. "We are changing course."

"Captain?"

"I waited until we were at sea. We will head to some islands for fresh food and water, then straight to a village named Illsenore. It is farther away than my original plan."

"Why the change, Captain?"

"Watchers at our backs. No doubt they were from Collenshore. Been there many days before we arrived, I think. Maybe they uncovered our destination, eh?"

He tossed the bowl at Odo, who fumbled with the thing momentarily.

Inoch continued. "I want no more surprises."

Looking up, Odo expressed his confusion at Inoch's revelation. "Captain? You think one of the crew spoke of our destination?"

"Perhaps," Inoch replied with a shrug. "Or one of my own. Too drunk. Too lusty. I never know which." Pausing for a moment, Inoch put his hands on his hips before scanning the seascape around him. When he was done, his eyes focused on the young man wedged against a wall of the foredeck, trying to keep all of his things together. "There are many rules of my trade, but one rule I keep above all of them. Do you know what it is, Odo?"

Odo's gaze dropped as he withdrew into his thoughts and memories, clouded by an inescapable obsession over the prospect of dying at sea. The only rule of freelancers that came to his mind was something to do with living long enough to spend your gold. Somehow, that didn't seem pertinent to their discussion.

"No, Captain."

Once more, Inoch looked one way, then another, though the gesture appeared for no apparent reason. When he did speak, his words came out cold and resolute.

"Trust no one," Inoch said. "Not even your own mother."

Then, with no additional fanfare or even a cursory glance at the young man he was protecting, he departed from Odo adding, "Come inside. Now. I do not need another large wave throwing my charge into the sea."

Chapter 13

From a spot at the ship's railing, Odo cast an envious gaze at the shores of the island in the distance. Snickers sat nearby, propped against the wall of the foredeck where their cabin was, keeping an eye on their most precious cargo. Bored, the mercenary occupied his time casting bones on the deck. The clicking and clacking of the tiny painted bones was the only reminder that Snickers was even present.

Out of a crew of twenty, only a small number remained on the ship, one keeping watch from the Crow's Nest, high atop the main mast. Another was situated on the aft deck where the ship's wheel was located. From time to time, he'd stand and pace, acting as a guard of sorts, though none were needed. The island whose harbor sheltered the craft was considered home for most of the crew. Trouble from land or sea was not much of a concern here.

The island itself consisted of two mountains that opposed one another. A gully connected the peaks, the land around them reaching out to the sea and the air warm for the autumnal season. Odo deduced that in their westward voyage they had also traveled south. It was a welcome relief from the stinging cold of the sea and the cutting chill of the winds that carried them across the waves.

For a good portion of his journey, the world around him was dying away; the welcoming green of summer had turned a dreary shade of tan. The thick verdant vegetation that spread out before him was a welcome sight, like a last deep breath before plunging below the waters. Palms, ferns, and wide-leaved brush covered everything, including the sides of the mountains. The fringe of the island was sand, made golden by the kiss of the sun. Rocks broke the border between the land and the harbor, up-thrust from the seabed. The stones were dark and pitted, worn from centuries of waterborne erosion. Somewhere past the screen of the tall bent palms was a village where Inoch and the ship's captain had gone to procure more supplies.

So little was known of the islands that dotted the Sorrowing Seas aside from those who occupied their shores. This was territory ruled by the Oncathar. Populated not long after the bloody schism that rent the mighty Cathar nation in twain, the islands were a sanctuary from further persecution by their heathen and savage brethren.

All because they broke from the dark and bloody rites demanded by The Four and took to the worship of the Allfather, the God of the West. In time, through determination, skill, and cunning, they came to dominate trade throughout the inland waters and to the southern seas.

As Odo stood there at the railing, his heart bristled. He had read much about the history of the Oncathar. Now he found himself deep in their dominion, only to be stuck on that accursed ship with a man who had barely spoken a dozen words since they met. Instead, he could be among the Oncathar in their village. To see firsthand their homes and their lives. To taste their food. Hear the songs they sang. Listen to their stories and lore for himself. To know more than what the dusty tomes told him and what he could imagine in his mind's eye.

Odo let out a sigh which resonated as much disappointment as it did disgust. Still, he could not tear his eyes away. Nor could he stop his mind from imagining what lay hidden in the bosom of those mountains, beyond the veil of trees and brush.

At some point, Snickers put away his bones and tended to his sword instead. He was a quiet man, saying little, with no express personality save for a blank expression and a seemingly mindless stare. In the long wait, he honed the blade, a well-worn puck of stone sliding and scraping along the nicked edges. Odo turned and stared while the soldier worked the steel, hypnotized by the mundane repetition of each pass of the stone.

A straight-bladed thing, the sword Snickers tended was decorated along the spine in a pattern of twisting vines with thorns running along their length etched beautifully into the gray steel. Brass adornments were riveted into the cross guard, a pattern of roses that encircled round depressions where gems were once set.

Yet, the nobility of the weapon had long diminished from neglect and use. The sheen of the metal dulled to a drab gray, dotted with tiny black specks of corrosion. The soft brass was rent and broken off in places, and the gems that once made the weapon proud had been plucked away by needful and avaricious fingers, traded for gold.

Pretty Boy conjured a story for the weapon in the long idle hours at sea. How Snickers won the blade as a prize at a game of dice, hustling another freelancer too inebriated to know any better. That the sword once proudly graced the mantle of a wealthy noble. That it was wielded by many generations of his family in times of war. Whether a believer or not, virtuous or not, the noble aligned his house and fortunes on the losing side of the last war. When they fell, the weapon was taken as spoil and the familial estates confiscated. The proud heirloom was stripped of all value, passed from one owner to the other in a game of chance. In many ways it stood as a ghostly reminder of the consequence of pride and folly. Fallen. Consigned to lesser men, in whose hands the blade would be used for all manner of bloody business. A thing no longer venerated or cherished but wielded and used until broken or spent.

"Tell me how you came by that sword," Odo said to Snickers, meek but curious.

Looking up, Snickers eyed Odo for a moment, wordless in his reply. He sniffed before preoccupying himself once more with his blade. A long, awkward silence followed as Odo awaited an answer that never came. Tired of waiting, and feeling a bit foolish, Odo returned to staring at the island.

Another night on the ship, and another day spent idle with nothing to do. Rojo came in the morning relieving Snickers, who went to the island to rejoin his comrades, rest and relaxation, as it was made out to be. The mercenary nearly threw himself over the side of the railing, so eager he was to leave the vessel.

And so the day went on. Idle and bored, Odo found a spot at the wall of the aft deck near the door. Rojo found himself a seat on the other side, his weapons at the ready, keeping a sharp eye on the crew as they went about their business.

"What do you know of the Watchers?" Odo spoke up.

"What?"

"Captain said we were being pursued by Watchers. He mentioned they were marked but said little else."

"I thought wizards knew all?" Rojo answered, the question itself mocking despite the lack of humor present in his thick, stunted accent.

"I am not a wizard," answered Odo, his face flushed. He was tired of having to repeat the phrase. "I had access to many books and scrolls in Remfrey's library. Yet, that was old knowledge. I am afraid I do not know much of recent events. I was hoping—"

"Fanatics," said Rojo, interrupting Odo. "Servants to some hidden god. If the world does not have enough madmen and their gods." After that, Rojo said no more. Instead, checking the wind first, Rojo turned his head and spat high into the air. The thick wet projectile arched, passing beyond the railing of the ship.

Odo waited in silence, expecting more. When it was not forthcoming, he pressed further. "Well?"

"What?"

"What were they like? Their customs? Their rites?"

"When you kill a man, you no ask questions," Rojo said, his speech clumsy and thick with his Cathar accent. His head tilted to one side and his eyes narrowed as he considered the question. Before long, he asked, "What know you of them?"

Odo thought on the things that Inoch told him, doing his best to not remember too much of that day. "Captain said they had a mark. That if there was true evil in the world, they were close to it. Little else."

"Aye," Rojo said with a nod, "they mark their skin like Rojo here." Extending his arm, he pulled back the sleeve to reveal black lines beneath brown skin. Given the distance, the lines were difficult to distinguish. As best as Odo could discern, they were a geometric design of some sort whose true meaning was only known by its owner.

Rojo pushed his sleeve forward. "And their priests? Eyeless devils. Pale skin like milk. Flesh cover the holes of their eyes. Them we made good sport."

"Sport?" Odo's brow furrowed.

Rojo sniffed. "First, we cut out tongue so they cannot make spells. And hands. We cut off hands. Then we hang them from tree by feet. Use them to practice bow, sling. Captain use his crossbow. Then, when Captain say so, we cut off their head."

Odo grimaced at the explanation Rojo gave. Rojo saw this.

"You think harsh?"

A certain reluctance to answer the question came over Odo. Still, he answered his guardian's inquiry. "It seems a bit...much."

"One put curse on Allois. Took Allois days to die. Flesh fall away. Much blood. Much pain. Because of Allois, we make blind priests suffer. They do the same to us if they could." Crossing those thick arms across his wide chest, Rojo shifted a bit on the deck. "Terrible war," he muttered.

"Allois?" asked Odo, confused.

"One of our brothers," replied Rojo. Pointing to his chest, he clarified. "Soldier. Freelancer."

Odo's eyes glazed over as his thoughts recalled recent events. Memories of the man he slew resurfaced, and his head twitched slightly as if he could somehow shake away the recollection from his mind. Even now, he had yet to reconcile his actions and his conscience, doing his best to bury the smell and the images somewhere deep in his head. A place that he could lock them away and forget them forever.

"We lost many in that war," Rojo said with a sigh. "Allois. Rohen. Sneaky Pete. Hammer Horos. Captain hate losing men. He hate Watchers much. Make them suffer when he can."

"And King Merrith allowed this?" Rojo's insights drew Odo from the spiral of guilt and doubt that was dragging him into dark places.

With a shrug, Rojo replied, "Don't know. Most times, we take them Watchers away, out of sight of others. Some of the men—men of Horunass—hate them as much as us. Say nothing. So long as none of them Bright Eyes see us, we do as we will."

"Bright eyes?"

Rojo lifted himself up, his head turning over to look at Odo. Pointing at his eyes, he spoke. "Bright eyes. Pale skin. Hair like gold. Armor like silver."

While frustratingly cryptic, Odo only knew of two peoples who had pale skin and golden hair. "Nolans?" he asked with bent brows.

"No," answered Rojo once more pointing to his eyes. "Bright eyes. Young. All young."

It finally dawned on Odo to whom the Cathar referred. "You mean, the Elanni?"

"Yes," replied Rojo, nodding his head and reclining once more.

"You fought alongside Elanni?"

Rojo folded his arms across his chest. "Yes. Bright Eyes. Many of them in the war. Rojo did not like them. They not like us, that is known."

Odo had read extensively on the Elanni and their ways. The wizard possessed a few tomes that spoke of that ancient race, Odo taking a keen interest. He knew them to be friendly to free peoples and to those who worshiped the God of the West. They were ageless, fair of face, best defined by their sharp features and long blonde locks. Though, the most profound feature of the Elanni were their piercing blue eyes, a hue and intensity unlike those of any mortal. It was said that in the absence of available light, the eyes of an Elanni almost glowed.

Rojo's story was intriguing to Odo. While generally friendly to those desiring peace, they did not entangle themselves in the affairs of men. For the Elanni to ally with men and engage in war was a profound revelation.

"Fascinating," Odo said in all but a whisper. "What were they like? The Bright Eyes."

Another shrug from Rojo. "I did not like them. None of us liked them."

"And Captain?"

Rojo's brows arched high. "Captain really not like them."

For a time, conversation between the two died, Rojo offering nothing and Odo preoccupied with a question in his head. Finally, out of boredom or curiosity, Odo asked, "What do you think of Captain?"

Rojo's head rolled along the tightly fitted planks until his eyes fell on Odo. "Captain?" he asked, as if he didn't understand the question.

"I mean…you follow him." Fearing he had crossed over a line, Odo tried to somehow double-back on the question. The way the words fell out of his mouth made it clear that his retreat was less than elegant.

"Captain and Rojo have been together many years."

"How long?"

"Longer than Maddie, Snickers, or Pretty Boy. Rojo is second in command. Captain give me orders. I give orders to others. That is how it is."

"Do…do you trust him?" Inside his head, Odo wanted to wince, having let his curiosity get the better of him.

"With my life." Rojo's response was unequivocal and resolute. "And Captain trust Rojo with his life. It is the way with soldiers."

Rojo studied Odo for a moment after answering his question. His face turned flinty and cold. "But you do not trust Captain."

Shamefaced, Odo looked away, and before long his eyes were on the decking, not knowing how to answer and fearing to say what he thought.

"Look at me."

Odo did not answer Rojo's request, ignoring it as if the words were never spoken. That did not satisfy Rojo in the least.

"You look at Rojo." The command wasn't angry or forceful, but it was persistent. Odo relented, slowly giving his attention to the Cathar.

"Rojo been with Captain at many battles, many wars. Each time, Captain see us through—he see us all through. He see us *all* through. Captain is cunning like a wolf. His will like iron."

Slapping his hands together, his top hand sliding off the bottom and launching into the air, Rojo added, "He say he do something, and so it is done. That is Captain. It is why we follow him. We trust him."

"Even Maddie?" asked Odo.

"Even Maddie," replied Rojo, the seriousness of his tone undiminished.

"But did he not say he would have you flogged?" Odo was far from convinced by what the Cathar was saying. "Back at Collenshore."

Rojo's expression intensified, and his demeanor turned serious and cold. He spoke like a father giving an errant son a lecture on the ways of the world. "The life of a soldier is not easy one. When soldier does not follow order, men die. Captain make threats? Yes. Captain keep threats? Yes."

"He had me kill a man," Odo said softly.

Dismissing Odo's concern with a snort and a grin, Rojo countered, "That is what soldier do."

"But I am not a soldier."

"With Watcher stalking you, does it matter? Or need you to learn as Allois learned?" He paused for a moment adding, "Hate what you have done, or what Captain made you do. You are alive. Better that than dead."

For a time, Odo was quiet, withdrawn into his thoughts. As troubled as he was over having killed a man, the clear logic of the Cathar—an unbeliever by all accounts—was hard to dismiss. In a way, it only deepened the conflict within him. When Odo did speak, it was soft and filled with shame. "But how do I live with knowing I took a life?"

"You just live. Sometimes that all you can do."

Knowing this, Odo only felt worse about what he had done. Hoping to change the subject and forget the charred corpse of the Watcher, Odo asked, "So, what will you do with all the gold you receive when you finally deliver me to Horunass?"

Clearing his throat, Rojo crossed his arms over his thickly muscled chest before shrugging his shoulders. "Rojo does not count his gold until battle is won." Rojo looked at Odo once more, the whites of his eyes brightly contrasting with the reddish-brown sheen of his skin. "When you enter Horunass, then I will decide. Until then, Rojo, like Captain, worry about why Watchers know to follow you before you reach Collenshore."

"Right," Odo said with a nod and a shy stare. In his head, Odo too wondered after the importance of the stone he bore, and why the wizard would entrust him to such a task.

CHAPTER 14

Four days they waited, taking on supplies before continuing westward. Odo came to the sober realization that, despite being surrounded by many men, he felt horribly alone.

Out here on the water, surrounded by strangers, the familiarity of home called to him. As the ship lifted and crashed through the waves of the dark sea, Odo would have given just about anything to return to the Crooked Tower. To sit again in the study of the wizard, all dusty and dim, and hear him lecture on the finer points of magic. To scrounge the countryside, collecting the herbs that Remfrey needed for his various concoctions. Even cleaning the stalls with old Jacks was preferrable to the strangeness of foreign peoples and the ever-present fear of the unknown.

It was moments like this, alone on the deck of that ship as the crew tended to their tasks, he began to question the lens through which he viewed his life. Was he truly alone? Or did he overlook the richness of what he had simply because he was different from them? If he should, along this uncertain road, stumble upon blood relations, would he find greater company among kin? Or would he continue to feel the same discomfort among them as he did the strangers who surrounded him?

At least in the morning hour, Odo found a way to assuage the homesickness that troubled him. As the dawn arrived, the captain of the Sarajwebo stood on the bridge. In a low and sonorous voice, he called the crew to worship and prayer. Odo sometimes heard the bellow of the captain as he lay sprawled out on the floor of his cabin. Other times, weak from lack of food, he witnessed the ritual as he sipped on hot broth. Now, however, no longer tormented by the oppressive sickness from the tumult of the sea, he decided to join the crew in worship.

It was awkward at first, shuffling up to the gathering, remaining in the rear. He was a curiosity to those among the worshippers who noticed his attendance. There were quick stares, though none that lingered. Odo knew some of the rudiments of the Oncathar speech, a pidgin version of Valelander blended with elements of their mother tongue. A few words, however, were mixed in that were still a mystery to his ears. Prayers were invoked by the ship's captain and sometimes repeated responsively by the crew. Odo followed along as best as he could, once more gaining attention from those in the back rows. At the end of each divine petition, the captain and crew called out, "It is true," with bold voices, something similar to his own prayers.

Then there were the hymns. The songs were foreign to him at first, and he sang them quietly and out of tune. With each day, he memorized them, in time singing them with as much finesse as his talents allowed. The words of the wizard wafted through his head.

Odo, when a hymn is sung to the glory of the Allfather, it is as if you pray twice. First with your voice and then with your words.

The change amidst the congregation was gradual. While he took his place in the back on his first day of worship, with each gathering, he found himself drawn into the mass of the crew. There was something comforting about finding himself enveloped by chanting voices and those raised in song. As his voice became more pronounced among the throng, smiles were directed his way along with welcoming pats. In a way, he had discovered a new family of sorts, if only for a short time.

All the while, he participated under the watchful eye of Rojo, who maintained his vigil from the back row. On occasion, either Maddie or Pretty Boy were dispatched to keep an eye on their eventual payday. But for most of the gatherings, it was Rojo who stood guard. He was easy to spot among the other dark-skinned men, standing nearly a head higher than the rest, arms crossed over his chest, a graven face filled with disinterest, and a small measure of disgust. While the others sang and chanted, he took no interest in blending in, even at times signaling his boredom with a sigh. Moreover, whenever one among the Oncathar stared at him too long, a stern and malicious eye was offered as a response. Odo managed to catch this exchange on occasion, noting Rojo's genuine sense of hostility towards the crew.

One day, as the service ended, and the crew dispersed, Odo asked, "Might I ask a personal question?"

Rojo grunted his answer, unfolding his arms and giving him an attentive stare.

"Why do you dislike the crew? Are they not your people?"

With a snort, Rojo looked as much amused as he was offended by the observation. "They not my people," he said with emphasis. "I not theirs."

Realizing how his words sounded, his manner softened and his words were less sharp. "Odo, keep your gods. I keep mine. Yes?" His brows lifted with expectation.

At first, Odo didn't know how to answer the question. He knew Rojo was a Cathar. He had never seen Rojo worship or offer prayer. Likewise, he had no desire to offend him, for—in his own way—he was kind.

"I only have one God," came Odo's reply, as clumsy as his answer was.

"Then you keep your God then," said Rojo, showing no hint of offense.

Left with nothing more to say on the matter, all Odo could do was acquiesce with a dumb nod.

Having found some sort of fellowship in a place of strangers, Odo no longer counted the days at sea. The air grew more chilled from day to day, indicating they were headed in a northerly direction. One day, a shoreline appeared, though he knew not if it was that of an island or the mainland shore. Regardless, they followed the line of the land for a number of days, four by his best recollection. Around noon on the fifth, the boats of various fishermen were spotted. In the distance, evidence of a settlement was proclaimed by the spotter in the crow's nest above.

"Illsenore," the crewman cried, the sound of it inept but nonetheless understandable enough given his native tongue. As word spread, the others of the company came out from their cabins, joining Odo at the rail as the Sarajwebo tacked its western course.

There was much excitement among the mercenaries, with Maddie even sporting a smile. "What of Illsenore makes you so glad?" asked Odo of Pretty Boy, who was standing next to him.

"Never heard of Illsenore?"

Odo shook his head. He had only seen Illsenore on a map. It was a village of no historical or strategic significance. Yet, even from a distance, there was something truly notable about the seaside town. Round walls poked up from the waves like sunken silos. Small boats tended these, lashed to some hidden posts along the sides, men climbing up and down the rocks like ants upon boulders.

"What a sheltered life you live, young lad," Pretty Boy chided with a smile. "Illsenore is famous. Kings and lords from all 'round spend gold a-plenty for the bounty they pull from the sea. Oysters bigger than your hand. Crab bigger than a dinner plate. Sea Bass and Red Perch as sweet as peaches. You see them?" He pointed at the conical formation of stone. "The villagers have dozens of them things built up all around here where the waters are shallow. They bring ice from the mountains in these great wooden wains and use it to store and send their bounty all through the west. When we pull into town, you'll see."

Indeed, Odo did see. As they neared the village, more of the stone pens peeked up from sheltered waters. Long sunken timbers surrounded by nets were tended by fishermen in their boats. As the wind lessened, the ship came to rest just outside an artificial harbor that was empty save for a series of single-masted boats unloading their catch. The anchor hit the water with a profound splash as the ropes streamed out from coils below, holding the Sarajwebo in place until pilot ships arrived. These lesser boats, manned by men at oars, came and hooked tow lines as the crew massed at the anchor lines to untether the Sarajwebo from the seabed. The next hour was spent waiting for the lumbering vessel to be dragged across the rugged waters by the pilot ships into the placid sheltering arms that protected the harbor from the rougher terrain of the sea at large.

While the ship was being towed, the freelancers drew lots to see who would attend to unloading and guarding their gear, Snickers drawing the short straw. Snickers cursed loudly, his face reddening with rage—a rare and unexpected show of emotion from the soldier. The others laughed both with relief and delight, knowing they would eat and drink well while their comrade was stuck with the drudgery. It struck Odo that despite his love of gambling, Snickers seemed to only be lucky with dice.

True appreciation of the place only came as Odo finally set foot on the solid wood of a dock. From a distance, the village, as it was referred to, was a bustling place. This was especially true seaside. Baskets of fish, oysters, and sea clams waited on nearby boats, lashed to the piers. Dogs barked from within the boats, seagulls glided and cried overhead. Men milled about on the docks, some labored, others—better dressed—inspected the incoming catch, haggling and bartering over price and quantity. Well weathered timbers groaned beneath their weight, the hulls of boats thumping against pilings as the waters rippled with activity. Everywhere, the smell of fish, sweat, and stink was so heady it nearly made Odo's stomach turn.

The freelancers who guarded him, however, laughed and jested. Hearts that were bitter and sullen suddenly lifted at the prospect of fresh fish and boiled crab with spice. Their boasts resounded amidst the drone and din of the docks of how many oysters each could consume before becoming physically ill.

Pretty Boy explained to Odo, "Kings and princes may pay a mighty price for such goods faraway. Here a pauper can eat like a king for a few coppers, if a pauper can be found among them."

It was as Pretty Boy said. Moving from the docks inland, Odo watched as streams of workers carried the catch to awaiting warehouses filled high with blocks of ice. Mounds of sawdust covered over the blocks, shoveled atop by laborers. Others attacked the blocks with axes and knives, breaking them into piles of broken chunks and chips. Another crew used shovels to fill dense wooden crates with the broken fragments, layering fish or crab atop and repeating this until filled. Great enclosed wagons awaited nearby where the crates were relocated, teams of hearty horses lined two-by-two to pull their massive loads.

While it looked like a village, having no high defensive walls to protect it like Collenshore, it was similarly large, sprawling from the shore, inland. Homes with thatched roofs, and others of split cedar shakes. Rude single-story dwellings of fieldstone mingled with taller dwellings with whitewashed walls and exposed timbers lacquered with pitch. Disorderly avenues where people moved to and fro—rich, poor, and those in between. While warehouses were located closer to the docks, as they traveled farther in, Odo saw the ramshackle huts and houses of the tradesmen— smiths, trawl makers, and menders. Boat builders with their large, covered shops. Chanting fish mongers whose open markets were crowded with people buying and selling. Women with cookpots making stew with their children as helpers. The steam from their outdoor kitchens rolled and shifted in the crisp breezes. On mud-slick lanes people passed, some stopping to smell the fragrance of what simmered within while others trudged on, preoccupied with weightier matters.

It was the mud Odo detested the most. As they moved from the waterfront, the grade of the land moved upward from the shore. His feet slipped with every step, despite relying heavily on his staff for support. The mud coated the hem of his robe and cloak, spattered his trousers, and caked his shoes. It came as a welcome relief when the group decided to frequent an ale house whose reputation they knew well.

Nestled between the open stall of a fish monger and that of the rude home of the proprietor, it was little more than a tent with a cedar shake roof. A small if not pathetic-looking place, it was nonetheless frequented by many. Shabby men sat in the mud outside the flap, mug in hand, drinking their fill, offering curious glances at the boy with his darker shade of skin.

A seedy place altogether, its split cedar roof was stained white with the manure of gulls that rested atop. The birds barked down at the occupants in protest, demanding the food served within. The flapping of wings and the shrieks of the creatures melded with the many voices of passersby, some soft, some rude. As Inoch pulled back the flap, an unwholesome smell assaulted Odo's senses. From within the dimly lit interior billowed out the stench of stale ale and the briny odor of cooking fish or crab, or whatever was in the pot that bubbled and boiled over the fire.

One by one the mercenaries filed in as their captain held the flap open. Maddie went in first, Odo following behind her. At the last moment, Rojo reached out and roughly pulled Odo aside allowing Pretty Boy to go in his stead. Stumbling at first, nearly losing his footing and sliding into the mud, Odo kept himself upright with the aid of his staff. He eyed Rojo as he recovered, only to note that the big warrior himself was scanning the crowd. A quick look over at the other side of the entrance and Odo saw Inoch doing the same. It then dawned on Odo that the order of their entry was purposeful. Two of the mercenaries went inside to make sure everything was safe while Odo and his precious cargo remained protected outside.

Shuffling his shoulders and straightening the strap of his satchel, Odo turned his attention back to Inoch. Slowly letting the flap fall from his grip, the mercenary captain fixed his stare on something in the distance. Like a hound tracking its prey, Inoch seemed tense, marking something in the roiling steam and moving bodies—both horse and human—along the muddy lanes.

"Rojo," Inoch muttered.

"Yes, boss?"

"You see what I see?"

Odo squinted, trying to detect what grabbed the attention of the captain. Bodies and mist, horses and carts. The rumble and slosh of people in close proximity, but nothing more.

"What, Captain?" Rojo's tone changed, his low voice having the hint of a growl.

Inoch did not answer. Instead, that cold stabbing stare of his remained locked on something. Odo still struggled to determine what it was.

"Get him inside." Inoch's hand reached again for the end of the flap, pulling aside such that Rojo and Odo could enter. This time, Odo went first with the big Cathar guarding his rear.

Inside, tables and benches were arranged as sets, all in orderly rows. A single candle, sometimes in pairs, was set on each table. Their pathetic light was barely able to illuminate the long serving tables. It was well past noon by now and few patrons remained within. Most were down deep in their cups, savoring their loneliness as they drank themselves into a stupor. There was nothing hinting of elegance in this place, for it was as shoddy within as it was without. Broken shells and crab littered the dirt, moist with the brine of the sea and the stink of spilled ale. The walls flapped with the gusts of the breeze, and the tallow candles let off a curious greasy scent, reminiscent of a time when fat was rendered for lard at the Crooked Tower.

"Best crab in Illsenore," commented Maddie.

They all gathered at the one table that was completely unoccupied, collectively sitting, dividing their numbers evenly.

As Odo went to find his own place to sit, Inoch grabbed at the hem of his sleeve. "You sit next to me." Then, thumb stuck out and using it to point to a place near Odo, the captain called Rojo.

Service was swift at this hour; an old man and his daughter came at once to ask for a show of coin before providing any food or drink. The proprietor was old and thin, shorter than any of the company that escorted Odo. Stubble graced his balding crown, and a thick shabby handlebar moustache covered the entirety of his upper lip.

From a small pouch tucked in his belt, Inoch opened his purse strings and pulled out five gold coins. Looming over the owner and pulling in close, he placed the coins in the palm of the man in a way to hide the transaction from prying eyes.

The proprietor of the alehouse looked down at his payment, his thumb caressing his golden bounty. With a nod, he closed them in his fist and turned to his daughter. In a thin, cracked voice he ordered the girl, "Crab and ale aplenty, child, and be quick about it."

The company had barely unloaded their gear at their feet before full mugs were placed before them in a cluster. A collective satisfied sigh rose among the company. Hands reached out for the mugs as each quickly claimed their own. Foam and beer spilt onto the table as the daggers came out, each of them setting their knives before them. The soldiers drank greedily, even Odo, who had grown sick to death of Ship's Biscuit and broth. Ale was a welcome, satisfying drink, as bitter as it was. The taste of it was superlative when compared to the biting taste of stale water and rose hip-infused liquor served aboard the ship. The dark heavy brew was as filling as a heel of dense bread. Odo drank it down greedily, relishing each and every mouthful.

A collective gasp was heard as the platters of crab were served. Crustaceans worthy of Pretty Boy's boasts, they were indeed near as big as a dinner plate, hard red and steaming. Each member of the group claimed one almost the instant the platter dropped. Like the warning call of a cluster of snakes, each hissed through their teeth, the hot crab threatening to burn the skin of their fingers.

Odo was hesitant, eyeing the crab with suspicion and loathing. Having lived in the bald hills and the open moors, Odo's tastes were more akin to mutton than flesh from the sea. He knew of crabs and other creatures which dwelled beneath the waters. Seeing one illustrated on a page and smelling the stink of it up close were altogether different. Coupled with the unwholesome environs in which they dined, Odo soon found his appetite rapidly sinking into oblivion.

As the others went about using the handles of the daggers to crack the hard shells, he pulled the last one to him. Observing Snickers and Maddie, he first went after the claw, banging on it with the handle of his dagger. Shell splintered, fragments flew as fluid sprayed, exposing the tender white flesh beneath. Using his blade, he went about cutting away a large piece of the meat. Slicing the flesh across the grain, he gracelessly pried it out with the tip of his blade. Holding it by his fingers, he inspected it as it steamed. It was creamy white, stringy, the cut end frayed like a tattered piece of cloth. Sucking up his courage, he closed his eyes and popped the meat into his mouth. He began to chew, and then stopped.

Distinctly fishy, the flesh breaking apart between his teeth like a bundle of threads, Odo found the flavor and the texture not only foreign, but abhorrent. Something inside of him wanted to retch, his first inclination being to spit the contents in his mouth onto the ground. The wizard had taught him better than that. His only recourse was to drown out the flavor with his ale and let the wretched thing slide down his gullet where he could taste it no more. Letting his knife fall to the table with a hollow thunk, Odo clutched his mug with both hands and took in a mouthful of ale with such speed he nearly bathed himself in the contents.

Swallowing hard, his face twisted in disgust, Odo set down his flagon. Eyeing the crab before him with revulsion, he used the tip of his knife to push the remnants of his meal away from him.

It didn't take long for the others to notice. At once, many sets of hands grabbed at the crab with threats and curses exchanged between the mercenaries as each vied for the extra meat.

"Crab not to your liking?" Inoch asked Odo, leaning in. He let the others fight, being content with his own share.

Odo nodded as the others broke apart his rejected meal, each taking what they could.

Inoch turned slightly, looking behind him. "More ale for the boy." Afterwards, he said to Odo, "Drink your fill, but keep your wits about you. If they have to carry you, then it will be by dragging you through the mud. Understand?"

Lifting the wooden flagon to his lips, Odo dutifully answered, "Yes, Captain."

Afterward, he drank deep, hoping to expunge the taste of crab from his mouth.

Prying out meat from the leg of his crab and sliding it into his mouth, Inoch turned his attention once more to the flap that covered the doorway. Odo wiped his mouth with his sleeve, noting the captain's preoccupation with the entrance. Those pale, passionless eyes of Inoch stared at the flap as if they could see past the barrier and into the street beyond. What they sought, Odo could only guess.

The look on Inoch's face and the intensity of his stare gave Odo an inexplicable sick feeling in his gut. As if he knew something was amiss but was unwilling to say. The gnawing fear that grew in Odo's heart was the second worse sensation he had that day.

CHAPTER 15

"Get up." Rojo's meaty hand shoved Odo awake. Eyes bleary, Odo yawned, wondering after the hour. It was dark in the room, a single tallow candle weakly burning in a stand of brass. He checked for his satchel, which he kept with him even at rest. Hands feeling the leather, the strap binding the cove of his shoulder, he exhaled loudly before rubbing his eyes.

After three large mugs of ale and ever cognizant of Inoch's warning about being dragged through streets, the trek to his room at the inn was challenging to say the least. While the draught made him full, the alcohol went straight to his head. The world wobbled and swayed for many hours before night finally descended.

His legs hadn't forgotten the bob and sway of the sea. Even now, hours after departing the Sarajwebo, he still felt the sea beneath him. Part of him wondered if it was some after-effect of the ale he consumed the night before, though he suspected it was not. The world did not spin, there was no haze in his thoughts. It must have been the long days at sea, or so he reasoned. Quietly, he wondered how long it would be before the sensation finally ceased.

The inn itself wasn't much, the room itself sparse. Two beds fit to house a single man apiece, their mattresses stuffed with hay and filled with unwelcome lumps. A plain wooden table large enough for the candle stood nearby, and not much else. Odo slept in one bed, Rojo in the other, with Snickers making a place on the floor for his bed. Despite the smell of crab and the unwholesome musk emanating from Snickers, Odo managed to nod off quickly, the ale he consumed the night before aiding in that endeavor. For how long he slept, he didn't know.

Now, however, it was dark. "What time is it?" inquired Odo, rubbing the sleep from his eyes.

"Before cock crow," answered Rojo, grabbing his sword that leaned against the side of his bed. No longer clad in clothes, his thick chest was covered by a shirt of rings. A leathery jacket overlaid the armor, hanging open. Around his shoulder, his blade hung all the way to his belt as he threw his cloak about him. The weapon he bore was different from the rest of the mercenaries, having a thick spine and a single cutting edge. Odo spied the weapon only twice, Rojo being diligent with its care. The edge was narrower near the hilt, and about midway along the blade bulged outward in a graceful curve, coming to a viciously sharp point at the tip. A *maranote*, as the Cathars called it, their traditional weapon of war. As Odo knew well, it was a weapon that, in the hands of a trained warrior, was brutally effective. This was part and parcel of why the nations of the Cathar were feared.

"Why?"

"Don't ask why," Rojo replied. "Just wake and we go."

With a grunt and a sigh, Odo slipped off his bed, grabbed his staff, and rose.

Horses and provisions were already waiting for them at the entrance of the inn, Inoch having secured them while Odo slept. Each member had a horse, with two pack animals to bear the volume of gold they carried with them, in addition to food and other supplies. As Odo mounted his beast in the pre-dawn dark, he took time to observe the scenery around him. The village, so alive with life many hours before, was dead still, the mud-filled lanes desolate, the constant rumble of traffic replaced with an unfamiliar silence. In the distance, a dog barked, the only sound to echo through vacant streets while the whole of Illsenore slumbered.

To Odo, the still was disquieting, though he could not explain why. He felt like a thief, sneaking away with valuable goods, undetected by spying eyes. It was dark, a thick veil of clouds moving in during the night, dampening the moon's pale glow.

Lamps were used to guide the way, the company riding in a single line. Inoch was in front followed by Maddie who had with her one of the pack horses. Odo rode behind her followed by Rojo. The order of the remaining soldiers Odo could not discern. Their departure was, for the most part, silent save for the snorts of the horses, the clinking of their bridles, and the slosh of heavy hooves in the perpetual mud that covered the avenues of Illsenore. A dog barked at their passing, another far off. Towards the outskirts, as industry gave way to agrarian homesteads, a cock's crow, the bay of a goat, or the remorseful mooing of a milk cow were rare but familiar sounds.

Their westward trek to Horunass took them along an east-west road. As the eastern sun crested the horizon, they doused the lamps, the dim and diffuse light of the sun enough for them to navigate their way. The chill of the morning was unmatched from days before, the breath of the horses coming out in great plumes. Odo's own breath billowed like a cloud. A thin layer of ice covered the various pools of standing water, the horses shattering the delicate creations of the waning autumn cold beneath their weight. All in all, they moved in silence, the road desolate at this hour. Hoods up, heads down, they appeared like pilgrims on a march to a holy site, the sound of their mounts providing the beat for a prayerful chant.

By noon, a covered wain passed them, heading towards the village they had just left.

Iron-shod wheels rolled through ruts and over stones, rocking and creaking on the uneven ground. Hollow thumps and rumbles resounded from vibrations through and within their empty holds. Save for the clank and jingle of the harness and yokes of the beasts that pulled the load, the wagons themselves sounded dull and heavy.

They spent the remainder of their first day putting ample distance between themselves and Illsenore, much to the dismay of the others. Flush with gold, more than one protested quietly about the rush. Another day of ale and feasting on the bounty of the sea was hoped for. Their captain, however, was stoic and quiet for a good portion of their complaints. One word too many was spoken, and before long he'd turn in his saddle to silence them, lacing every other word with profanity.

"Have you forgot what we fought here?" he asked of the others coldly.

It was later explained to Odo by Rojo that Illsenore was not far from the lands where they fought in recent times. The memory of the Watchers and their deeds were still strong in these parts.

For most of the trek, the terrain was open, reminding Odo of home. Closer to the village, farms dotted the countryside and large pastures were partitioned by timber fencing, much of it well maintained. In the distance, thatched roofs covered long stony walls of granaries where the summer wheat was stowed for the oncoming winter. Great swaths of open ground neatly trimmed by a reaper's scythe spoke of a recent harvest. Herds of sheep gathered in great woolen packs as they grazed, their fleece grown out and ready to insulate them from the frigid nights to come.

As dusk neared, they approached the farmstead of a man and his three grown sons. The patriarch was thin with a weathered and tan face, his body wrapped in wool. The farmer eyed them suspiciously as they passed, a timbering axe in hand when the company approached. It was a silly gesture as neither he nor his sons were a match for freelancers. A few gold coins dropped into his palm outweighed any fears the homesteader had, his long, cracked fingers wrapping around his prize after the last one dropped. That night was spent in the confines of an open barn, a fire in a stone-lined pit, far from the combustible hay, being the only warmth as the night descended. As the wind blew, Odo said his prayers at the far end of the barn. He did so in the darkness with the mules who grumbled and snorted while Odo made petitions for a safe passing. While he prayed, the others drank, quietly mocking him in his nightly ritual.

Yet, Odo was cognizant enough to hear the whispers stop when Inoch drew near.

They were gone by daybreak the day next, continuing their trek on the long road west. The terrain around them changed little, save for the stands of trees that now popped up along the path. Most were bare, the many-colored leaves layering the ground. Jagged branches reached up skyward like gnarled fingers, Odo taking a fond dislike to the late winter in lands where trees grew thick. Only a lonely oak held its leaves, though they were now all brown. Some wafted to the ground, pushed from their high places by the breeze. Tall grasses rose where the ground was open—high thistles whose brown and broken pods had gone to seed many days past. Rushes near streams and marshes were the only exception to the dying time of fall, being the only green things amongst dying vegetation.

Fording a river by ferry, they made camp several hours after, finding a spot frequented by travelers now long departed. A ring of scorched stone was filled with the remains of charred wood and leaden ash turned hard from soaking rain and frigid air. Segments of fallen trees were placed around the pit as makeshift benches, though time and the elements were having their due. Nearby, a shallow stream ran, its banks covered over in spots by a brittle veil of cloudy ice under which frigid waters flowed.

The air grew chill as the sun descended, all of them working with haste to gather wood for a fire, run a highline across the limbs of trees where the horses could be tied, or setting hobbles about their hooves. Each breath they made in the crisp air reminded Odo of the stories of dragons. Great exhalations of smoldering smoke, sparking flame, reeking of Sulphur. Creatures, he remembered, that were used to great effect in the Great War.

What became of them little was written, though it was believed that some still troubled the mountains to the east.

"Odo," Inoch called out. "Set the flame."

"Captain?"

Inoch was unburdening his horse when Odo answered. He stopped, turned, and gave the young man a disbelieving eye. "Did you not hear me? I said to set the fire."

Odo looked around. "Do any of you have flint and steel?"

Dropping an armload of wood on an ever-growing pile, Maddie unfolded and brushed fragments of bark, wood, and leaves from her coat of rings. "You got magic. Use that," she grumbled.

"What was given to me should be used only at need," Odo protested.

"We need fire," replied Inoch brusquely, lifting his saddle off his horse. "Now," he added.

Putting her weight on her back leg, Maddie folded her arms over her chest. With a hard look and sneer, she added, "You heard the captain. It ain't getting' any warmer out. Now get to it."

Staff in hand, Odo knelt next to the fire before setting it aside. Removing the satchel from around his shoulder, he placed it near the staff. Picking through the piles of dead wood and twigs, he "built the tent," as old Jacks would have put it. Reaching down into his clothes with his right hand, he pulled the amulet and chain from about his neck, wrapping it around his hand and pressing it into the flesh of his palm. Taking up the staff with his other hand, he closed his eyes as he chanted the words softly.

"Arros el saidu inflama."

Thrice he spoke the words, eyes closed, while Maddie loomed over him, watching intently. Silence followed. Nothing happened. Not a spark nor a single tongue of flame. Not even a thread of smoke.

Odo's eyes opened briefly to check his progress. Inhaling deeply and closing his eyes once more, the tenor of his voice like the drone of a monk in deep meditation. He spoke the words again, four times over before going silent once more.

Still nothing.

Passing by and slowing, Pretty Boy snickered, one hand on his hip as he casually witnessed Odo's failure. Maddie snorted.

Odo repeated the words once more, the third strain broken by Pretty Boy's sniffing. His face turned flush as his fingers gripped tighter around the amulet, his hand almost shaking.

Eyes opening with a snap, Odo was caught by surprise as Maddie sniffed loudly, rubbing the back of her hand under her nose. As he looked up at her, he noticed a wicked grin on her face, fully amused at his failure.

"Need me to light that for you, child?" said Maddie as she removed her hand from her face, her mocking tone more than enough to set Odo's teeth on edge.

"Right," Pretty Boy mumbled. "Maddie, get me a striker—"

"No!" Odo exclaimed. "Wait."

"Ain't got all night," Maddie replied low and gruff. "Make me a fire now or move."

Air moved swift into his nostrils as Odo's eyes shut tight, his lungs filling quickly. He looked the fool, and he knew it. His ears buzzed as he concentrated. The words came out more forceful now, the purposeful chant anointing each syllable with the oil of ire and frustration.

"Arros el saidu inflama!" He spoke the words through gritted teeth, the sound of each syllable seeming to scrape the back of his throat as he uttered them. With a roar, the cone of tinder exploded in flame, sending a wash of warmth over Odo's face. As his eyes opened, a slow smile rose on his lips.

Maddie's taunting tongue went still, the corner of her mouth slipping down as her eyes grew in amazement. Pretty Boy's scoffing also drew silent.

Odo tilted his head and eyed Maddie. Her answer was a hard, hateful stare. Before long, she turned from him and departed the fire, leaving him to tend his creation.

"I might be more impressed if you had gotten it goin' the first time," Pretty Boy remarked, wearing that smart smirk he always used. What little flush of victory Odo felt fled in the presence of the others. He grumbled as he rose, taking up his satchel once more.

Such was the camaraderie, or lack thereof, between Odo and the mercenaries for two more days of travel. Two more days of Odo wishing the journey would *finally* end.

CHAPTER 16

Odo awoke with a start. The covers fell from his chest as he reached out for his staff. Sounds in the night, sounds in his dream, alarming enough to wake him from his deep slumber and fill him with dread. As he rose from his bed, a hand reached out and grabbed him by the shoulder, halting him at once. From the odor that wafted to his nose, Odo knew it was Snickers.

"Stay still," Snickers said, kneeling next to him. "Cap'n's orders."

His blade out, Snickers clutched tight the hilt of his sword, the tip of it cutting the ground, his stance and his demeanor indicative of how serious the mercenary was.

The horses neighed and cried, reminiscent of the sounds Odo heard in the dream. Something clearly had the beasts spooked. Those with hobbles about their hooves reared, the others pulling on their high lines, threatening to snap the line or break the branches to which they were tied.

"You know a spell to calm the horses?" asked Snickers.

"What?"

"The horses. You know a spell to—"

"No. Magic does not work in that way," replied Odo with narrowed eyes. "But I can—"

"Right," Snickers interrupted, his eyes fixed on a spot past them in the night. "Then stay where you are and keep silent."

Snickers was normally quiet and absent emotion, leading Odo to wonder if he was somehow dim. The only thing Odo knew of the man was that his name came from his favorite game of dice. Yet, the man who knelt by his side, that man whom he observed over many days at sea, was radically different. Keen-eyed, serious, Snicker's tone and words reflected a man whose business was war and the shedding of blood. Whether it was something dormant within or cleverly hidden, his hard, aggressive nature was there at the fore.

In the distance, there was a glow in the midst of a sparse clustering of the trees, accompanied by shouts, and an anguished cry that rolled out like thunder. This Odo recognized as the voice of Rojo. He scanned the campsite and found Rojo missing. Inoch was gone. Maddie and Pretty Boy were absent. Only he, the horses, and Snickers were present in the dim glow of the waning campfire.

"Where are the others?"

"Quiet," Snickers answered softly. His gaze never wavered as he knelt there as still as a statue.

In the distance off in the dark, the beam of a lamp flashed and flailed. Shouts of familiar voices resounded through the trees, Inoch's harsh voice spewing curses in some foreign tongue. Contesting with it came a screech and yawp that sent a shiver down Odo's spine. It was shrill and wordless, almost primeval in a way. His mind didn't have to race to know from whence the call came, nor did his eyes need to see such a beast. His reaction was primal, instinctual. Whatever the two mercenaries had in their midst, it was not natural. It was something else. Something as frightening to hear as it was to behold.

"By the gods," Snickers mumbled.

"We should go help them," Odo said, reaching out for his staff once more.

The fingers of Snickers pressed deeply, painfully into the flesh of Odo's shoulder, causing him to wince and grunt. "You're not goin' anywhere," the mercenary uttered with a snarl. "Cap'n says stay? You stay."

Odo feared Snickers and what he might do. He also feared the wrath of the captain for his disobedience. Yet, there was a part of him—the not so courageous part—that had no real desire to see what Rojo and Inoch were fighting. Odo relented, and the painful grip of Snickers loosened.

More shouts, and then another terrible wail, this time anguished and shrill. It was a pathetic screech whose rending cry was interrupted by the continual shouts and curses of both mercenaries. Then, as the sounds fell away, there was a troubling silence as dense as dead stone.

Anxious moments ticked by while the pair waited in the waning light. Once more, Odo protested. "Should we not—"

"Shut your hole," Snickers growled, his eyes staring straight at the source of the disturbance. Tension hung in the air, bitter and cold. The pair stared off into the darkness beyond the furthest extent of the firelight's glow. In time, their patience was rewarded. The beam of a lamp cut the night, bobbing and dancing to the motions of the hand that held it.

The tramp of heavy feet through brush and the low, sharp murmur of curses preceded the two men that broke from the night's veil. Rojo was first to appear, grunting as he moved, the firelight painting his rugged face. Slung over his shoulder, the lifeless body of Maddie hung, Rojo's thickly muscled arm curled around her waist. Her ragged blonde locks bounced with each stride he took, her head swaying in a manner that reminded Odo of a freshly slaughtered chicken. In the other hand, Rojo clutched his sword, dark stains running down from his sleeve, glistening with blood. At first, Odo thought it might be the blood of Maddie, that he might have slain her for some offense known only to the mercenaries. But then he noticed the torn leather of the upper arm, rent from the sleeve of the leather jacket he used to stave off the cold. The blood was that of Rojo, trickling down from the wound beneath the worn hide of his outer garment. Whatever thing the big Cathar tangled with in the woods, it got a piece of him before it was slain.

Inoch was next to appear. The flames of the fire painted him with orange light and shadow, the lazy lid of his one eye almost completely hidden in darkness. His sword arm out before him to keep his balance, the other hauled something behind him. It was heavy by the noise it made as it scraped through low underbrush and along the frozen ground. As Inoch drew it closer, he turned his back to the others as he clutched his load with both hands. Heaving and grunting, he yanked with all his might as if returning to the camp with a downed stag. This was no stag, however. As the fire revealed more, Odo spied a long arm mottled both hard gray and green. Inoch hunched over, his hands wrapped around the wrist. With a final effort, the mercenary captain laid a body alongside the firelight.

At first, Odo thought it was some unfortunate stranger that stumbled too close to camp. That assumption was dispelled as he got a good look at what Inoch brought back from the dark.

Casting away the arm he used to drag the corpse of his victim, Inoch let the limb bounce and fall to the ground with a thud. Bent over, hands on his knees, he breathed heavily, exhausted from his labors. Unsteady when he rose, he moved away from the thing, rounding the fire at the center of the camp, giving Odo a clearer view of what it was the two mercenaries slew in the wilderness.

To Odo's eyes, the creature was long and sinewy with skin a mossy sort of green and gray in the amber firelight. A huge gash dissected a good portion of its torso, a blade having bit deep beneath its long, lanky arms, cutting its way to the breastbone. Short and bowlegged, the creature's fingers were long—abnormally long—and knurled, the joints profoundly round. It had a bulbous sort of head atop a short neck, and large round eyes bulged from their sockets beneath pinched and exaggerated cheeks, the orbs covered entirely by thin lids. Hanging open, a wide maw sported sharp yellowing teeth painted with red blood. Bits of flesh were wedged between the gaps along with tiny shreds of brown leather. It was clear the creature managed to sink those bony points into soft tissue, no doubt what created the wound spied on Rojo's upper arm. Sparse threads of black hair adorned its crown as if this was all that remained of its former self. Odo noted impressions where one arm met the shoulder and near where the neck met the head. Beneath the skin, however, the meat was dark and red, and crimson blood glistened almost black in the dim light.

Yet of all the strangeness of the thing, the one feature that stood out most was a bronze dot that sat proud in the center of its forehead. Around it, a ring of skin formed, fusing with the metal as if it were a part of its body and not some foreign invader to brain and bone.

"Come, Odo," Inoch called out between heavy breaths.

Odo was slow to respond, the horror and oddity of the dead creature holding his rapt attention.

"Odo!" barked the captain.

Pulling himself away from the creature, Odo turned and joined both the Cathar and Inoch. Inoch pointed clumsily to the prone body of Maddie laid out on the ground. Odo stared at the frame of the lumbering woman. Her chest did not heave, her hands did not twitch. Her head fell to one side, immobile. Maddie was dead.

Kneeling, Odo laid his fingers on her brow and used the end of his staff to prop her head up to inspect her face proper. The dancing flames of the fire and the shadows they cast only highlighted the horrifying visage of the warrior maid. The very sight of her made him gasp and recoil. Distended near the point of popping from her skull, Maddie's eyes were wide open, red, and fixed in a terrific death stare. A bloated and purple tongue ballooned from her mouth and blood ran in thin streams from the corners of her lips. Below her chin, deep bruising formed—red, blue and purple, evidence she had been strangled.

"Quiet down those beasts," Inoch shouted in frustration, Snickers rising at once to meet his captain's demands.

Odo felt the neck, the flesh of it yielding to his touch. Warmth still remained within her, that he could tell.

As he pulled away his staff, Maddie's head fell to one side, lifeless and without mooring. He wasn't sure if her throat had been crushed, her neck snapped, or both. It mattered little as she was most definitely gone.

"Bring her back!" Winded, the captain still spoke with rigid authority. A hand went to his forehead, wiping the sweat from his brow.

"No," Odo answered with a shake of his head.

"Bring her back," Inoch shouted.

"I...I cannot," Odo blundered.

"Can't, or won't?"

"I do not have that power."

"But you can kill all well and good?"

To that, Odo had no answer save, "Only at your command."

Inoch turned away, cursing quietly, kicking the soil in frustration.

Odo, however, continued. "There are those who can raise the dead, or so I have read. Yet, the wizard has never taught this skill to me, nor do I have the power."

A long, tense silence hung over the group as Inoch stood there, a hand on his hip and his head bowed and still. Pulling his sword from his sheath, he turned to the monstrosity he'd dragged from the darkness. Pointing with the tip he asked, "What is this? What is this that killed Maddie, eh?"

Odo followed, leaving Maddie behind and coming at the captain's command. For a moment, he stared at the bronze disc on its forehead, lost in thought. Something about it rattled loose in his memory—an obscure scroll he had read many years prior.

Odo looked around for his dagger. Having removed it from his belt before going to bed, he had forgotten its whereabouts.

"What?" said Inoch.

"My dagger," replied Odo. "I need my dagger."

"Use this," answered the captain, pulling his own dagger from his belt, flipping it in the air to catch it deftly by the point of the blade. Stretching out his arm, he offered the weapon by its handle.

Horses grumbled and neighed, still riled and upset. Inoch snarled his displeasure, shouting in the air for all to hear. "I said, silence those beasts!"

With a moment of misgiving, Odo took the blade with a muttered word of thanks before kneeling at the crown of the creature. Blade out, he started to trim away the raised flesh around the metal disc. He could feel the blade cut, the edge grinding against a metal post beneath. As he progressed, he discerned that what lay beneath wasn't round but had four distinct sides.

"I think this is a nail," Odo said.

"A nail?" answered Inoch.

Once the surrounding flesh was cut away, Odo used the edge of the blade to pry out the remainder of the spike. As he did, the body of the creature began to twitch. The more he tried to work the nail free, the more the body moved and convulsed.

"Help me," Odo pleaded softly, the fingertips of one hand gripping the outer fringes of the disc, another on the hilt of the knife twisting it like a pry bar.

Inoch's actions were swift, thrusting his sword straight into the abdomen of the creature and burying the point into the hard ground as far as he could. After this, he knelt, pinning one long arm with his leg, placing one hand on the opposite shoulder and wedging the other hand beneath the dead creature's chin, his fingers clasping the flesh of its neck like a vice.

"Be wary of the teeth," Inoch warned.

Odo shifted moving around the head to keep his hands and arms away from the mouth before trying again. The horses fussed and cried with increased anxiety as he started once more, the beasts sensing something, a primal wisdom the others lacked. As Odo redoubled his efforts, the unique voice of Remfrey drifted through his conscious memory.

Every natural born beast was made by the hand of the Allfather. Heed them and what they say. You will learn as much from them as any musty book or dusty scroll, Odo.

Slowly the deeply embedded spike started to work itself free. With each miniscule gain, the body of the creature spasmed and moved with more violence, Inoch struggling to keep it pinned. The eyes opened and the mouth snapped as Inoch grunted, pushing down harder to maintain his grip. As the last few inches were pulled free, the thing made a hideous shriek as the flesh of the rent creature writhed its hardest and its last.

Almost at once, the horses became calm, their nickering and snorts ebbing like a sudden breeze.

What Odo held beneath the blood and gore looked like a long carpenter's nail, if not longer than most. Square on all sides and with a rounded cap, it looked mundane by all accounts. Yet, as he studied it by the dancing flames of the firelight, he saw something beneath the blood and bits of flesh that still clung to it. Standing at once, he looked around for a moment before his eyes fixed on one of the leather sacks that held their drinking water. Letting the dagger fall from his fingers, he retrieved a flask from near his bed. His fingers slick with blood, he pulled at the stopper with haste.

"What is it?" Inoch asked as he relaxed and sat up.

Fingers still covering the wound on his upper arm, Rojo knelt, though it did not look purposeful. He was breathing heavy and his eyes looked sleepy.

Water splashed over the edges of the nail as Odo worked to clean away the blood and bits of brain. Stoppering the flask and tossing it aside, he wiped the nail on his sleeve, caring little for the stain it might make. Then, from the fire, he pulled a half-burnt branch, using the flame to more closely inspect the curious object.

Revealed by the light of the dying flame, was a strange, harsh looking script in the metal of the nail—one he had seen before. An ancient tongue long forgotten by men and wisely so, forbidden, reserved only to be remembered in books and scrolls. A language locked away from the rest of the wayward world by wiser minds.

Inoch called out, impatient. "Odo!"

Odo's answer was soft and ominous. "I know of this creature. It is an ancient thing made from the remains of dead men. Buried beneath cursed ground for a turning of the moon."

"What is the name?"

"Togoloshi," Odo answered. His gaze slowly turned to Rojo, who knelt on the ground not far from him. A giant of a man, his arm still bled, rivulets of blood streaming from the wound. His face was pained, the wound vexing him more now than before.

"According to the lore, the bite of a Togoloshi is poison."

Chapter 17

"Give me one reason to not slit your throat," growled Inoch, the cold steel of his knife pressed against the neck of Pretty Boy. Captain closed quickly with his subordinate when he appeared from the darkness, approaching from behind the horses. Wrapping his fingers in Pretty Boy's hair, Inoch pulled him down to the ground with the speed and deftness of a man who had done this many times before. Pretty Boy let out a girlish yelp before his back pounded the hard ground with a reverberating thump.

Now Pretty Boy was prone beneath the mercenary leader, a dagger wedged hard at the crease in his neck where it met the jaw. Blood trickled as he struggled, the edge of the weapon cutting into the first few layers of skin. Snickers approached casually, his dagger looming above the pair, ready to aid his captain should the need arise.

"I...I heard a sound," Pretty Boy pleaded, teeth clenched, eyes slammed shut.

"Aye, we all heard a sound," replied Snickers, unimpressed by the young man's excuse.

"I...I went off, to see what it was," answered Pretty Boy, his voice strained.

Odo witnessed the scene from afar, his attention divided. Tending the wound on Rojo's arm, he couldn't help but watch as the two mercenaries bore down on their comrade. Rojo knelt on the ground, bare-chested in the cold. On the ground next to him was the shirt of rings he normally wore, the thick undershirt that provided a buffer between the armor and his skin. Atop them, the leather jacket that he wore draped over both. His shirt was untied and hanging around his waist, the shirt and jacket bloody and torn in the area of the upper arm where the teeth of the creature attacked his flesh. Rojo's armor covered his abdomen well enough, though it left his arms unprotected, an oversight for which the Cathar paid a regrettable price.

With a small amount of liquor from a flask provided by the captain, Odo used a stick to grind and mix a mash of herbs on a crudely carved bowl, a mash to be applied to the heinous wound rent by the fangs of the Togoloshi. The upper arm was a mess—flesh torn and blood coating the limb past the elbow, the wicked teeth of the creature having sunk deep into the tissue. Rojo, for his part, made a good show of things. Despite his marred flesh, he remained stoic, revealing little of any pain or discomfort he felt.

"You were on guard when Maddie was slain," Inoch shouted angrily, spittle flying everywhere. "Twice now, you abandoned your post. You had best do better than that." Inoch's cold, pale eyes scanned the face of his subordinate, looking for a lie. Killing for him was as easy as drawing a breath and it was clear—at least to Odo—that Pretty Boy was half a breath away from being the second casualty of the night.

"Just kill `em, Cap'n," Snickers said with a sneer.

"Quiet," Inoch answered, not bothering to look up. After a moment, his head tilted to one side as if some innate sense within was trying to perceive the final thoughts of his soon-to-be victim. "You had best loosen that tongue of yours," he added, pressing the blade of his dagger harder into the soft flesh of Pretty Boy's neck.

Strained as it was, Pretty Boy started to speak, "There was a noise. The horses. The horses were nervous. I went to go look."

"Leaving us alone. Asleep."

"I thought it was a fox! Or a stag!" His voice pitched high, Pretty Boy voiced each word as if he were pleading for his life.

"Have you forgot where we are?" Captain replied, a hint of anger in his tone.

"Them Watchers are all dead."

"You forget who tracked us all the way to Collenshore?"

"That's across the sea," answered Pretty Boy, his pitiful voice squeaking.

"Fool," Captain growled. "Chasing maids left your brain soft, I think. What else happened then? Be quick!"

"I followed the noise," Pretty Boy continued. "Kept going deeper and deeper. Cross the stream. Then…then…"

"What?"

"Gods, Captain, don't cut me!" Fear now crept into the strangled tones of Pretty Boy's voice.

"What then?" Inoch's voice turned harsh again.

"I had The Call."

"What?" Snickers said, as if he could not believe his ears.

"The Call."

Inoch grumbled and Snickers turned away, as if the whole incident was an ill jest.

"It was dark, and my trousers were down when I heard the shouts. I swear it, Captain! I swear it on my life, I do!"

"You stink of a lie," answered Inoch through gritted teeth.

"I was gonna hold it until my time was done, but I was out there—you can go see for yourself. I swear, Captain. I swear!"

As pathetic as it sounded, it was convincing enough. Even Rojo agreed, saying it softly to Odo, "That's what happened to Maddie. Left for The Call in the night."

Grinding away in his crude bowl, Odo set the mash down on the ground. From one of the saddlebags that lay nearby, he pulled a large folded square of linen and started to unravel it. Drawing his knife, he cut the cloth to make a wrap, pondering silently what he had heard and seen.

Quickly, Inoch pulled his dagger away and stood erect.

Hands to his throat, Pretty Boy lay there for a time, rocking on the ground. A soft sound issued from the prone man. It sounded like sobbing.

"Do you think Pretty Boy was led away from camp?" said Odo loud enough for only Rojo to hear.

"Do not know," answered Rojo as he tilted his head to see what Odo was doing. "Or he lies. One thing is known. Come morning, Pretty Boy had best left something out on the trees. If not, Captain will leave him here."

"Leave him here? What does that mean?" Odo looked up at Rojo, his fingers working the cloth in his hands.

Putting his index finger to one side of his throat, Rojo dragged the digit across the skin of his neck, tracing a line from ear to ear.

Odo understood the meaning at once, his brows lifting. "Oh!"

"Get up," snarled Inoch, the tip of his dagger pointing at Pretty Boy. Pretty Boy lay there, still rocking and clutching his throat.

"Get up, damn you!"

Pretty Boy rolled over slowly, pushing himself up to his hands and knees. As he finally started to rise at a half crouch, Inoch kicked him hard on his buttock with the side of his boot. Pretty Boy was sent flying into the dirt and debris.

Afterward, Inoch turned to address them all, arm extended straight, dagger out. "As for the rest of you, no leaving camp. Is that understood?"

The rest replied in unison. "Yes, Captain."

"You need to answer the Call? Leave it in your pants. Understood?"

"Yes, Captain," they each answered, one after the other.

Turning to Pretty Boy, Inoch barked at him as he turned on his back. "As for you—you get the honor to wrap and bind Maddie."

"Why not just make a pyre here," asked Snickers, uncharacteristic in his curiosity.

"Take too much time, and this is a poor place for a pyre. We tend to her at Pellinore. `Till then, put her in a blanket, and tie her around her horse. Understood?"

"Aye, Cap'n,"

Having doused the wound with water, Odo wet a pad of linen with liquor and applied it to the wound. Rojo hissed through tightly clenched teeth, the sound of it like a furious snake. Pulling the pad away, Odo leaned in closer to inspect the rent flesh. The dim light of the fire did little to aid him in his task, his naked eyes seeing little in the shadows.

Odo set the linen pad on his knee and started smearing the mashed herbs onto the center of a long strip of cut linen. As he worked, Inoch approached and squatted down next to the pair.

"How goes the mend?"

Odo was slow to respond, concentrating on applying the mash and bandage on the wound. Odo hesitated for a moment before answering. "The flesh is torn badly."

"I had worse," Rojo answered. This was true. Several scars blistered his skin. The most notable of them was a long, hideous scar that ran the length of his left side along the ribs.

Odo offered silence as he wrapped the bandages around Rojo's upper arm, making sure they were tight. It was a tense taciturn moment and all three of them knew it.

"And?" said Inoch.

"Perhaps we should speak more when I am done."

Inoch reached in and grabbed Odo's chin tight. Turning Odo's head to look at him, he made sure the young apprentice made eye contact. A cold fire roiled behind Inoch's pale and poisoned gaze, his anger not yet abated. "We speak now," he said gruffly as he withdrew his fingers.

Odo paused his work as his gaze fell. "You know the bite of the Togoloshi is poison."

"Speak plain, Odo, and do not try my patience further. One of my men is dead, and I have little stomach for false words."

Continuing his task, Odo inhaled deeply before letting out a troubled sigh. "The only cure for the poison of which I am aware necessitated the use of an herb named Melwort. It can only be found growing in the eastern mountains."

"Use a spell. You know magic," said Inoch.

"I was never taught such a spell," answered Odo, shamefaced.

Inoch's head fell with a discontented sigh.

"I know of other ways to treat such venom and I have the herbs. I am applying a mash," offered Odo, "but I do not know if it will work. Rojo is strong. He may be sick, but he may survive." Then with a much softer tone, he added, "That is my hope."

Head lifting with a snap, Inoch used his dagger to point at the dead Togoloshi that lay nearby. "And what of that thing?"

"What of it?"

"You said it was made of dead flesh," replied the captain. "Can someone bring it back to life?"

"The nail I took from it was the source of life."

"But *could* it be restored to life? Another nail, perhaps?"

Odo hesitated. "I...I am not sure. If I had to speculate—"

Inoch didn't wait for Odo to finish. He rose swiftly, returning his dagger to his belt. Walking over to the dead thing, he pulled it to a nearby fallen log. Fetching his sword, he drew the weapon from its sheath, casting the covering away.

At once the sword rose and fell, rose and fell again as Inoch hacked at the joints of the fallen Togoloshi. Each strike hewed flesh and bone, ligaments and tendons, rending the thing down into bits and pieces. When he was done, he cleaned his blade with a cloth he pulled from his belt before fetching the sheath and returning the weapon to its holder.

Tying the knot tight on the bandage, Odo shuffled around on the ground. Looking at what Inoch had done, he asked, "Captain?"

Inoch turned to the rest of them and said, "None of you leave camp. If this thing can be brought back, then its master will have to scrounge for the pieces. Stay here."

Rojo flexed his arm, noting the bandage with a measure of satisfaction. "Good bandage." He paused for a moment, raising his hand and wiping sweat from his brow.

"Sweats are a sign the poison has taken effect," said Odo. "You will feel weak and sick."

A sad sort of resignation overcame Rojo, his eyes shifting left and right as he wondered in silence. "How sure are you of cure?"

"Truth?" replied Odo with quizzical eyes. The tenor of his voice was far from confident.

"Truth," said Rojo.

"Not sure," he answered with a slow shake of his head, his gaze avoiding that of Rojo. Then, as if to reassure the Cathar, his head lifted. "But you are big and strong. There is that."

Yet, as hopeful as he tried to sound to the stricken Cathar warrior, Odo could not deny the sickness welling up in his bosom. Not that his words were a lie. Only that Rojo's fate was uncertain and dangled precipitously on the few things Odo learned.

He wished he had studied more. The wizard would know what to do; he always knew what to do. And in understanding this, Odo realized just how helpless and ineffectual he truly was.

Why had Remfrey send *him* out into the world?

CHAPTER 18

"Perhaps, if we return to Illsenore, I might find an herbalist there."   Odo followed Inoch as the freelancer made for his horse. The sun had yet to break the eastern horizon. The world was grainy and gray, the forms of the others less distinct in the pre-dawn light. The smell of pungent smoke and wet leaves wafted on the air, mingled with the sweet aroma of flat cakes cooking on coals. Snickers knelt next to the fire; a plank of wood cradled in one arm filled with several flat cakes. He waited patiently for the last of them to cook through.

"There is nothing in Illsenore other than ale or fish." Inoch's words were short, and his tone sounded cross, perhaps more than before. In his hands was a bundle of blankets rolled up and bound with leather thongs. These he would tie to the rear of his saddle. Bit and bridles on the mounts, the camp had been broken, and all of them were near ready to leave. The captain didn't want to waste another second at the campsite, preferring to be mobile.

"We have been there enough times to know. There are even no decent women there for the men. You are as likely to find rare herbs there as you are a courtly concubine," he added.

Pretty boy was tending to the body of Maddie, struggling with her bulk, and rigor was beginning to set in. The horse snorted and swerved as he lashed hands to feet, her shrouded body bent over the saddle.

"Make sure she's bound tight," Inoch barked at Pretty Boy. "I don't need her falling off along the road."

Pretty Boy replied with a soft, "Aye Captain." Head down, concentrating on the loops of loose rope in his hand, he clearly was avoiding eye contact.

Inoch stood there for a time, looking his scorned subordinate up and down. Pretty Boy made a strong effort to avoid his captain's murderous glare.

Something in Odo's head made him wonder if the mercenary captain might kill Pretty Boy right then and there. Only when Inoch continued walking did Pretty Boy flash a glance at him. The look was brief but struck Odo in a significant way. Dark eyes looked to him furtively, a placid face with narrow lips speaking less of regret and more of fear of what the future might hold. Looping the fibrous rope in his hands, he returned to his task. Odo continued to follow Inoch.

As Inoch threw his bundle over the back of his horse, Odo continued his plea. "If not Illsenore, then what about the city further south? There must be—"

"The Port of Rosseun is a nine-day ride," Inoch countered, fiddling with straps on the back of his saddle. The tail of his horse waved almost responsively as he went securing his blankets. "Horunass is six."

"Captain—"

"Enough!" Inoch snapped, turning at once. The horse of the freelancer snorted and stomped a hoof, alarmed by the sudden noise. His face glowered as the distinct look of frustration and anger flared in Inoch's eyes. "If what you say is true, there is a dark conjurer at our backs. One powerful enough to make a familiar with dead flesh and cursed iron. And you would have me turnabout and go back? Taking us further from those who will offer us safe harbor?"

Speechless, Odo's lips moved, but nothing came out. His mind tried to come up with a response that sounded remotely reasoned and thoughtful, but he quickly understood it was pointless to say much of anything.

"Captain is right," Rojo said as he approached the pair. "We go back? More trouble. Forward is best."

"How is the arm?" Inoch asked Rojo.

Rojo made a good show of things, flexing his wounded arm without showing a hint of pain. Yet, Odo spied the droplets of sweat on his brow and knew that his show of bravado was just that—a show.

"Apologies, Captain," Odo said after a time. "It is...just..."

"Your mash is working," Inoch proclaimed, turning to affix his bedroll once more. "Let us hope it works well enough. Now, get ready to ride. I want to be off when those cakes are done."

"Yes, Captain," Odo answered, adjusting the strap of his satchel across his chest.

As the captain so desired, they were off not long before the first rays of sunlight painted the thick veil of clouds on the horizon. They ate as they moved, each taking three cakes to consume while they rode. Everyone was offered their share, with Pretty Boy being the last. What remained on the plank were the cakes no one wanted, often charred but still edible. He took them, flashing a disquieting glare at the others as he did.

Leaden skies and bouts of cold rain followed them on the westward trek. The road they traveled was deeply rutted from years of traffic. Water collected in the grooves and depressions, mud making each stride forward questionable at best. When they could, they took to those lanes less traveled or along the grassy fringe where the trees allowed. Overall, it was a miserable day of travel where fear and gnawing doubt were palpable. The animals were driven hard when possible, in the hope they could outpace whatever followed behind.

Maddie became Pretty Boy's burden, the disgraced soldier having become a pariah among the group. Wrapped in her blanket—a makeshift shroud—her corpse lashed over the back of her horse. It was an ignoble end to a fierce and independent woman, even if she was altogether unstable.

They camped while the light still reigned, their first task to gather wood for a pyre. Inoch and Odo remained in the camp while the others gathered what they could before the darkness descended. Odo watched his patient intently, looking for signs of Rojo weakening. Outwardly, the Cathar labored and moved as he always did, though there were subtle signs that things were not well. He moved slower than the others. From time to time, he coughed. Small things that gave Odo cause for concern and undermined what small measure of hope he fostered. Five more days still remained ahead of them.

The wood piled high, their campfire was a pyre for Maddie. By now, rigor had set in, and it took a few strong arms to remove her from her mount. Her body bent like a horseshoe, the only dignity provided to her was the fact they left the blanket wrapped about her. Pretty Boy and Snickers laid her atop the haphazard pile of fuel they gathered, a good portion of the wood rotted and most of it wet. It took Odo and some magic words to light the fire and keep it going. There was no ceremony to the act. No reverence. Just a gathering of men standing in somber silence, most of whom had broken into flasks of hard liquor. They drank as they stared glassy eyed into the flames, the rain falling upon them with dismal repetition. Torrents of smoke billowed, first white, then black and greasy as Maddie's body caught fire. The smell of it repelled Odo as he raised his wet sleeve to his nose in the vain attempt to cover the stench.

The others seemed unfazed by the odor. Instead, they just stood there staring at the flames, transfixed as their comrade burned. Collectively, they seemed lost as Maddie was delivered to whatever afterlife awaited her. Someone who had fought by their side. A soldier who survived battle in its most heated and desperate moments now food for the flames. Odo wondered how many of them secretly worried they too might come to the same end. To continue forward on this journey, only to become a grim bonfire for their comrades.

No one spoke. The only sounds heard were the patter of rain and the roar and crackle of the fire. Men, standing and drinking, perhaps lost in thought, perhaps trying to divine their own fate. Evening eventually fell and weariness took them. The night passed without incident with two men on guard and no one daring the dark to answer The Call.

Rojo's cough continued the next morning, the hacking furious as he rose from his bed. Despite the respite from the rain, a deeper cold settled in. Puddles and depressions filled with water were capped with a thin layer of ice. Odo made haste to change the bandages before they left, preparing another mash. The look of the wound was questionable. Rojo's skin appeared inflamed and the stains on the bandages had a sickly greenish tinge. More liquor was applied to clean the wound, the sting and burn making the jaws of the great Cathar clench. While he stifled a growl in his throat, his face clearly echoed his pain.

Despite Odo's concerns, Rojo started their trek high in the saddle, showing no weakness as the sun broke the eastern horizon. That night, with two members alternating guard, Odo heard subtle moans come from the Cathar while he slept. While he started strong again the morning next, by midday he was slumped forward in his saddle, his strength seeming to fail him. It was then Odo knew, despite his best efforts, he had failed to contain the venom. As the day wore on, the poison in Rojo's veins moved swiftly. By the time they reached the outskirts of Pellenore, the Cathar swayed listlessly atop his mount, bending and weaving to the rhythm of the horse and its motion. As they made camp, Rojo required assistance dismounting, lest he fall from the saddle. Both Inoch and Snickers moved in swiftly to offer aid.

Their camp was established in an abandoned garrison just north of the main village, if a village it could be called. Pellenore was once a city of stonework and high defensive walls. A prosperous mining town in its golden years, it had fallen on hard times when the precious resources of the earth ran dry. After that, absent the wealth the mine provided, the town went into a long period of slow decline before being all but abandoned. There was a slow revival at some point before the Watchers took quiet control of the region. Pellenore, with the underground tunnels of the mine and strategic position along the Horunasian border, was a location greatly desired by the cult. Soon it became a center of their activity in the region. In the end, the Watcher threat was cleansed by blood and steel in a war where Inoch and his men played a part. And once the Watchers were expelled, the town fell once more into quiet obscurity.

The garrison was a ghostly reminder of a better time. Set upon a rise not far from the entrance of the mine, it was a place that guarded a high bluff. But that was long ago. The main house was ruined as were the walls and the towers. Most of the outer buildings were gone, leaving a large open space in a courtyard where they made camp.

Odo attended the dying man. A blanket covered the Cathar, fir boughs his bed, insulating him from the cold hard dirt. Changing his bandages once more, Odo applied a different mash to the wound, binding it over with fresh cloth. By now, the wound had gone septic, the rent flesh having a strong odor similar to cheese. A part of Odo wished he had inquired more of Remfrey and the healing arts of wizards. All he had was the knowledge he gleaned from the wizard and those curious nuggets of wisdom he uncovered from books and scrolls. Clearly, it wasn't enough. Wiping Rojo's brow with his sleeve, stained bandages in his hands, Odo resorted to prayer. Silent petitions were offered to the God of the West, hoping against hope his prayer might be heard. Even as he called for the healing of the big Cathar, more than a silent thought passed through his mind as he whispered the words of his petitions. A thought that left his heart cold even while it wafted around in the tenuous and untamed vapors of his thoughts. It was a question that pestered him since Maddie's cremation. With Maddie gone, and now Rojo, at what point would the others abandon him? Where was the line when the bounty awaiting them in Horunass was no longer worth the risk? How easy would it be to take what gold they had and leave him to rot?

"Praying again," Inoch said as he took a seat next to his suffering comrade. Knees up, he made a place near Rojo's shoulders. Snickers lay on the ground across from them on the opposite side of the campfire, covered by a blanket, propped up on his side. Pretty Boy sat not far from Odo, a dagger of sorts in his hand. The blade was long and thin, the cross guard just large enough to prevent a finger from slipping off the handle, but little else. He tended it carefully, sharpening both sides of the blade with a stone. In a way, he was surprised to see the weapon, for this was the first time he had laid eyes upon it in all the days he was with the mercenaries.

Eyes shut as if slumbering, beads of sweat formed once more on Rojo's brow. Watching Rojo's head rolling side to side as he softly moaned, Odo concluded that either an ill dream had befallen him, or—worse yet—he had succumbed to delusion.

Once more, Odo used the sleeve of his robe to wipe away the sweat from Rojo's forehead, placing the back of his hand on it afterward to gauge his temperature. As he feared, Rojo's brow was hot. With his thumb, he lifted the lid of one of Rojo's eyes, spying a dark iris and pupil surrounded by bright red. Likewise, bloody spittle drained down from the corner of his patient's mouth. He didn't need a book or a scroll to tell him that soon Rojo would be breathing his last.

"I have done all I can," Odo answered, all hope having left his voice. "It is for the Allfather to determine his fate."

"Which is why you pray," Inoch said. "You know Rojo is done for."

After a moment of silence, Odo answered softly and unsure, "While he breathes, there is hope."

For a time, there was silence. Late in autumn or early winter—Odo did not know which—the wilderness was usually silent save for the distant baying of wolves in the hills. Tongues of flame hissed from the campfire, pockets of gas trapped in the fibers of the wood snapped when the fire found them. Only one other sound could be heard among the others—the wet and labored breaths of Rojo as he lay there in his death throes.

"There is only one thing left to do," Inoch said, breaking the quiet. Extending his hand, he motioned to Pretty Boy, fingers out, waiting to receive the knife the soldier possessed.

It took a moment before Odo realized what was about to transpire. As he started to stand, he was grappled from behind. From the smell and the stink of his breath, he deduced Snickers was upon him. In all his preoccupation with his patient and the captain, Odo hadn't noticed Snickers had risen from his bed, and snuck behind him, waiting for the captain's signal.

Pretty Boy handed Inoch the blade, handle first, his fingers lightly and carefully gripping the point. Too thin to be a weapon of war per se, it had a singular purpose Odo would discover, much to his dismay.

"No, Captain. No." Odo protested and screamed, all to no avail. Snickers held him tight, knocking the staff from his hand before pinning him to the ground. A knee pressed upon his back, his arm forcibly bent behind him, Odo was all but helpless as he squirmed.

"Stay down, boy,' Snickers grunted. "It's better the Cathar go this way than choking out his last."

Tears began to roll down Odo's cheeks as he lay in the cold broken grasses, one side of his face scuffing the dirt. He protested loudly, his voice warbling, the sounds barely words.

"Do it, Cap'n," Snickers said strained, struggling to keep Odo pinned.

Managing to wrangle one arm free, Odo started to chant, fruitlessly at first, looking to conjure a spell that might help him break free. The words started to come as he splayed out the fingers of his free hand.

Snickers saw this. In an instant, he thrust one hand over Odo's mouth, looking to silence the chant. For a time, the two struggled, Odo attempting to repeat the words. Snickers was too quick. One finger found its way up Odo's nose while a few others pressed down and over his lips.

"Do it quick, Cap'n," Snickers grunted through clenched teeth.

Even as the pair wrestled, Inoch was calm, lifting the thick arm of Rojo enough to sink the blade. Grasping the blade tight, he tensed to drive the blade home. As he went to do the deed, he hesitated while Pretty Boy looked on, curious.

"Do it Captain," said Pretty Boy in a dispassionate whisper.

For a time, Inoch looked at Rojo, who lay there lost in his delirium. While Odo wept muffled sobs, the eternal cold in Inoch's eyes warmed, a moment of emotion flooding his sight. Brief and poignant, the moment passed.

With a singular, resolute thrust, Inoch stabbed the pit of Rojo's arm, cutting deep, the tip of the blade piercing Rojo's heart.

Rojo shuddered and gasped, and in a matter of moments went still. Inoch twisted the blade and made it dance in the thick flesh of his second-in-command. After a time, Rojo's arm and body went limp as a long gurgling exhale escaped his lips. A final, terrible sound rippled from the big Cathar.

Rojo was gone. His suffering was done.

Blood spilled out of the wound as the captain withdrew the blade, handing it to Pretty Boy not long after. With a certain reverence, he laid the thickly muscled arm of the dead man next to his lifeless body, pulling the blanket over his head as a final acknowledgement of the warrior's passing. With that, he tumbled to the side, sitting upright, knees up once more. Running a hand through his hair, Inoch let out a resolute but somber sigh as his head bowed.

"Let him up," said the captain with a voice that hinted of sorrow.

As Snickers lifted from Odo, he wiped his nose with his sleeve and muttered, "Squirms like a netted fish, that one," before turning away.

In the quiet of the moments to follow, the only sounds that filled the night were the snaps and pops of the campfire combined with the soft pathetic sobs of Odo as he lay there defeated.

In the end, despite all his learning and all the things the wizard taught him, Odo discovered a hard, unfeeling fact of life. That, sometimes, power and knowledge have their limits. That, sometimes, prayers dutifully offered are not answered. Bitter tears spilled from his eyes, the intensity matching his heaving sobs. His studious and reasoned mind seized with sorrow and guilt. And as he lay there in his wretched state, words of Remfrey echoed through his distraught and scattered thoughts, repeating endlessly as if in an infinite loop.

The world is as it is, and all the power any may possess will not change it.

CHAPTER 19

Inoch pulled one stone after another from a pile, letting each fall to the ground with a crack. Broken pieces of masonry along with found stones from the ground and trailings from the nearby mines choked a doorway hidden deep inside a patch of virgin woodlands.

"There are tunnels beneath us," explained Inoch. "It took half a moon to clear the mine and these tunnels. Wodemen were brought in to collapse the mine. It took nearly a full moon to fill this spot in."

"Why an entrance out here?" asked Odo.

"This doorway was a secret. Allowing some to come and go and not be seen. My men and I were tasked to fill in this place. Back during the war, the Watchers used Pellenore as a holdfast. From here to the mines, there are tunnels that run beneath the village and all through this forest."

Tufts of moss and dead grasses fell as the gaps in which they rooted were disturbed. Squirming their discontent, their hibernation disturbed, earthworms tried in vain to find cover once more. Dead insects and leaves fell as debris, both having died away as summer fled. A covering of earth hid the entrance from the opposite side, appearing as nothing more than a curious mound in an otherwise lonely forest, a perfect place for Inoch to hide his gold.

Odo had set aside his staff and worked with the mercenary to excavate a pocket in the heap of rock and earth. Given the events of the night before, he had little desire to do much of anything. Yet, he was wise enough to know that if the captain gave him an order, telling him no was not an option. He heaved and grunted with the larger chunks of rock, creating a neat pile a few paces away. The pair worked in isolation, doing little to announce themselves or their task. One of the horses snorted, and somewhere in the distance a sparrow sang as the sun climbed the sky. It was a cheerful song well received in the hearing, one of the few heartening things Odo had heard or seen in a while.

His mind burned with a question, though he lacked the heart or desire to ask. Rojo's demise, while secretly expected, still affected him. The guilt and shame of failure hung heavy on his heart. Perhaps if he had asked more questions of Remfrey, or read more of the wizard's books, he might have found a cure that did not require some rare and obscure weed as an ingredient.

Inoch paused and clapped his hands together as he stared at the wizard's assistant. Odo retrieved two more stones from the great pile of rock in that doorway.

Halting his work, Inoch stood straight up and scanned the terrain. Hands on his lower back, he stretched and groaned before continuing his labors. "It is a fine place to hide gold. No one comes here. Huntsmen and farmers keep to the lands south of the village."

When a large enough pocket was made in the pile, Inoch set about dividing up the gold. Two horses bore the lion's share of their fee, the others—Snickers and Pretty Boy—consenting to leave their bounty in a place they all knew was isolated and secure. They were more preoccupied with creating another pyre for Rojo, one more fitting for the last rights of one of their own.

Scattered clouds troubled an otherwise clear sky that morning, though the forest in which they labored was far from dry. Odo constantly wiped his muddy hands on the fringe of his cloak. The dirt had packed its way beneath his fingernails and clung to the cuticles. He wasn't used to this type of work, and he tried to recall where he had laid his gloves. That aside, the labor was a welcome distraction from the troubles which plagued him. He felt drained emotionally. Lost. Powerless. And, most of all, he wanted to return home.

Remfrey would have been able to save Rojo. He would have known what to do. And yet, despite the power and training the wizard provided, Odo found himself impotent and utterly useless.

"Why fill in the tunnels?" Odo's voice was soft and touched with subtle notes of remorse. Despite how he felt, he hated the silence and gave in to the impulse to ask.

"Rumors, I think," Inoch said with a sniff. He wiped his nose with his sleeve and added, "A few of the men who cleared the tunnels below returned with strange tales. Part of the reason why we buried this place, I think."

"What were the rumors?"

"Strange things. Unnatural things some said," answered Inoch, the sweat dripping from his brow.

"Do you believe that?" asked Odo, checking his hands and casting a watchful eye at his satchel that lay nearby.

"I do not know," Inoch answered. "I have seen too many strange things in my time. But when an order is given, it is to be followed."

Unfolding a large oilcloth, Inoch set it inside the depression they had made in the pile. Then it was a matter of placing the sacks of gold within. The fibers of the burlap sacks groaned at the strain of the mass they contained, Odo fearing one might break. One after another, the mercenary fit them carefully together, finally folding the fringes of the ruddy oilcloth over them covering the stash completely.

In his head, Odo tried to calculate the staggering fortune amassed in that burrow of stone. It led him to wonder once more where the wizard came by such a mass of gold. As soon as the flaps of the water-resistant cloth were folded over, the task of burying the treasure began.

"Tell me, Odo, when you prayed, was it for Rojo?" Inoch's words were uncharacteristically soft as he spoke.

Leaning in and picking up a stone, Odo handed it to the captain. "Yes, Captain."

"Did you pray that your God heal him? Or did you pray for a swift, merciful death?"

"Healing, Captain." Odo picked up another stone and handed it to Inoch.

"Because Rojo is strong, and no doubt because he would protect you, eh?"

Odo didn't know how to answer the question. "No, Captain," he answered, but thought better of the words he spoke. "In part, perhaps. I prayed for the wisdom to heal him. I have no desire that any might die to save me."

Inoch stopped and straightened himself, one foot high on a pile of stones, the other one on the ground. He was a striking figure, and imposing, as his cool gaze turned to Odo, staring at the young man for a time.

"Why else would the wizard pay us so much gold, if not to ensure that we die for you? Why this is half of our reward, eh?"

"While you slept, the others spoke. They think we should leave you here, take the gold and go." Inoch's revelations were offhand and nonchalant, but they struck the homesick wizard's assistant like a hammer blow to the brow. At once, he stopped his work, holding a sizable stone in his hand. Fear flooded his breast and the blood in his veins went suddenly cold. Eyes growing in their sockets, he stared at the freelancer not really knowing what to say.

Then it struck him. "Captain? Why then are you burying the gold?"

Inoch sniffed, lifting himself up. A small stone in his hand, he playfully tossed it in the air, almost like an unconscious habit. "I will say this—you are brighter than you look."

For a time, the two exchanged glances, each expecting the other to talk and neither of them doing so. Inoch, still as the surface of a mountain lake, broke the silence.

"When I give my word, I keep it," answered Inoch, casually tossing the stone on the pile with the others. It clacked and snapped as it tumbled over the other stones, coming to rest in an awaiting crevice.

As if he was feeding a lion by hand, Odo delivered another stone to place on the pile. Slow, deliberate movements, tense, his eyes fixed on the expression of the mercenary.

Taking the stone with both hands, Inoch continued, "A man's word is all he has in this world. Why else would the wizard pay so well if he thinks—even for a moment—that I might break and run under threat? No one hires a freelancer if they think the enemy could pay a few more coins to fight for their side."

Pausing his work, Odo inquired further. He spoke as if he dreaded asking the question, but he asked it all the same. "What if the others—"

"They are soldiers. They will do as I command," answered Inoch bending down and laying the stone in the gap.

The conversation died, and the pair went back to the task at hand. In time, the bundle of gold was hidden from view, though the mound had yet to be fully reformed. Comforted somewhat by Inoch's admission, Odo grew bolder.

"Captain?" Odo held out a stone for Inoch to take.

"What, Odo?" Inoch said without thought, taking the stone from Odo.

"Why did you kill Rojo?"

Unfazed by the directness of the question, the mercenary replied. "I did Rojo a mercy. As I would want him to do for me if I was stricken as he."

"Could we have—"

Inoch did not let Odo complete the question. Once more he straightened. "Two men down. I have a mission to deliver you for which I was paid...and paid well. You know as well as I that Rojo was a dead man. It was only a matter of time." His voice was grim and cold, and his commanding stare bore down on the wizard's assistant hard.

Odo shrank slightly at first, then relaxed. Inoch's observation sickened his heart. A sudden rush of sadness and guilt swept through Odo, his cheeks hot and flushed as he stayed the emotions roiling within.

The mercenary was not done. "Rojo was a fine soldier. He was with me for many years. He would agree with what I have done."

There was a pause, then Inoch's expression changed ever so slightly. The cold, certain stare turned passive, indecisive. As he bent down to pick up a stone to put on the pile, he spoke in softer tones. "Loyal. Bold. A better end I gave him than choking on his last breath."

"What comes next, Captain?"

Inoch paused his work. Through narrow slits for eyes, he surveyed the land around them. Clearing his throat, he answered, "The land of Horunass lay across the river. Three days ride to the city, I think. Open road, and patrols frequent as we near the city. Out here, soldiers will be few, so we take caution."

Once the hole was filled, they set to the task of replacing some of the moss and weeds they excavated from the pile to try and camouflage the recent work they had done. Inoch jumped down from his perch on the rock pile. Odo was quick to retrieve the satchel he set aside as well as his staff. As was his habit, he checked the contents of his bag after slinging it across his shoulder.

Satisfied everything was in order, he closed the leather flap and tied it shut.

Cradling his staff in the hollow of his arm, Odo wiped his hands once more on the fringes of his cloak while Inoch retrieved the crossbow and bolts that lay nearby.

Odo waited while Inoch set his foot into the iron hoop at the front of the crossbow's stock. Bending down, placing both hands on the bowstring, the captain tensioned the weapon, the trigger receiving the bowstring with a click. From a nearby quiver, Inoch plucked one of the bolts, holding it in his other hand before the pair wandered to where the horses waited.

As Odo took the reins of his horse, Inoch strode over to him. In one hand, the mercenary grasped the dart and the wooden stock of the weapon. "Tell me, Odo, what more do you know of these…these…Togo…Togomo…"

"Togoloshi," answered Odo.

"You say a dark wizard makes them, eh?"

"Yes," Odo replied with a nod. "From dead flesh. Sometimes parts, sometimes in whole." Cradling his staff in his arm, his hand motioned the procedure he described. "A nail is enchanted and is driven into the skull. Then the body is buried—"

"A dark wizard does this, yes?"

"Yes. It takes the full turn of a moon before they rise."

"They only move at night?" asked Inoch, lifting his head and surveying the land once more.

Head down in thought, Odo searched his memories. Uncertain, he answered, "I am not sure. Though it is known that most things made with dark craft favor darkness and night. Yerch, of course. Morgurs and Attin as well. But both are known to wander and trouble the land in daylight."

"Given the chance to fight in day or night, what would this Togoloshi choose?"

"Oh, most definitely night," answered Odo with a scholarly tone.

"Tell me then, once made, do these things roam as beasts? Or do they work the will of their maker?"

"The will of their maker, no doubt," answered Odo. It only took him a second to see what Inoch was trying to glean.

"You suppose a sorcerer is behind the attack? That one is following us?"

"What do you think?" replied Inoch. "A dark wizard dies, you think his creations run stray?"

"It is possible."

"With the merchants and travel between Illsenore and Horunass, you think none came upon this Togoloshi in the night? A thing like that might kill a few in the dark, like Maddie. Then stories of ghosts and peril start to spread."

With his free hand, Inoch pointed at the countryside around them. "Much gold is spent keeping the roads free from bandits. A few dead men means armed patrols up and down these roads and into the forests. Trackers and huntsmen. You see any on our journey?"

Odo thought on this for a moment, recalling any and all they passed from Illsenore to Pellenore. A few merchants and their guard, a covered wain or two, but nothing that spoke of force. "No, Captain."

"Then it means only one thing," replied the captain.

"A sorcerer," said Odo, his voice wistful and riddled with fear.

"A sorcerer," parroted Inoch. "Or a Watcher priest."

Chapter 20

It was the smell that caught Odo's attention as they neared the campsite. The smell of roasting meat and burning flesh along with the tingle of pine and oak fueling the fire. Then, as the trees cleared, he witnessed a dark pillar of smoke rising into the sky. The ruined walls of the abandoned holdfast obscured the source of the fire. The smell and the sight of it made clear that Rojo's remains were in the fiery throes of being consumed.

The sight and the stench struck Odo as being profoundly sad, the second such funereal right practiced along this terrible trek west. Two souls lost for a golden payday that, for them, would never arrive. A sobering feeling and one that troubled his waking thoughts. They died protecting him. Their lives were lost for a mysterious stone in a satchel, a rock covered by seals and runes whose origins were far beyond his understanding.

Slowing, Inoch spoke to Odo as they rode. "Speak nothing of what I said to you, Odo."

"Yes, Captain."

"I trust my men, but only so far. Snickers is loyal enough and will follow orders if I give them. Pretty Boy is too new for me to know where he stands. All of them have been tested by battle, but fear does strange things to men."

"Yes, Captain," answered Odo.

"Good," Inoch added with a nod.

Passing through a tumble-down gate, their path took them through the main archway, or what was left of it. Inoch rode slow, his horse in tow. Odo rode next to the captain. When they entered the open expanse of the common grounds, they found a wide flaming pyre, Rojo's body laid out on top, the ground cleared to the dirt for some distance all around. Tall dead grasses lay trampled beyond that, covering ruins and scattered stone that were once walls. Burning hot and hard, the flames rose high, thick, gray plumes rising like a menacing specter. The remaining horses were quartered nearby in a half-collapsed stable. Absent from the scene, however, were Snickers and Pretty Boy.

Halting the horses, Inoch handed off the lead of the pack horse to Odo. Taking up his crossbow, he slid from his horse. Plucking a quarrel from the quiver that hung down the saddle of his mount, he set the dart on to the stock. Cautious, he moved forward through the mess of stones and logs and dead fauna, suspiciously scanning the surrounding terrain.

"Snickers! Pretty Boy! Call out," commanded Inoch. His answer was stillness and silence, save for the roar of the pyre. Fallen timbers and chunks of masonry cluttered the ground, making a level stride troublesome, Inoch briefly scanning the ground before each step. He called out to them again, with only the rustle and sway of dead grasses on the lonely parade grounds answering his call.

"Captain, look!" Odo pointed to a spot beyond the pyre. Suspecting something was amiss, he let the reigns in his hands drop as he lifted his leg over his saddle. Sliding off the back of his horse, staff in hand, he landed with a thump and a crunch, grinding lifeless stalks beneath his feet. Leaving the horses, he waded through the grasses, following where the captain trod.

In the distance, the pair saw Pretty Boy rise slowly from the fauna and debris. His movements were clumsy, his stance unsteady as if drunk or stunned. Rubbing his head, he looked around before spotting the pair approaching from far off. "Captain," he yelled. "Captain! We were attacked!"

"Captain?" Odo said unconsciously as if mindlessly repeating Pretty Boy's call. There was no real question, just confusion.

"Stay there, Odo." Inoch's command was said without bothering to look back. Crossbow in hand, quarrel waiting on the stock, he slowed his approach. The sight of Pretty Boy alone was not enough to get him to lower his guard.

Hand on his head, Pretty Boy stumbled forward weak. "Captain, it came at us—one of those things. One of the things that killed Maddie!" The shuffle turned into a stumbling gait as the mercenary continued his trek towards his captain, all the while pleading words stumbling out of his mouth. "It...it took me unawares, and when I woke? Snickers. It...Snickers."

Closing the gap between them, Inoch lifted the crossbow, making a bead on Pretty Boy before halting. A click of the lever and the twang of the string rang out as a bolt went flying.

In the blink of an eye, the quarrel slammed deep into the chest of Pretty Boy with a dull thump, knocking him back. Stumbling, Pretty Boy fell to the ground hard along with the cracking of fragile stems. Thereafter, a panicked cry arose from the wounded soldier. Bewildered. Agonized. Wracked with fear.

Inoch took the initiative, letting the crossbow fall with a clunk and drawing his sword without a moment's hesitation. Closing the remaining distance with a dash, the captain let his sword rise and fall. Just above the tops of the grasses, Pretty Boy's hand thrust up in the fruitless attempt to block each blow.

Thrusting and slashing, Inoch grunted with each strike. Pretty Boy bleated out, "Captain, Captain," protesting, screaming. The voice that was so sly and seductive and so beguiling to the ladies now squawked and squeaked mindlessly as his captain set about cutting him to pieces.

Odo froze in his tracks. The horror of the events unfolding before him sent a chill through his frame. His heart seemed to skip a beat, his limbs paralyzed by bewilderment. "Captain?" His voice was little more than a whisper, the words he meant to say losing all meaning as he witnessed murder in its most cold-blooded form. His mind went blank, and his fingers turned numb as they clutched tightly at his staff.

When the screams of Pretty Boy ceased, Inoch straightened and stood there for a time looking down. Finally coming about in full, his eyes leveled at Odo. Blood spattered his face and garments, that cold dead stare he saw when they first met returning like a vengeful ghost from an icy realm. A realm where those condemned to damnation dwell.

In an instant, something spoke to Odo. Something primal. It told him to turn about and run. Just run.

"Odo!" barked the captain.

He didn't wait for context, nor did he care. Odo spun about, set eyes on the arch where they entered this field of slaughter, and made a path to escape the inevitable. Running mindlessly, heedless of the terrain, he gripped his staff with both hands. There was no plan. There was no thought about what he'd do once he got there. Fear drove him. His legs moved with the same swiftness as a rabbit pursued by a hungry fox. Had he the time to reason or kept his wits about him, he might have thought through his hasty plan better, perhaps making for one of the horses and riding away instead of fleeing on foot. Or being mindful of the clutter that lay hidden by the high vegetation.

Something caught Odo's foot. Before he knew it, he felt the weightless sensation of flying. A queer thought occurred to him in that split second where gravity ceased to be, something along the lines of being the quarrel that cut down Pretty Boy, cutting the air and striking home. The hard ground came up to him and a light flashed behind his closed eyes. When they opened again, the world was a blur. It spun much in the same way it did when he had a belly full of ale in Illsenore.

Illsenore was one of the more pleasant moments in this journey, or so he mused in his stunned stupor. His head ached and the ground moved like the waves of the sea again.

Crunching grass was heard, footsteps heralding the approach of the captain. A vague notion came to him that this was his ending. That the last thing he'd feel was the cold steel of Inoch's blade. Instead, what he felt was a hand gripping his robe, rolling him on his back, and a sharp pain as Inoch slapped his cheeks.

"Get up." Inoch's words were soft but even his softer tones were still orders. "Come, Odo. Get up."

Immediately a hand went to the top of Odo's head as he felt the tug of Inoch's arm. Instinct took over as the top of his head began to throb from the wound on his crown, his legs remembering how to stand. Unsteady, he wobbled like a drunkard, the strength of Inoch's arms steadying him.

"What do you think you were doing?"

Odo pulled his hand from his head, the tan skin of his fingers and palm painted a dark red. Blood. At once, his senses returned to him as he winced from the newfound pain.

"You were going to kill me," Odo answered wincing, returning his hand to his head. He still wasn't thinking clearly. Nor was he in any condition to defend himself.

"Why would I kill you?" Inoch growled, annoyed. His tongue came out and licked his lips, both top and bottom spattered by blood. In disgust, he turned his head and spit. "You are worth far more alive than dead." Then, gripping the collar of his cloak, Inoch pulled him along as he muttered, "Come with me."

Struggling to keep pace, Odo was helpless in resisting the mercenary's pull. His mind fixated on maintaining his balance, instinctively fearing that one misplaced step might send him stumbling to the ground. Across the uneven terrain they went, near to where the bodies of Pretty Boy and Snickers lay. Arriving at the spot, Inoch halted, throwing Odo to the ground next to the still body of Snickers.

"Look at his throat."

Hand on his head again, Odo replied strained, "What?"

"Look at his throat," Inoch commanded again, this time pointing with the tip of his sword.

Sprawled out spread eagle in the grass, the expression that remained on Snickers' face was one frozen in perpetual fear. Tongue blue and swollen, it protruded past his lips, his face a ghastly shade of dark violet. Eyes red and bulging out of their sockets, it was a sight reminiscent of what he saw in Maddie. And yet, the only thing that passed through Odo's mind in that moment was how Snickers smelled as bad in death as he had in life.

Drawing closer, he gingerly pushed the dead man's head to one side. There, running below the chin and along the length of his neck, a line of bruising showed, bleeding in places where something abraded his skin. It took a moment before he saw the pattern—a thin dark line, quite pronounced amongst the bruising.

"What am I seeing, Captain?"

Wiping his blood-speckled face with his sleeves and spitting again, Inoch answered. "He always liked to use a cord on his victims."

"Snickers?"

"Pretty Boy, fool!" scolded Inoch.

Slowly, Odo rose and turned to face the captain, mouth open, words escaping him.

"That sewer rat has been a spy in our midst since the beginning." Inoch's words were hard and harsh. Yet, as he went to use his sleeve again to wipe his face, Odo noticed a tremor in his hand. A subtle tick, easily missed by less observant eyes. But a tremor all the same.

"I should have slew him when Maddie died," Inoch said, his tone hot but his face absent any sense of fury. "An error I will not make again."

Rubbing the top of his head with his hand, Odo asked sheepishly, "What do we do now?"

Thrusting the tip of his sword into the ground, Inoch set about pulling away Odo's hand from his head. Having all the grace and patience of an angry bear, he twisted and pushed Odo's head around to view the wound. For a time, the mercenary captain studied the cut, pulling at Odo's hair and probing the gash with his fingers. The young man grunted and yelped from pain needlessly inflicted. Inoch, however, seemed oblivious to Odo's suffering.

"I've seen worse," Inoch said before letting Odo's head loose. "Go back to the horses. Clean it and get a bandage on that. When you are done, make ready to leave." With a disgruntled sigh, he added, "I will take care of the rest here."

"Yes, Captain," Odo answered meekly. Hand once more to the top of his head, Odo made his way through the open courtyard, shambling more than walking. Somewhere along the way, he picked up his staff, which lay on the ground dejected and seemingly forgotten. It was then his mind returned to the stone he carried. With anxious hands, he felt the strap of the satchel around his breast. Fumbling with the ties on the flap, he pulled back the covering and reached within. Feeling around, he felt the stone and the paper around it, touched the letter handed to him by Remfrey. Pulling the stone from the leather enclosure, he checked the seals, breathing a sigh of relief when he found them undamaged. Back into the satchel it went.

A man's word is all he has in this world. Why else would the wizard pay so well if he thinks—even for a moment—that I might break and run under threat?

Inoch's own words bubbled to the top of Odo's thoughts as he bandaged his wound. He used water first to clean the area, the liquor that followed to sanitize the wound burned like fire on his brain. The lids of his eyes slammed shut as he hissed through his teeth as the sensation hit him. The noise he made sounded like water cast on hot coals. Something in his head noted the philosophical nature of Inoch's statement as if a part of his mind was detached from the searing pain he was feeling at that moment.

Even now, Odo had a hard time thinking it was only gold involved. Yet, he wasn't about to inquire as to the motives of the mercenary captain.

Having acquired a wad of cloth from his saddlebags and pressing it to the wound, Odo moved swiftly to consolidate the gear they might need. Food, water, and blankets were prioritized above all. Inoch still had a large bag of gold with him to be used out of necessity. Everything else was left and the extra horses set free. Four mounts remained—two for the riders and two to carry supplies.

Inoch, for his part, threw Snickers on the pyre as best he could. Pretty Boy, too, ended up in the flames, though not all of him. Taking a fallen branch and hewing it with points on both ends with an axe, Inoch made it a makeshift pike, and planted it deep into the ground.

On top of this pole was impaled the disembodied head of Pretty Boy, whom Inoch hewed from the body of the traitor with an axe. Lids open, the bright eyes that once excited the ladies were now rolled back into his head. The lips and mouth that once held a cunning sure smile hung open, his tongue lolling out of the gap. Blood ran from the grisly thing, staining the pole and the grass beneath it. Had it been only a few days before, Odo might have retched at the site. Now, he could only stare at it in grim wonder.

Odo poured water over the blood-stained hands of Inoch. The mercenary spared their precious water to wipe away the last vestiges of a traitor, as if the taint of it could infect him as well. Unfazed by what he had done, he rubbed his hands as the crimson fluid dripped away. It was at this moment Odo dared to ask the latest question on his mind.

"Captain?"

"What?"

"Why—"

There was a reluctance to finish the question, his inner sensibilities returning to him.

"Why did I do that to Pretty Boy?"

Inoch held out his hands once more and shook them, beckoning Odo to pour more water.

As the water flowed again, the captain rubbed his hands together once more. As he did, he answered Odo's question. "Because now the priest will know that we know."

"And what will that do?"

Inoch shook the remaining water from his hands. "If fortune is with us, it will put fear in his heart. Or send him into a rage. Now, put the water away and make ready to leave. Daylight burns. We need to find shelter before nightfall."

CHAPTER 21

Slow and cautious, Odo placed a few strands of hay over the marks he made on the dirt of the stables where they were quartered. One of the horses snorted in the back, threatening his concentration. He set another ward in the ground like he had done on their march from the Crooked Tower, a deadly snare for the unwary. This time, however, he was not as hesitant as before. The only overwrought worry he had was a concern a stray goat might wander over the mark and ruin all his work.

At least they would have goat to feast upon that night. The prospect of fresh meat didn't sound half bad.

Odo slowly backed away, treating the rune like a loaded bear trap, fearful to even breathe lest the snapping jaws be sprung. He was alone at the entrance of the stables, the rising moon bright behind a haze of overcast clouds threatening rain.

The farmer who offered accommodations was an amiable sort. Even to rest in the stable was a blessing. Providing them a half a loaf each for an evening meal was beyond generous. That and the three gold coins Inoch offered for the homesteader's hospitality. Yet, it was nonetheless a simple kindness that Odo planned to thank the Allfather for in his evening prayers.

Odo stepped back a pace, crouched down, and carefully lifted his staff from the ground, being wary to keep it far from the fringe of the rune. Straightening, he turned and headed back to a nearby heap of hay where their gear was piled.

"Done?" asked Inoch. It took Odo a moment for his eyes to adjust to the dark. The captain took a position on the other side of the hay, resting against a wall of timbers that separated the front of the stables from the back. He preferred the shadows as his blanket, keeping a clear line of sight to the entrance. Nearby, the stock of his crossbow lay propped up against a supporting timber, tensioned and within arm's reach. Next to it, a succession of quarrels—four in all—their heads thrust into the dirt floor, made ready at a moment's notice.

"Yes, Captain," answered Odo as he laid his staff down against the mound of hay. He bent down, his fingers clamping on the edges of a bucket filled with water. With a grunt, he lifted it, moving it aside. The chilled water within sloshed, numbing his fingers, which he wiped dry with the fringe of his cloak.

Many such buckets were placed strategically around the interior, mainly at the behest of the homesteader. He no doubt feared the feckless regard of two strangers who might spark a fire on a cold autumnal eve. He was a friendly enough man with kind eyes and a graying beard that was in desperate need of a good combing. More than one bucket was provided. The farmer placed them about the interior with a smile and a nod, choosing not to speak openly of what troubled him.

Turning, Odo took up his staff once more and had a seat at the base of the dry hay. The dead grass crunched and squeaked as he leaned back, cradling his staff in his arms and stretching out his legs. A musty smell arose, wafting to his nostrils as the strong scent of horse and their manure permeated the very wood of the structure. As unwelcome a stench as it was, it was far and away preferable to fish or the reek of those cramped quarters he occupied on the Sarajwebo.

"Make sure you do not block my view," said the captain.

"Yes, Captain."

"How is the head?"

Instinctively, Odo reached up and felt the wound on his head. The area was still tender and slightly wet, a scab not yet formed over the wound. "Fine, Captain."

It was quiet that night, despite the rustling and snorting of horses in the rear of the structure and the rare baying of a goat in the pens not far away. To Odo, it was a nervous sort of silence.

The type that led him to wonder, over and over, how things might go horribly awry.

"What if the ward sparks the hay?" said Odo, concerned.

"Let it burn for all I care. I will give him gold enough for three stables more."

Odo grumbled, pulling the fringes of his cloak tighter around him.

"Just do not block my aim," warned Inoch.

Odo thought for a moment. "What if they come from other than the doorway? What if there is another way in?"

"I closed and barred the doors and checked the outside. We will hear them well before they make their way in. The horses will tell us of their approach."

Odo thought back to the night Maddie was slain, the grumbling and whinnies of the horses, even as Inoch dragged the dead thing back to the camp. The words of the wizard rang out from his memory.

Blessed be the beasts of the world. They are always the first to note danger and the first to smell evil when it is near.

"What about the farmer?" inquired Inoch. "When the beasts start to call—"

"I placed another rune on their threshold," answered Odo. "They will sleep until I remove it."

"Good thinking," replied Inoch.

Reaching over to the packs, he grabbed his hunk of bread and began to pick away pieces, placing them into his mouth before chewing. The bread was dry, near to the point of being stale. Still, it was better than having to dig through the saddle bags for something to eat.

"Strange," Odo remarked.

"What?" Inoch's tone signaled a general disinterest, despite answering Odo.

Odo eyed the rafters and noted the size of the structure. His eyes tried to pierce the gloom, merging memory with vague, grainy features obscured by night. Large timbers hung overhead, fitted with a craftsman's precision and eye, individual stalls with sturdy walls and thick gates to quarter animals. It was far from a hasty ramshackle building made for a lonely homestead far from the cities. "It is a large stable for only three horses."

Inoch was quick to answer. "It is a decree of the king that homesteads near the road must have a stable to house ten horses or more. Those that don't raise one will have a portion of their land taken for such purpose."

"Seems strange," noted Odo."

"It is to house those that patrol the roads."

"Why?"

"Bandits," answered Inoch. "They were a problem during the war."

"How far is it to Horunass?" said Odo as he chewed.

"Three days, I think," answered Inoch.

"When we get there, what then?"

"You go and meet with them. I get my fee. You will like them, I think. They are like you."

"No," Odo replied, "I mean, what will you do with your payment? Where will you go?"

For a time, there was quiet. Odo probed further. "What will you do with the gold?"

"First, I go to Pellenore, get the gold I buried. Maybe hire a few men to guard me as I do."

"Is that all? Is there nothing more to life than gold?" Odo pulled another hunk of bread from his ration and placed it in his mouth.

Another long silence followed, Inoch not so easily giving up his secrets. "Tell me, Odo, will you keep that stone the wizard gave you? Or will you give it back?"

"The one I carry? That I am to give to the king."

"The one around your neck," Inoch quickly corrected. "The one that gives you the power to draw wards and cast spells."

From beneath his robe, Odo pulled out the talisman and held it up slightly to inspect it. The moonlight gave a new life to the dull stone, the diffused silvery light refracted within the matrix of the crystal. "Yes," he replied after a time. "It was never mine to keep. Only something to use at need."

"You intend to tell the wizard all you have done with that power, Odo?"

This time, Odo fell silent. His mind reached back to the beginning of the trip and the wards he cast. The smell of the charred flesh of the man who was the victim of his work.

"Yes," replied Odo sheepishly.

"And what will the wizard think of how you used the gift that was given to you?"

"You ordered me to lay those runes."

"Aye. And they took a life. Something that sickened you if I remember."

"Captain," Odo piped up, turning his head slightly. "Do you mock me?"

"Answer the question, Odo."

Reluctantly, the young man replied with the only words he could summon. "I do not know."

A pause settled over the two with Inoch breaking the silence. "I know little of the life in that crooked tower. Yet, the world beyond? It is not a simple place. Sometimes you do as you must to survive."

Inoch's head fell back slowly, finally resting against the wood of the stall. "Do not condemn yourself, little wizard. Had you not done what I commanded, you would have been left alone in that open plain. Or dead. Hard to say."

Odo pondered the words Inoch spoke, remembering the threats to abandon him if he did not set the wards as commanded. A harsh thing to say at the time. Now, having witnessed the horrors that beset them on their journey west, the need for that cold resolve had become abundantly clear. War and death either bred hard men from the soft or broke them utterly.

Yet, as Odo recalled those first uncertain days of his journey, an odd thought struck him. A question of sorts drifted through his mind like an unexpected draft in a room. A sudden, unwelcome chill in warm confines whose source eluded detection. It came in the form of a question he wanted to ask and yet feared to do so. Curiosity eventually outweighed caution.

"Captain?"

"Yes, Odo?"

"I have a question to ask of you."

"Speak," answered Inoch.

Odo, hesitated, doubt invading his reason. "It is just...it is something I have wondered—"

"Ask your question, Odo, before I die of old age. Or before you annoy me," chided the mercenary.

Odo's tongue was still as he reconsidered the words he was going to use. "It is, well...you were willing to abandon me so easily when we began this mission. For far less than what we face now. Yet—"

"Because I did not know you. And I did not know what I had in my midst," replied Inoch, surprisingly unfazed by the inquiry.

"Then why remain now? You have more than enough gold as none of it needs to be shared," followed Odo.

"Aye, true," replied Inoch. "I could live like a king until my final days with the gold I possess. And a sharper man might do just that, or one less true to his word.

Some say the reputation of a man is greater than gold. In what I do, being true to your word, even when it means your doom, pays well. But that is not why I stay."

Odo's thoughts returned to a dark night in another barn not so well maintained as the one that sheltered him this night. "You are using me as bait once more."

"I see now why the wizard takes such a liking to you," answered Inoch. "You are brighter than most, without need for guile. Yes, Odo. You are bait. If not you, then us both."

"And what if the threat we face is greater than us both?" Odo turned his head slightly, as if doing so, Inoch's words might be more insightful and clear.

"I started with a wizard and my best men," replied Inoch. "Now, only you and I remain." Inoch halted for a moment before asking, "What do you know of these priests? Of the Watchers?"

"Very little I am afraid. Only what you and Rojo told me."

"I put a few of them to the sword," continued Inoch. "Eyeless freaks and their dark powers. I made sure they spit their curses through bloody lips and broken teeth before I hung them from a tree." He paused once more to reflect on the past. "If any of the deeds I have done trouble me, it is not wiping their lot from the world. The things I have seen."

"So, this is about vengeance? For Rojo?"

Inoch sighed, answering softly at first. "Maddie was who she was. Her anger had its use. Snickers kept his own company. Yet Rojo? If ever

I had a friend in this life, it was he." His voice trailed off for a moment, the question asked and unanswered.

Odo's head dipped as he retreated into his own musings. For the first time ever, he saw something soft and vulnerable in the stony heart of the man with dead eyes. Yet, the captain was not done with his explanation.

"I want you to say a prayer for me, Odo. Like you did for Rojo."

"Captain?" Odo thought back to his many quiet petitions for the burly Cathar in his final days.

"I want you to pray to that God of yours. I want you to petition His favor. That I might live long enough to wring the life from the eyeless son of a whore who took the life of my men. Who killed Rojo. You will do this for me, yes?"

Odo's answer did not come quickly. "I...I will pray for our deliverance."

"The only way we will be delivered from this, Odo, is if the priest lay dead. His life poured out onto the ground. You pray what you pray. But your God or no, I will have my vengeance. For my men. For Rojo."

"Yes, Captain."

After that, another sullen silence returned, Odo taking his time to silently mouth a prayer to the Allfather. When that was done, he picked up the crust of bread that remained, wishing he had an appetite. This time, it was nerves that robbed him of hunger, not the sick feeling of his past deeds. Deeds that haunted him like an angry ghost.

"A powerful thing you have hanging about your neck," Inoch piped up. "Seems strange that the wizard would so freely lend such power to someone he did not trust, eh?"

"What?" asked Odo with a slight turn of his head. He let the bread fall from his hand.

"What I am saying, Odo," Inoch spoke up, "is that such power is not given away lightly. To have done some of the things you have done since we left only means that he has placed a trust in you."

"How many wizards have you known in your time?" said Odo.

"Two," Inoch replied. "Three with your master. More if I include those dark priests."

"Who?" Odo's heart began to beat hard in his chest at the mention of dark wizards.

"One named Gregor. A counselor to this King Merrith you seek. Another named Faradyn."

"How well did you know them?"

"Well enough to know that their secrets are jealously kept. What power they had was hoarded like gold and like misers, rarely spent.

What I am saying, Odo," Inoch continued, "is if the wizard did not trust you, you would not have that stone. No one pays the sum he paid for you to be delivered safe and alive. A princely ransom we were paid. He did not even haggle."

"Do you blame me? For the loss of your men?"

"We kill for a living, Odo," Inoch answered. "In what we do, Death is a frequent guest. I have lost many over the years. Few freelancers live to see old age. If it wasn't here and now, it would have been in some petty squabble between two spoiled princes over a useless patch of land." He paused for a bit, letting loose a sigh. "Losing Rojo was hard."

"Why don't you just stop then?" Odo inquired, confused by how one could live in such a way.

"To do what?"

"What, then, is the purpose of all that gold?"

Inoch was not so quick to reply. "In the south, there are islands. The water is blue. The air is warm and the people there know little of war. I thought that I might build a home there. Buy an island for myself and forget death for a time."

"Sounds nice."

"Aye. It does."

When the conversation died, the pair remained in somber silence for a long time, sitting in the dark. Over the span of hours, the diffuse moonlight dimmed. In the distance, the low rumble of thunder was heard and the rumor of a breeze made itself known. Cold air rushed into the stables, setting some of the stray remnants of straw to flight.

"A storm approaches, I think," remarked Odo. The observation went unanswered by Inoch.

Moments after, the horses in the back began to grumble and the baying of the goats drifted from their pens somewhere outside the stables. The noise the animals made was low at first and almost went unnoticed. However, the restlessness continued, making it hard to overlook.

"Captain?"

"I hear," answered Inoch as he lifted from his place against the stall. Quickly, he pulled out his crossbow and plucked a quarrel from the ground, setting it in the stock.

The animals snorted and grunted, their fear and panic creeping upwards like the low rise of a flooding river.

Something began to move in the dark outside the barn, Odo catching it in the corner of his eye. Then came the voice, as jagged as broken ice and twice as cold. A wicked, mocking tone whose words were like the edge of a jagged knife.

"And what do we have here? A wizard's cub? Protected by men whose swords slay for gold? And how much did the wizard pay for such loyalty? A hundred Talens? Two?"

Odo heard rustling behind him as Inoch drew close enough to speak without raising his voice. "Odo, you answer him. Speak carefully. I do not think he knows our true numbers."

"How much of that gold will you spend when your life spills out into the dirt and the light fades from your eyes?" said the voice once more. The very words struck a cold dagger of fear in Odo's heart. How did he know about Remfrey? How did he know about him? Or the mercenaries that Remfrey hired?

Then, he remembered. Pretty Boy.

Soft and low, Inoch spoke to Odo, giving the young man a measure of confidence, as feeble as it was. "The priest fishes. He knows little. Tell him little. And keep clear of the door, lest I put a dart in your back." With that, Inoch crawled back into the obscuring dark, kneeling near his sword.

Seeking to keep the item he guarded safe, Odo slung the satchel across his head and around his shoulder, the strap of it slung tight across his chest. Using his staff, he lifted from the ground. Looking back at Inoch in a moment of indecision, He turned once more to the door of the barn. "What is it you seek?"

"Ah, the cub has a tongue," came the reply. "Yet the mewling of a cub interests me little. I speak to those with greater understanding. My offer is simple. Hand over the boy and what he carries and you will walk free to spend whatever meager portion that accursed wizard offered you."

"Proclaim yourself," commanded Odo.

In the night, amongst the alarmed noises of the beasts, Odo strained to hear the low, grating cackle as his unseen pursuer laughed at Odo's bold inquiry.

The voice continued. "Three of your number have died already and you have taken to turning on your own. How many leagues lay between you and the walls of Horunass? How long do you think you will last? This night? Another? How long before my servants take you all in the bosom of the night while the others sleep? Speak now or share the fate of the one you protect. I await your answer."

There was a long pause, the only sound being that of the horses, the baying of the goats, and the cackle of hens in a distant coop. Soon after, a new sound was heard. A scratching against the walls somewhere near the back. The alarm of the horses in their stalls greatly increased, the thudding of anxious hooves and the pound of the hindquarters of the horses as they banged against the stalls. In the growing chaos of that space came the clacking of shingles over top of them. This was not some sort of nighttime rodent as it scrambled to and fro along the roof. It was heavy. Its footfalls made the cedar shakes crack and groan beneath its weight. "Click clack. Click clack." Up and down it went over the top of the peak and back again. Forward and back and around.

"Captain?"

"Quiet," barked Inoch, kneeling and sliding along the hard ground of the barn, the fibers of the hay tearing as they ground beneath his knee.

Odo gripped hard his hazelwood staff, knelt at the ready with both hands. The two defenders had their eyes cast upward as they followed the noise, debris falling from above, tracing the path of the mysterious thing that stalked them from on high.

Seconds passed in what felt like hours as Odo's heart thumped hard in his chest. Thunder boomed again, the ground beneath him trembling as his fingers wrung the dense wood of his staff.

Strength began to wick away from his legs, his knees trembling slightly. In his head he vainly searched for the words of a spell he could use to counter an assault should it come. His lips moved without sound as he practiced the words of power, praying silently that when battle came, he would not fail or falter.

Then came those chilling words from outside. "So be it. You have chosen your fates."

CHAPTER 22

The clicking and clacking continued along the roof, coming to a stop somewhere behind the pair. After that, only the neighs of frightened horses and the baying of the yard assailed their ears. Their attention drawn to the rear of the stables, Odo and Inoch prepared for an assault from behind. Anxious and wary, each of them tensed, waiting for an attack.

Just then, an explosive crack and a bang thundered from the entrance behind them. A bright flash lit the interior like a strobe, a cold, white light like lightning striking from the sky. The graying timbers of the structure lit up on their faces. In an instant, Odo could see the passage to the stalls, the pegs where tack and gear were stowed, a pitchfork propped up against the far wall and lengths of rope nestled on the ground like large immobile serpents.

As suddenly as it came, the light was gone, shadows reclaiming the space. Odo's ears rang from the sudden sound.

An ear-rending screech filled the air, the sound of it like a shockwave. The flash left him temporarily blind, his eyes struggling to adjust. He stumbled clumsily until his vision restored, though darkness no longer filled the stables. A warm orange glow crept in, dancing in the dark as he turned to face the source of the blast. The ward at the entrance had been tripped. Before him, the grim picture of a Togoloshi burned at the entrance, victim of the full power and effect of Odo's enchanted rune.

Wreathed in fire, a form danced and spun around, long arms flailing in the dark, flames dancing along their length. Amidst the shrieks and screams, a sweet and acrid smell wafted to Odo's nostrils. An unwholesome odor smoked as the thing cooked, vainly trying to rally against its inevitable fate.

For a time, Odo stood there dumbfounded, left immobile by the shock of it all. Never since that fight in the tumbled-down barn on the outskirts of Collenshore had he seen first-hand the work of his meager skills. He stood numb, unable to comprehend the damage done as the nameless creature sizzled beneath unquenchable flame.

Returning to his senses, he tried his hand at another bolt of energy. Leveling his staff at his hip, Odo began to speak the words of power. Before the first word came out in whole, the sound of a dart cutting the air came to his ear and a blur tore through the shadows. When Inoch's bolt landed home, it struck with such a force that the creature was knocked backwards, hitting the ground hard, flames and cinders jumping from the burning thing on impact.

The cries of the animals grew more intense. In the dark, Inoch reloaded as Odo looked on, paralyzed. Toward the back, the splintering of wood was heard just below the manic cries of the beasts in their stalls.

Small tongues of flame grew from the dirt floor of the barn. Odo immediately dropped his staff and rushed to one of the many buckets nearby. The water sloshed as he lay hands on the swollen wood of the buckets, huffing as the weight of the water within them resisted his efforts.

"Forget the fire," barked the captain.

The words went unheeded by Odo as he spun, haphazardly throwing the water at the many growing flames that began to sprout like weeds from the scattered hay. Into the air it went like a spray, landing hard, the bucket falling free from his hands. It hit a patch of orange and yellow tongues, weakening some, dousing others, and missing the rest altogether.

As his eyes looked towards the entrance of the stable, he saw movement from the creature that burned. It rose from the ground, blackened skin beneath fire, a dart sticking out prominently from its chest. Long gangly arms thrashed. Warped bowed legs strained to stand straight. As it unfolded upwards, another quarrel cut the air, hitting the thing center mass once again.

Realizing his error, Odo immediately rushed back to where he dropped his staff. In his haste, his feet slipped on a swath of hay and he tumbled to the ground, the satchel he carried slipping beneath him as gravity had its way. The lump of the item he carried hit him square in the middle of his abdomen, briefly knocking the wind out of him. A moment or two passed before he was able to scramble to his feet. As he did, he saw Inoch, sword in his hands, race to the fore, closing on the burning creature. As Odo reclaimed his staff, he turned just in time to witness the cleaving blow of Inoch's blade. The weapon left a fatal wound between neck and shoulder, the beast vainly defending itself with a swipe of its claw and missing.

As the captain pulled his blade free, the Togoloshi fell to its knees. From there, the fiend fell on its hands. Without a second thought, Inoch gripped his sword with both hands, raising the blade high in the sky and letting the edge cleave another path at the base of the monster's neck. The severed head fell, bounced, and rolled along the ground, setting alight more of the straw.

In his momentary victory, Inoch stood straight, taking a moment to collect himself. Then, from the dark beyond the barn, a blue bolt of something cut through the night. It hit Inoch on his right side, knocking him back into the barn, the impact sending his sword flying from his hand.

Collecting himself, Odo focused his thoughts, leveling his staff and aiming at the spot in the darkness from whence the blue bolt originated. The noise of the animals and the growing flames around him hampered him as he spoke the words of power. *"Yen. Girin. Mar."*

Nothing.

This time, the young man closed his eyes and tapped his panic and rage. Speaking the words again, he placed behind them a voice with confidence and purpose. *"YEN-GIRIN-MAR!"*

From the tip of his staff, a purple ball of scintillating flame shot forth, cleaving through the dark. In the distance the power of the missile connected with something unseen, crashing and spraying like a rush of water against unyielding stone. Behind it, something cackled, the sound of it mocking, malicious, sending a chill through Odo.

Inoch recovered, stumbling though still stunned. Finally, he lifted himself erect. Odo moved quick to help the captain.

Inoch at once looked around for his sword, his eyes catching something in the dark behind them.

What happened next unfolded quickly as if Odo was all but a helpless witness to the events that transpired. In the confusion that reigned, a form dropped down from the back of the barn, hitting the ground with a hard thud. Unnoticed by the defenders, another Togoloshi had torn away the shingles that covered the roof of the stables.

Through the hole, it dropped down while Odo and Inoch were preoccupied. Wounded, it moved with an awkward shambling gate as it rushed forth, the fall damaging one leg. Long gangly limbs outstretched, it sprang from the shadows, letting out a shriek as brittle and hard as broken glass. Even with a damaged limb, the strength it possessed seemed impossible as it flew headlong at Inoch, who stood discombobulated from the blast that clipped him.

Odo watched, stunned and helpless, mouth agape, eyes widening as he witnessed the creature lift and arc, colliding with the mercenary. The two combatants hit the ground in a heap, a pronounced thump rumbling through the cold hard dirt.

Lightning flashed, and in the blinking of an eye, night seemed to give way to day before retreating just as quickly. The flames inside the structure continued to grow, the scattered straw making ready fuel for the spreading fire. Inoch wrestled with his attacker on the ground, one arm underneath the thing's chin pushing its head upward. The digits of the Togoloshi struggled to make contact with the mercenary's flesh, the fiend making a high-pitched growl. The pair rolled in the dirt and hay as Odo watched, paralyzed and fascinated. Arms thrashed and legs kicked as one rolled on top of the other and back again. In his stupor, words wafted to his ears as if from a distant place on some misty plain.

"Odo!"

Shaken from his stupefied state, Odo moved to action. Pulling a dagger from his belt, he closed with the grappling mass, raising his weapon in the air. His eyes watched as the Togoloshi finally rolled atop, leaving Inoch on the ground, exposing its bare back. Odo shouted wordlessly as the dagger fell with all the strength Odo's arm could muster. Biting deep into the mottled green flesh, the blade halted halfway in, the kinetic motion of the cut stopped by bone. A rending wail followed. An elbow connected with Odo, knocking him back hard. He stumbled, tripped, and fell to the ground.

As Odo scrambled to his feet, Inoch somehow got a foot under the fiend, and with a grunt, kicked the creature off him. A minor victory, it was unfortunately brief, both combatants rising as quickly as they could. The Togoloshi was faster. Before Inoch could stand, it lurched again, this time its fangs finding a home in the nape of Inoch's neck.

The captain roared in pain as the teeth cut through leather, cloth, and flesh, the head of the Togoloshi twisting and turning, rending muscle and sinew. Somehow, Inoch managed to pull a blade from his belt, stabbing repeatedly at the creature's ribs and the softer parts of its abdomen. Its teeth bore down even harder, as if killing the captain was now its only purpose.

Odo recovered as well, grabbing at the knife he left in the creature's back, pulling it free as Inoch fell back, taking his attacker with him. With little else to do, the young man manically stabbed at the thing, both hands on the dagger, each thrust mindlessly in its destination. Over and over the blows repeated, both above and below as Odo and Inoch set about cutting the thing to ribbons. Eventually, the creature weakened enough for Inoch to push it off again.

This time, the Togoloshi fell on Odo, his left arm flexing tight as Odo fell back, the force of the impact and the weight of the monster pushing the air from Odo's lungs. His blood up and his mind focused on a single task, Odo suddenly remembered a spell. A moment of inspiration, the words repeated over and over in his mind as one hand clutched the throat of the monster. His fingers dug into cold flesh as he shouted the words with purpose.

"LITENISMA MOROG VOLUE!"

The creature shuddered, twitched, its eyes bulging from its sockets as a powerful electrical charge flowed from Odo's hand. Then, in a second surge of electrical power, the Togoloshi was knocked away, its body flying backwards in an arc, landing on its back. As the vile thing squirmed and twitched, its nerves garbled, its limbs tensing uncontrollably, Odo scrambled to his feet. Dagger in hand, he let not a moment pass before he fell on his assailant once more. His dagger rose and fell with a startling savagery, the young man screaming uncontrollably as the blade bit into his opponent's head and neck. His impulses were running on pure adrenaline, all rational thought gone as his primal side was unleashed.

There was no counting the number of times he stabbed at that bow-legged fiend, nor did he lay a keen eye where the dagger pierced flesh. As quickly as the beast within him came, it vanished. What he left behind was a ruined, bloody mess. The thing still twitched, though weakly. Gurgling noises came from its throat. Not long after, its limbs relaxed and there was sound no more. Odo rose, unaware of the cold blood that spattered his face and ran down his cheek. He breathed hard, his lungs unaware the immediate danger had passed. Vaguely aware of a droplet of the creature's cold blood running down his cheek, he reached up with the back of his hand to wipe it away. It was then he realized his hands were slick and painted a dark red.

Horses screamed and cried in the back. Smoke rose and the fire sizzled, the stink of it filling his nose. Should he douse the flames? Should he attend to Inoch? What else awaited them in the darker recesses of that barn?

A thump rumbled along the ground and a familiar voice groaned. Spinning about quickly, he caught the prone form of Inoch out of the corner of his eye. At once he rushed to the captain's side.

Dropping to his knees, he looked his fallen protector up and down. His clothes had been rent in the melee, though the mail that covered his torso looked to be intact. On the left side of Inoch's neck a grievous wound bled. There, cloth and leather were shredded and torn, the side of Inoch's face painted with streaks of red. It didn't take Odo long to realize just how deep the teeth of the Togoloshi had dug. Dark blood poured out in an alarming stream. A nicked artery, perhaps, deep beneath the flesh.

"Captain?" Odo vainly called out. At once, his wits returned to him. Dropping his knife, he pressed a hand against the wound in the fruitless attempt to staunch the bleeding.

Despite the state he was in, Inoch was all too aware of his condition. Blood formed on his lips. In a voice both weak and wet, the captain said, "Odo. Flee this place."

Heedless of Inoch's command, Odo looked up and around him, seeking something to press into the wound. Spying a crumpled blanket nearby, he grabbed Inoch's left hand and placed it against the wound. "Press hard. Here!" he said, the urgency of his words cutting through whispered breaths.

"Odo."

Ignoring Inoch's pleas, Odo rose, dagger in hand. Moving swiftly, disregarding the growing danger about them, he set about cutting a large strip of cloth from the nearby blanket. Taking time to warily scan the interior of the shelter, he returned to Inoch with the cloth, falling hard to his knees. With trembling hands, he moved the captain's hand away from the wound, only to see it was completely covered in blood. A cold sick feeling entered Odo's limbs. Pulling away the tatters of the rent cloth and leather, he scanned the wound to no avail. Blood pooled as it spilled out, making it near impossible to evaluate the extent of the damage. Acting quickly, he pressed the dingy green swath of cloth into the wound and pressed hard.

"Odo," Inoch said weakly. "I am done for. Flee this place."

"Quiet," Odo replied, unable to think of anything else.

"I won't die like Rojo," answered Inoch. "Leave me here to burn."

"I will not leave you here to die," replied Odo in a senseless shout.

"Blood, fire, or poison, I am dead. Now flee." The blood bubbled from Inoch's lips as he spoke, his eyes rolling back into his head.

Odo had given little thought to Inoch's plight other than the wound he sought to mend. Odo's mind began to stir. Stifling smoke wafted into his nostrils, causing him to cough as it invaded his lungs. Soon, he realized how true the mercenary's words were. A moment of clarity came to him. A quicker death by bleeding-out was a far greater kindness than what was to befall him. And yet, the words of the wizard came swiftly to him.

All life is precious, Odo, no matter how long or how brief. Remember this above all things and the Allfather will bless you in return. For where there is life, hope remains.

"Quiet," Odo said with a false smile. "There are still many miles to go to Horunass."

In a moment, Inoch's bloody lips turned up in an uncharacteristic grin. Blood spat from his mouth as a croaking chuckle rose from deep in his throat. "Fool of a wizard," he mumbled afterwards.

Even as they spoke, the fire in the barn grew, the heat of it now felt on Odo's face and back.

Heavy wet drops of rain began to hit the ground outside the barn, the noise of them squelched by the screaming of the horses and the sizzling sound of the fire. Yet one thing that was heard rising just above the din was the cracked, haggard laugh of the sorcerer waiting somewhere outside of the stables.

Odo's head lifted and looked about, scanning the interior. One Togoloshi was dead, its head severed from its body, the other lifeless, its blood pooling on the dirt of the stable floor. The only threat that remained lay outside the wooden wall that defended him, somewhere in the dark of the night.

Once more lifting Inoch's hand, Odo set it against the cloth that covered the wound in his neck. "Press here as hard as you can," he ordered. Eyes set on the entrance of the barn, he reached beneath the cowl of his robe and dug out Remfrey's talisman. Winding it around his left hand and burying the stone in the flesh of his bloody palm, he rose to his feet and set his eyes on his hazelwood staff.

Inhaling deeply, a defiant flame burned in his breast. Odo voiced a bold prayer, seeking aid from his unknown, unseen God. "Allfather! Everlasting God of the West. Hear me. Aid me. And let us be done with this chase."

For good or for ill, Odo was done running. Summoning as much resolve as he could, he made for the entrance of the barn to confront whatever remained out there in the black.

CHAPTER 23

Stepping out into the gloom of the night, Odo paused. Cradling his staff with one arm, his right hand pulled up the hood of his cloak over his head. The rain was still sparse, coming down in large drops, heralding the onset of an approaching storm. Stepping out further and leaving the clamor of the horses behind him, he gave little thought to anything but the night. His focus was ahead of him, confronting the danger awaiting him in the encircling black, his breath steamed in the biting air, reminding him of a story about a sleeping dragon. His heart thumped wildly and his blood-slick fingers anxiously wrung the dense wood of his staff. The harsh smell of the fire behind him still lingered in his nostrils, the dim light aiding his sight in the night. He gripped tight the stone in his bloodied hand as he spoke the words the wizard taught him.

"*Aleosensigthia.*"

He repeated the phrase with growing vigor until the night's sky no longer cloaked the threat that awaited him.

The shade of night lightened before him. Many paces away, a dark figure stood, situated halfway between the goat pen and the coop where the chickens cackled in alarm and fright. There was no fox in that hen house. The threat that raised their beastly fear was standing on open ground, patiently awaiting the young man like some sentinel of doom.

The smoke from the barn wafted its way to his nose once more, and heavy drops of rain peppered the cloth of his cloak and hood, suddenly growing in frequency. Striding forward a few paces, Odo stopped, and for a few tense moments the duo faced each other in the silence of the night. Odo, his mind a swirl of anger and confusion, remained immobile, unsure what to do or say next.

"What is it you want?" shouted Odo.

The form cackled, low at first, growing more and more maniacal as the seconds passed. When the laughing ceased, the form spoke to him with a voice as cold and harsh as winter's ice.

"So, only you remain." The stranger's tone was grating and sinister.

Odo clutched his staff, his fingers trembling as his heart pounded in his chest. His legs felt weak, his knees threatening to give way. It was a mixture of adrenaline, terror, and sheer will alone that kept the young man upright in the face of an evil he could almost feel.

Yet, in spite of the fear and vexation he felt, there was courage still in his heart. His face turned stony. The lids of his eyes narrowed as if his wrathful stare was a weapon itself.

"What do I desire?" questioned the figure. "Why you, of course. You and that which you carry."

His lips pressed tight together, each breath passed hard and harsh through his nose. "Show yourself," demanded Odo.

The sorcerer was silent at first. "You are in no position to demand anything, child. What fool of a wizard sends a cub into a world ruled by lions?" Then, with a tone that stuck Odo in the gut like a knife, he added, "You are no match for me, boy. You know this."

The rain fell hard and fast now, penetrating Odo's robe, the ground beneath becoming slick with a thin layer of mud. A million things rushed through Odo's head, the events of his life passing like a cloud of Meadowlarks bound for warmer climes. Images moved, turned, and twisted in a mass, seemingly chaotic but with purpose. Thoughts of home. The sound of Remfrey's voice, soft and scholarly. Things he had read and the images he conjured of them. Spells and counter spells, none of them appropriate, his mind grasping desperately for a solution, as if this encounter were simply a puzzle that needed to be solved. Yet, as his mind buzzed in thought, his heart sank as the words of the dark sorcerer repeated themselves over and over somewhere in the back of his mind.

You are no match for me, boy.

Now, in this hour of his greatest need, the voice of Remfrey was strangely silent. The wise words fondly and dutifully remembered failed to come. His protectors slain, one by one, Odo stood alone against an unknown threat. A threat keen to the knowledge of dark spells and vile lore. Rites forbidden and deep, such that it could raise three minions to plague and ruin them.

Behind him, in the burning timbers of the barn, Inoch lay dying. Poison in his wound and a nick in an artery bleeding away what little life remained. A man cold and unyielding whom Odo had grown fond of over time. The man who once threatened to leave him for gold and commanded him to do the unthinkable. A man who, in the end, remained true to his word.

Odo's heart despaired. Grief welled up in him like a geyser. His soul called out to the God to whom he prayed, hoping after hope for aid to arrive in this dark hour.

The end of his staff thumped the wet soil, his right hand letting go to reach around and grasp the strap of his satchel. Pulling it clumsily over the cloth of his hood, he lifted the leather bag he carried close to him all these days. Holding it up for the sorcerer to see, he offered it silently for a time. The dreaded thing Remfrey entrusted to him. The secret and the burden that embodied the trust and confidence of the wizard in his pupil. It almost made him physically ill to yield the bag and the stone. His insides melted like jelly, his gut raging against his acquiescence.

"This is what you desire? Here it is." The young man shouted, his chin trembling as he gave voice to the words. Pulling his arm back, he tossed the satchel towards the sorcerer. The weight and pull of the stone pulled the strap from his fingers, the bag arcing in the air before falling to the wet ground. The momentum made the satchel slide an inch or two before coming to rest midway between the two opponents.

As soon as the bag hit the ground, Odo lifted his staff, thumping one end hard to the ground. "ARAMACHA!" he shouted, the force of his voice expressing his will, a sudden wellspring of valor in his heart giving power to the words. In response, the tip of his staff pulsed with a scintillating violet light, leaving behind a dull ultraviolet glow. Once more, he leveled the staff, his right hand gripping it like a weapon. Feet apart, he set his stance and prepared for a fight even as a tear fell from the corner of his eye.

"Take it, if you dare," growled Odo. "But you will leave Captain and me alone."

Lightning flashed once more, thunder rolling behind it like the voice of an angry god, the peals of it filling the silence. Odo's vision began to darken, as one spell was traded for another. As the grumble in the skies waned, he heard the cutting laugh of the sorcerer once more. This time it was long and condescending, his head thrown back, dismissive of the threat Odo posed. For a long time, the dark master continued this way, beyond amused at the prospect of some sort of wizard's duel.

"So, the cub has claws?" His hands spread far apart as the cloth of the sorcerer's dark robe grew like wings of shadow, making him seem larger than before. He took one step forward, then another.

"I will take what you carry, little cub. I will strip you of the wizard's stone. And, if I am merciful, I will let you live on…as one of my pets."

He took one more step forward then stopped, his arms falling.

From behind Odo came a voice barely audible above the din. "Odo! Behind you!"

Odo spun about, barely in time. Approaching rapidly, a dark form charged, the features of it hidden by the night's shadow, backlit by the amber light of the burning barn. Without a second thought, Odo leapt aside, stumbling, falling back, hitting the ground hard, his staff flying from his hands. The pounding of panicked hooves thundered through the ground as the form passed by. Crossing his arms in front of his face instinctively, he dared to lift one arm to witness his approaching doom.

The form in the night passed by him, barely missing the young man, then another form rushed out from the barn, this one screaming. Horses.

They were horses escaping from their stalls, fleeing the now burning carcass of the stables.

Thinking quickly, Odo pulled himself up into a ball, his hands and arms covering his head, fearful of the tromp of hooves as the beasts raced past wailing in mindless fear. The ground rumbled as Odo gritted his teeth and closed his eyes, anticipating the pain of many pummeling blows. Their cries and grumbles louder now than before, the horses were driven by sheer terror, stoked to a fever pitch by the greedy flames. With them, along with the confusion, was heard a loud thump like the sound of a heavy sack falling from a great height. With it came the cracked and stifled screech of a man, the nature of whose voice was all too familiar to Odo by now.

Seconds passed. The sky roared, the echoes of it roiling, fading into oblivion. The freezing rain fell harder now, dripping unwelcome onto his face from the hem of his hood. He waited, holding his position on the ground. There was no sound save the falling of the rain and the cracking of timbers in the stable as they yielded to the fire. Hooves still thumped but they were distant, the sound growing less as the seconds ticked on. Odo held his shape for a moment before relaxing some more. Peering out on the world past his raised arms, he scanned the terrain with a healthy measure of trepidation, expecting the rush of some crazed animal running at him full bore in its madness. When that didn't happen, he slowly lifted his body, the golden links of the talisman drooping from his hand. Eyes skyward, he saw only darkness and the haze of the rain. Hands into wet earth and mud, he pushed himself up and quickly scanned the field.

There were eight beasts quartered in those stalls, Odo remembered—seven horses and a mule. Flames consumed the aged and seasoned timber of the stall far beyond the ability of a few buckets of water to quench. Smoke began to enshroud the structure, the fire protesting the driving rain from above. The satchel which Odo tossed at the dark sorcerer lay exactly where it came to rest, undisturbed. He wiped his hands on his woolen robe now slick with mud, his eyes tracing a line from the satchel to where the Watcher priest once stood. Where a shadowy figure once loomed, a heap of something rested in its place. It moved slightly, lying on the ground. A weak groan made itself known above the din of the storm and roar of the burning barn.

Odo wrapped the talisman around his hand once more and sought his staff. Pulling the hazelwood stick from the damp ground, he inspected it quickly, praying it remained intact; it did. He could smell the mud on himself and feel the pull of it on his robe and cloak. Nonetheless, he was unharmed, the only one still standing. Or so he thought.

From the blaze of the barn, another figure appeared, this time moving slow. Silhouetted against the orange and amber glow of the fire, it was the tall form of a man shambling forward.

Arms down and behind, he struggled with each step, two burdens seeming to drag behind him. In one hand, he clutched a sword, though he had not the strength to lift it. In the other, saddlebags. His head was tilted to one side, a large clump of cloth wedged between neck and shoulder. It took Odo a moment, his eyes focusing and his mind still addled.

It was Inoch. It could only be Inoch.

A few steps forward and the figure fell to its knees, struggled to stand, then finally gave up the fight. The sword and the bags fell from his hands, Inoch finally collapsing to his side.

"Captain," Odo shouted before rushing to his side. His feet splashed on ground that grew slicker as more rain fell. Approaching the fallen mercenary, he let go of his staff and dropped to his knees, almost sliding across the ground.

Odo shuffled and turned in the gathering mud of the farmstead. His hand reached around, cradling the head of the captain in his lap, one hand pressing against the wound. Tears momentarily halted now began to leak out the corners of Odo's eyes, the trails they left on his cheeks all but lost in the drenching rain.

Inoch's eyes blinked furiously trying to bat away the droplets that fell from on high. In a weak voice, haggard and half shouting, he called out to Odo, "The priest?"

"He is down," Odo replied with a half-hearted smile.

Inoch swallowed hard, breathing heavy now. "Odo," Inoch said in a weak cry, "Finish it."

"No, Captain," Odo answered in protest, his voice tremulous in his grief. "I will not do it. I will not end your suffering, like Rojo."

"Not me, you fool," Inoch said in rebuke, his failing strength and resolve returning to him in a waning instant. "The priest. Take my sword. Finish him."

"But—"

"Do it, damn you," commanded Inoch, his voice haggard and his skin turning pale.

Eyes lifting, he looked past the crumpled form of Inoch to the sword that lay in the mud near his feet.

"While there is breath in him, we are in peril," Inoch added, his words halting through labored breaths. "Slay him and end this."

Gently, Odo lay the head of Inoch back on the ground, making sure the cloth was still pressed against the grievous wound on his neck. Pulling up Inoch's near lifeless hand, he placed it on top of the cloth saying, "Press here." It was a useless gesture at this point and Odo knew it.

Rising, Odo strode around the captain, eyeing the blade. He reached down and took the hilt from the gathering mud, the weapon heavy in Odo's hands as he lifted it from the ground. The rain and muck made the hilt slick in spite of the leather wrappings. Clutching it tightly with both hands, he lifted the weapon clumsily as if it were a heavy burden. Head turning in the direction of where his foe lay, his body followed, both slow and purposeful. Feet splashing in the water that collected on the ground, Odo made furtive steps forward. In his head, the events of the past days repeated themselves over and over in a maddening cycle. The burnt body of the Watcher. The hot eyes of the denizens of Collenshore. The attack at the orchard, the Togoloshi, and the terror and sadness they left in their wake. Rojo's fate and Pretty Boy's betrayal. The bulging eyes of Maddie as they stared blankly at a cold autumn sky. Swaying with each step forward, Odo felt his grip on Inoch's sword tenuous with the downward pull of the earth threatening to wrench it from his grasp. His heart beat a furious rhythm in his bosom, pounding on his breastbone as if trying to escape his chest. A numbness settled into his fingers as he clutched tightly the hilt of Inoch's sword, not knowing what might come next and fearing the worst.

Moans and muffled curses came to Odo's ear as he approached the downed sorcerer. Half dead, the wretched thing still defied the darkness of oblivion. For a moment, Odo halted, partly summoning up the courage to do what must be done and partly desiring for it to be over. One foot reached out and set itself on a shoulder beneath the black garb. A pained cry issued from the broken man, if a man he still was. Lightning flashed as the head beneath the deep hood turned. In that instant, with the cold white burst of illumination from the lightning, Odo finally got a good look at the vile conjurer that hounded him since Illsenore. Wisps of light hair pulled back from a withered brow, dark blood staining skin so pale it seemed as if the man had not seen the light of the sun in decades. Deformed slightly from the unlucky strike of a hoof, a portion of his face was swollen and purple. Yet, in the sockets where his eyes were supposed to be, flaps of skin were overlaid, fused to the cheeks and brow.

Odo's heart thundered in his chest as he stood there, his emotions a mixture of pity and revulsion. It passed through his mind to let the Watcher priest lay undisturbed, his fate already sealed. Yet, even now, the conjurer's spite and wickedness persisted, defying the embrace of death. Swollen lips spit blood, slurring the words of a curse upon the young man. Even now, as death neared, he spoke words filled with venom and spite.

Heart hardened, Odo wrung the hilt of the weapon, lifting it high, his hands and arms trembling. In the strobe of another lightning strike, he let out a primal yell, letting the pull of gravity and the anger in his limbs drive home the blade. Piercing flesh and bone, the blade cut through the withered heart of the foe.

The dark priest screamed as his body shuddered. Odo heard none of this. Holding down the body with his foot, he wrenched free the blade and thrust it through again. Then again, and once more. A mindless, wordless yell issued deep from Odo's gut, driven out by his angst, fear, and pain.

Pain hidden since birth, multiplied by the events of the journey and the ever-present loneliness that plagued him. Again and again, he drove the blade home, a sudden madness blinding him to the fact that his foe was already dead. With one last thrust, every fiber of his being drove home the keen steel with such force it unbalanced the wielder. Losing his footing on the slick earth, Odo fell back into the mud.

Chest heaving, Odo lay there inactive, stunned in a way. As if reluctant, the young man rose to his knees. There was no sickness in his gut this time, no regret. Rising to his feet, he shambled back to where Inoch lay, leaving the mercenary's sword in the carcass of their foe. His gait was like a man drunk on too much wine, stumbling the entire distance back. When he reached the fallen warrior, he found Inoch motionless, mouth open, face absent expression. Rain, icy and hard, poured down upon the man he called Captain, Odo looking once more to those cold dead eyes. Yet those eyes no longer returned his stare, fixed skyward, lifeless, the lids no longer caring to shield them from the rain. No more did the billows of warm breath escape Inoch's nostrils. Inoch was gone.

The strength of his limbs failing, Odo fell to his knees defeated. In a rush, the emotions came pouring out of him like the bursting clouds above. Tears fell. Sobs came slow at first as his face wrinkled with grief and pain. His body convulsed as his voice cried out in the night—wordless, raw, without contemplation or thought.

The man who threatened to leave him behind so many days past remained—in the end—faithful to his task. Unto the bitter end.

CHAPTER 24

Shivering as he sat there on the stoop of the farmhouse, Odo held his staff upright in one hand, wiping away the tears from his cheeks with the other. Blood crusted beneath his fingernails and cuticles. Skin the color of tanned leather was stained black and gray from ash. His face was streaked by hands caked with soot, the result of the many hours of attending to all the things that needed to be done.

The top of his head throbbed. A wet sniff followed as he stared at what remained of the farmstead. The sun had already crested the tree line, the day already underway. Behind him, on the worn, wet wood of the farmer's threshold, a large sack lay. Inside the folds of the rough burlap, a small fortune in gold coins resided, taken from Inoch's saddlebag. A few coins were deducted for necessities, the rest left behind as recompense for the stable he helped destroy. It was, after all, the only decent thing to do.

Wet wood made up the pyre on which he laid the fallen body of the man he called "Captain"—a title spoken with far less fear and resentment than at first. Magical fire was not as encumbered by the elements as natural flame, though it took Odo several tries before the pyre was alight. A large stand of trees nearby supplied most of what he needed. Odo did his best not to take from whatever stocks the farmer and his family needed to keep warm during the winter.

As Odo thought back to the events of the night past, he started to cry once more, his face pinched in sorrow, a squeak escaping his lips. The outburst was short lived, the young man reining in his feelings. Yet, even after emptying his sickened heart for many hours, he was cognizant of what still needed to be done. He sat on that stoop alone, wrestling with the dreaded images of the recent past and an uncertain future. An incessant fear gripped him, nourished by former days filled with death and betrayal.

In that uncertain time, awkward memories of home returned to plague him. The quiet discomfort he felt from time to time came back to him in a rush, hounding him again, like old regrets ladled atop new.

Then, like now, he returned his anguish and sorrow to a place in his heart where he'd locked them away. With his composure restored, his keen mind and studious sensibilities returned to the tasks ahead of him. There was still a package to deliver and a mission to complete. If grieving needed to be done, it would have to wait.

To his side, he picked up a piece of cloth cut from the robe of that eyeless sorcerer. Within the folds lay two nails, both pulled from the dead Togoloshi, one from the creature that killed Maddie and Rojo. The other from one of the assailants that came at them during the night. He unfolded the cloth and inspected the spikes he had extracted from their skulls. They didn't seem like much, save the fine writing inscribed on each side of the spike. Angry letters written with a precise hand and cunning skill. He wondered after the source of such dark lore. Knowing legends and myths of days gone by was one thing. Understanding from whence they came was another.

Too much time was wasted grieving over the death of Inoch. He had exhausted himself dragging that foul conjuror into the interior of the burning barn. The stink of burnt Togoloshi, all charred and smoking, made him retch at first. He had intended to brave the flames to extract both nails; the heat and the smoke made that impossible. A sharp crack from within the structure was warning enough to leave the hungering flames to their business. Instead, he had kicked the head of the first fiend out into the open ground and withdrew. His stinging eyes had witnessed the steam rolling up from his clothes, evidence of the intensity of the heat within.

The fire still burned even now. The grand carpentry of the stables collapsed upon itself. What remained was blackened timbers, smoke, and scattered flames. The Allfather, in his blessing, had brought the rain, preventing the fire from spreading and consuming the livelihood of the homesteaders. Odo would have to remember to offer thanks for this in his prayers.

The spikes and the cloth were bound around the center with a stray thread. No doubt Remfrey would want to inspect these dark things when he returned home. Depositing the grim trophies into the contents of his satchel, Odo inspected the wrapped stone, and the sealed letter which he was to hand the king upon his arrival. That was *if* he arrived. There were still many miles to travel and much uncertainty of what else may be stalking him from behind.

Horses milled about the farmstead, dispossessed of shelter. Two chestnut plow horses and a sable rider gathered together with a grazing mule. Of the four horses he and Inoch brought to the farm, he could only locate three. The saddles and all their gear were all consumed by the blaze save for the saddlebags that Inoch dragged away from the stables. Odo knew he'd have to go bareback. That meant mounting a beast that was as tall as him without the aid of stirrups or a seat to grasp onto. Remfrey provided lessons to the young man, teaching him how to speak to animals, though that was a long time ago. If that didn't work, Odo would have to improvise. That was the least of his worries.

Sitting on that stoop, watching the flames of the pyre consume the body of Inoch for a time, he fell into his own thoughts, ignoring the creeping cold of his soaked attire. Mud caked his cloak, robe, and trousers. Mud, now dry, encrusted the dark curls of his wild mane. No doubt he stank to high heaven, even worse than when he pounded out sulfurous ash. His appearance, however, was the least of his worries. The smoke would undoubtedly attract other homesteaders. He needed to be off, and soon. What gave him pause was the unknown. Was there another of these eyeless conjurers out there searching for him? What other sinister surprises awaited him at the approach of night? Even as he labored to dispose of the dead and ensure those foul Togoloshi remained absent life, he was ever fearful that more remained. Could the dark wizard have laid a trap for him in the event of his demise? Like a gnat buzzing in his ear, the thought plagued him all night. Even now, exhausted and dreading a long day's trek, the fear of what might lie ahead kept him alert and awake.

Ashen hands wiped the ward of sleep from the door of the farmer's abode, Odo chanting words to deactivate his spell. In a few minutes, the family would wake, find the gold, and look on in horror at the mess he left behind. The words he used to speak to his horse—a calico mare— worked well enough. She came as he instructed, and he lashed the saddlebags to her hindquarters. Throwing the satchel over his shoulder, he instructed the horse to kneel, which she did with a grumble and a snort. Setting himself on the back of the mount, his hazelwood staff balanced across her back, he prodded her and spoke once more. As commanded, the beast took the path from the farmstead to the road where he continued his mission.

The farmer could keep the other horses. It seemed only fair.

From that moment on, his journey west was a long, tense, if not lonely affair. Teeth chattering from the damp cold, he shivered most of that morning, his clothes still far from dry. His condition made it difficult to balance on the back of the horse and more than once he nearly slipped off. Clutching in desperation to the mane, he was able to steady himself. His situation got better as the day went on, the rays of the sun beating down upon him and the warmth of his body doing its part to dry his things.

Remembering something Inoch said about a main road, he found a wide thoroughfare, following a setting sun to his destination. A pitiful looking thing in some regards, he wandered a vacant stretch of road all day. It was a lonely business, the travel along that desolate highway. From time to time, he had a dangerous tendency to nod off. All it took was the croak of a raven or the cracking of a limb broken by some unknown beast in the forest to get the adrenaline flowing through his veins. He stared wide-eyed, looking to and fro as trees rose around him, his fear only abated with the passage of time and sleepless exhaustion. Despite all his nervous trepidation, nothing came at him along that well-traveled track. And despite his wariness to close his eyes, sleep found him as night approached. A small fire that night was the only thing preventing him from freezing to death in the terrible chill.

After breaking camp the next morning, the fire all but dead, Odo extinguished what remained. The sound of horses on the road, the rattling of chains, and the clunk and creak of wagons came to his ears. He was quick to gather his things, withdrawing hastily with his horse further into the surrounding woods. Finding a good screen behind a stand of firs, Odo wrapped one arm around his horse's neck and whispered to her as he watched the road from the gaps in trees.

Slow and lumbering, a convoy of three covered wagons passed before him on the road, each pulled by a train of four horses. A fair number of men rode with them, surrounding the carts. They carried what looked to be crossbows, the hint of a sword or two made themselves known from beneath the cloaks. Hope welled up within him, thinking this might be some armed detachment of Horunasian soldiers. Perhaps they might be able to escort him to his destination. Yet, he could not see the surcoats beneath the drawn cloaks and a voice in the back of his head warned about trusting strangers on the road.

The assemblage of horses and men moved on at their deliberate pace, oblivious to Odo's presence. He worried plumes of his breath would give him away, but in the end he remained hidden. No one halted. No one strayed from the road to investigate the still warm coals of the fire or the matted grass where he once lay. They had no interest in him; in that he was partly glad. Yet, fear and suspicion gnawed upon him. He had no idea how many miles lay ahead, riding alone on the road and ill prepared for a trek longer than a handful of days. Likewise, he had no idea if more Watchers were on his trail looking to finish the task the eyeless conjurer started.

Waiting until after they had long passed, Odo mounted his horse and continued his anxious journey. He held to the fringe of the road for most of the day, ready to move into the cover of the forest should anyone approach. Where the forest cleared, he strayed from the main track, following his own parallel line.

On his own now, with no others to defend him, his very senses worked against him. With each pace forward by his horse, he felt the tickle of hidden eyes on the back of his neck. Real or imagined, it felt all the same on the barren road, his head constantly turning, his eyes seeking movement in the lifeless trees and praying he found none. No matter how far he went, it wasn't far enough. No matter how much he urged the horse forward, it wasn't fast enough. A forest road was not only lonely but foreboding in its silence, like the constant whisper of rumor that foretold some imminent threat. It wore on him with each stride. In the pitiless wilds he was exposed, vulnerable, and ripe for misfortune to strike.

Yet, if misfortune were to unerringly find him, it was not this day. The travel was slowed near evenfall, the road showing signs of life. Moving off into sparse, slumbering forest, he followed the setting sun. Here the terrain was harder, and he was ever cognizant of skirting scattered homesteads to avoid detection.

His wandering brought him to a rise. From there he dismounted and scanned the terrain, noting a road and traffic. On an opposing hilltop, fortifications were erected, the land about it cleared to the road. It was a fortified encampment buzzing with activity. Merchant wagons and travelers of all sorts stopped for inspection, some choosing the spot as a safe location to stop for the night. The smoke from many fires rose in the still air, dark curls against a sky fading from amber to violet as the sun retreated in the face of night. Odo debated for a long time as to the wisdom of approaching the settlement. Furtively trying to recall some sage words the wizard imparted over the years, he sought his guidance, only to find that comforting voice stilled. Nothing Remfrey ever said or did covered the dilemma presented to him, save for one.

The Allfather speaks to all of us in our time of trial, no matter how great or small the challenge.

Odo looked for that still, small voice in the back of his thoughts, the one that spoke comfort and assurance even when everything seemed bleak. There was nothing. Nothing but his inclination to make straight for the fort and ask for aid. Straight through a crowd of strangers into another crowd of strangers with swords and spears, not knowing who among them might be a spy or an assassin for hire.

Heaving deeply and eyeing the dying sun, he found reason overruled the leanings of his heart. Night was approaching and with it the dark. With the dark came the terror that haunted them all the way to the homestead. He'd need to find some place to encamp. Withdrawing from the hillside, Odo found himself a place to bed down in a wide partition of trees between two barren fields. Harvesting what forage there could be found for his horse, he used the remaining hay as tinder, overtop laying a few scattered branches to feed the meager flames. Flames that he hoped might not attract any attention.

Settling in with his blanket and cloak, he kept his staff and satchel near should trouble come. His dagger was laid out on the ground within ready reach.

Night was even lonelier than before, the silence of a winter's eve absent the welcome songs of crickets or even the hoot of a hidden owl. At best he got the ominous rattle of leaves that clung tenaciously to their limbs, long bereft of life, pushed by a gentle breeze. His meager fire burned and snapped defiantly at the onset of night. The cold and the quiet left nothing other than time to reflect and remember his journey and leave his mind to wonder what horrors might still await him in the deepening dark. Somewhere in all of that, better memories of home were fondly recalled. The Crooked Tower. Remfrey and his gentle but mysterious nature. Jacks and the songs he hummed as he worked. The smell of herbs and fresh baked bread in the kitchen. The warmth of the hearth as he whiled away the night, reading by the fire.

Here, alone, he felt oddly ashamed of all the sorrows he harbored in the years he spent under the guardianship of the wizard. A boy with sepia skin among the fair and aged. A clear outsider accepted within. Yet for all his differences, he was never made to feel anything other than belonging to that place. His homesickness renewed with a virulent vigor, he now understood what it was like to be *truly* alone.

Was this a lesson Remfrey was trying to teach? Why did the wizard send him? These were the last questions he pondered before drifting off to sleep.

Cold steel on his chin made for a rude awakening. Night still reigned and the fire was not yet dead. As his eyes snapped open, he pulled back from the sensation, shifting on the ground beneath his cloak. Looking upward, he found himself surrounded by six figures clad in mail, bright helms covering the features of their faces. The dim light of the fire cast shadows, making it hard to see within the open spaces of the helms.

Reaching for his staff, he found it pinned to the ground by the foot of the soldier who loomed over him. His sword poised at Odo's neck, it was close enough that one quick thrust could end any struggle Odo might be able to muster. As Odo's eyes focused, he became aware of the others, four of them with bows at the ready, white-fletched arrows nocked into slackened bow strings and another whose sword was out.

Odo's hands slowly went up and out, signaling his submission. Then he heard the figure that stood over him speak. It was a strange voice, gentle and yet commanding. From the inflection of his words, Odo knew the tongue he spoke was not native to that of the region.

"Well, what have we found here?"

CHAPTER 25

Flanked by two of the Elanni soldiers that captured him, Odo sat in a chair. Across a well-worn pine table stood a man his captors called Commander Belthan. Several brass lamps lit the interior of the commander's quarters, the room itself Spartan and lacking many comforts. The table in front of Odo doubled as the commander's desk, now cluttered with many items. There was a quill for a pen and a jar that held ink, along with the contents of Odo's satchel—the wrapped and warded stone, the nails, the letter addressed to the king, and the bright feather from the Nightarie he and Inoch slew.

In addition to these items was Remfrey's talisman, the dull stone hidden beneath the coils of the golden chain from which it normally hung. His captors having examined the contents of the saddlebags, there also was laid out the meager remainder of the mercenary fortune. Resting on the ink-stained pine top sat a worn burlap sack whose golden contents spilled out before the commander, each imprinted by the wizard's mark.

As the commander reached for the talisman, one of the Elanni soldiers in the room spoke quickly. "I would advise caution, Commander. If our guest here is to be believed, there may be some risk in laying hold to that device."

An imposing figure of a man, the commander was tall and lean with a menacing glare. Clean cut, he had dull brown hair peppered with gray at the temples, trimmed short atop his crown. He wore mail beneath a surcoat of crimson and blue, and a golden gorget hung from his neck—the symbol of his authority. Embossed with a wreath of thorns and the image of a bow, it bore the royal standard of the ruling house of Horunass. Behind him hung a banner on a stand whose fields were also crimson and royal blue. Trimmed with gold thread and matching strips that hung from the fringe, the banner displayed two crossed spears and a wagon beneath, both embroidered in white. The block letters below the standard said, "8th Traveler, Bandits Beware."

No doubt, he was a man who knew war and a soldier's way of life. The hand of his shield arm was missing the middle finger. A terrible scar marred his hairline and forehead. His manner was formal but gruff and direct, hallmarks of someone comfortable with commanding men in the confusion of battle.

A fire smoldered in a simple hearth next to the desk, the commander's quarters inside a building made of horizontal courses of logs. Next to where they gathered stood the doorway to a separate room with a bed and a stand that held a ceramic bowl and pitcher for washing. A few implements were also set there, bare necessities for a man more concerned with mobility than comfort.

The hand of the commander withdrew. Soon after, the commander gave the Elanni with the satchel a questioning glance.

The soldier to the left of Odo motioned to his captive. "He claims it will burn you if you touch it." Under the soldier's arm was the empty satchel Odo carried with him nearly the entire journey.

"Magic," added the other Elanni to Odo's right as if to clarify the true meaning of the warning. In his hands was Odo's staff, which he inspected closely.

While all three of Odo's interrogators were soldiers, the dress of the Elanni differed from that of Commander Belthan. With their proud helmets removed, long flaxen manes hung down, pulled back into braids that ran the length of their backs. Both wore shining coats of mail finely wrought, the fringe hanging down to their knees. Over their armor, surcoats of gold and green covered their torsos. The moss green cloaks they once wore were removed, offering Odo a full inspection of those who captured him only an hour or two before. Odo speculated they were a remnant of the army that fought in the war Rojo spoke of on the ship.

"Captain," said the commander in an abrupt tone, "what do you make of this parchment-covered item?"

Nearing the desk and leaning in to inspect the stone, the Elanni pried himself away from his own activity to answer the commander's inquiry. Scanning the stone for several moments, he fixed his mesmerizing blue eyes on the wax seals along the seams. "They appear to be the wards of a wizard, though these I have never seen before."

To Odo, it seemed the voice of the Elanni hinted of song and mirth. A strange thing to note, given the seriousness of the situation he found himself in.

"Meaning?" said the commander.

"I am no wizard. Only one of their brethren will know for certain."

"Some are there to block scrying spells, I think," Odo added, almost sounding enthusiastic. "The others are protective, I suspect. I do not know what they do."

Lifting the staff, the Elanni captain added, "Hazelwood."

"Captain?" The commander said, his attention immediately pulled away from the items covering his desk.

The other Elanni with the satchel answered quickly, "Often used by wizards and their devices."

Motioning to Odo, the commander asked, "You mean to say we have a wizard in our midst?"

"Unsure," answered the Elanni holding Odo's staff. "He may not appear as such." Briefly looking over at Odo he added, "He certainly has the trappings of one."

"Tell us again, what became of this Captain Inoch and his men?" Belthan said, glaring at Odo stern and cold.

"Dead," answered Odo directly. "A dark sorcerer and his creations."

"And these nails?"

"I pulled from two of the dead Togoloshi."

"And you say there were four of these...these..."

"Togoloshi, Captain. And there were three." Odo nodded as he spoke.

"Commander," Belthan corrected.

"Apologies," Odo said with downcast eyes, avoiding the commander's stare.

"I seem to recall a freelancer named Inoch," said the Elanni with the satchel. "Ruthless. With a tall woman—"

"Maddie," interjected Odo.

"Yes, I remember her," Belthan added. "The woman was cracked. Pried teeth from some of the slain, I recall. No forgetting her."

The Elanni with the staff neared the desk and picked up one of the nails. For a time, he inspected the implement, noting the foul script etched into the metal. "Togoloshi," he said quietly. "I remember these creatures. Cunning things, prowling the dark, strangling their victims in the night."

"So, there is some truth to this tale?" The commander's countenance changed, turning inquisitive for the moment.

"Perhaps. Only one way to be assured." For a moment the two exchanged glances—the Elanni captain and Belthan—with the Elanni motioning to Odo. Speaking the words Odo cringed to hear, the captain voiced what the two were undoubtedly thinking. "Have him cast a spell."

Just then, all eyes turned towards Odo. In an instant, a-piercing unease overtook the wizard's apprentice. With the sudden, undivided attention of the others, he felt all of three inches tall. Even with all he had been through, the prospect of performing on demand seemed an insurmountable task.

"I...I would need the crystal. And the staff," stammered the young man.

The Elanni holding the satchel was quick to speak. "I have known a few wizards in my many years. None of them needed their staff for a simple task. Nor a crystal."

As the eyes of the others bore down harder on Odo now, the scattered thoughts in his head whirled like sand scattered in a violent storm. He waited for a question to be asked, finally realizing the expectant eyes spoke more than words at that moment. His protest was pointless at best. "As I have said, I am not a wizard. Merely an assistant."

With a disgruntled sigh, Commander Belthan looked at the objects laid out on his desk. Frustration and indecision were clearly expressed on his face. His eyes went to the letter, his hand following after. Taking the document by a corner, he inspected the seal on the back first before turning it over and scanning the neat script Remfrey had inked on the front. By now, the paper was stained, stray drops of water having made their way past the oiled leather of the satchel.

Holding up the letter, the writing facing forward, Belthan asked, "Captain?"

"It is our script, yes."

"What does it say?"

"It is addressed to the king."

"And the seal?"

The Elanni captain shrugged his shoulders slightly. "It is not difficult to forge a seal." He paused for a moment adding, "There is only one way to be sure."

Extending his arm, Belthan offered the letter to the captain. In turn, the Elanni soldier gently laid Odo's staff on the desk, allowing it to settle before taking the folded parchment in his hands.

Thin and nimble fingers turned the note back and forth, the captain feeling the weight of the parchment, his keen eyes scanning the lettering, focusing on the color of the ink and the minute details of the wax seals. Then, with a look that signaled both curiosity and reverence, he snapped the wax of the crimson seal with both hands. Cautious so as not to ruin the parchment, he took his time making sure those parts still bound by the wax were separated without rips or tears. Unfolding it finally and holding it open, he turned it right side up before reading.

Odo watched with anxious anticipation while the captain's eyes shifted left-to-right as he read the first line. The frame of the Elanni twitched as a sniff and snicker followed quickly after. The captain closed the ends of the note and handed it back to Belthan.

"And?" said Belthan, an intense curiosity washing across his face. The note dangled in the air for a moment, the commander's gaze alternating between the Elanni and the note.

"The work of a wizard."

Belthan gingerly took the note and inspected it once more. "How did you—"

Repeating the words of the first lines, the Elanni captain spoke with an air of dignity, chin up, eyes looking down his nose. "It said thus, 'I did not pen this note for an Elanni captain. The contents herein are for the king and queen alone.'"

The soldier with the satchel bowed slightly, amused as the captain crossed his arms over his chest. "No doubt in my heart, Commander. The work of a wizard."

Belthan's expression changed quickly from certainty and resolve to that of befuddlement and indecision. He looked over the note again, a muted sort of awe in his stare, before gently laying the object back on the yellow knotted wood of his desk.

Belthan cleared his throat, his commanding presence returned. He leaned forward, his hands splayed out on the pine top. His thumbs thumped the desk as he considered all he had learned. Head bowed slightly, he looked both ways before saying, "Thoughts on this matter."

Odo watched in a moment of nervous anxiety. Something in his stomach twitched, fearing things might take an ill turn despite all he had heard and seen. The Elanni soldier looked to his captain. The captain's head was bowed in thought.

"I think his story genuine," answered the Elanni captain.

"Agreed," answered the other soldier.

Staring down at his desk for a moment, Commander Belthan inhaled noisily, breathing out with a grumble. Odo was on the edge of his seat, the actions of the man before him seeming uncertain.

In a sudden flurry of motion, the hands of the commander lay flat on the table with a thump as he sat in his seat before leaning back. "Agreed," he answered.

Odo relaxed, his body reclining slowly as if deflating. Allowing the back of the chair to catch him, he let out a long and relieved sigh.

"Suggestions?" asked Belthan.

The captain spoke, extending a hand in Odo's direction. "I could assemble a detachment and we can escort the assistant of Remfrey here to Horunass."

"In secret?" inquired Belthan.

"Yes, Commander."

The ends of Odo's staff wobbled up and down as Belthan beat the palms of his hands softly on the table. "Agreed," said the commander with a note of finality before pushing himself away from the table. The legs of his chair rumbled and scraped the slate floor beneath their feet as Belthan made space to stand.

Rising, Commander Belthan looked down at Odo and said, "My apologies to you, young man. While war is behind us, we are ever vigilant of those that might do evil in our midst."

Motioning to the Elanni captain he added, "Captain Roendel will see to your needs. I bid you, offer our apologies to the king and queen for the manner of your treatment, and for the breaking of the seal on the letter. As always, we are ever concerned for their wellbeing."

Turning his head towards Roendel, the commander said, "Captain. You are dismissed."

"Yes, Commander," both Elanni said with a shallow bow.

As the commander made his way to his personal quarters, Roendel turned to face a wide-eyed and visibly relieved Odo. With a shallow smile he spoke. "Well, as a first order of business, how does a warm meal sound?"

A slow grin crept across Odo's face as he answered softly and relieved, "Like heaven, Captain."

CHAPTER 26

"The courtly rules are as such when speaking with the queen," said Chief Councilor Caryndyn, his words soft but official. "Speak only when spoken to. Always address the Queen as 'Your Highness,' or 'Your Excellency.' Eyes always down unless otherwise directed. When we approach, you will follow me. When we near the platform of the throne, you will kneel at the bottom stair until commanded to rise. When we depart, you will step backwards four paces, bow, and then turn. It is important you never turn your back on the queen."

"Yes, Captain," answered Odo. He didn't catch himself this time, and quickly corrected his mistake. "Apologies, Lord Caryndyn."

Caryndyn straightened himself, pulling at his robes, making sure all creases were tended to. Garbed head to toe in white, he had long golden tresses that fell from his crown along with the characteristic blue eyes of the Elanni. Across his chest, worn shoulder to hip was a sash of green and gold adorned with a golden eight-pointed star. His beautiful features and kind countenance gave him an almost angelic appearance, his soft but commanding voice doing little to spoil the image he portrayed. "Wait here. It will be a moment or two before the court is cleared. Then I will return to escort you to Queen Hertress."

Odo looked on with a feigned disinterest as he watched the Elanni counselor make his way to a set of heavy double doors. Cast from bronze and emblazoned with the scene of a lion with a strange sea creature in its jaws, they looked as ponderous as they were. Two Elanni guards in polished decorative armor flanked each door. Setting aside their spears and each laying a shoulder against the portal, they strained to push open the doors. Hinges groaned when the door gave way, as if in protest, revealing the well-lit interior of the throne room beyond. From where Odo sat, the room itself looked round with a white pedestal in the room and the hint of steps that led upward at the center.

The sun shone bright that day. The white marble of the hallway seemed to reflect and diffuse the rays of the sun as they streamed in from skylights above and windows set high on the wall. Candle stands of black wrought iron stood unused in the corners of the long rectangular space, the same being true of the sconces that hung from the gleaming stone fascia. Seated on an intricately carved bench, Odo lingered at the spot where important petitioners were to wait until the Crown was ready to hear their cases. Save for the guards and the councilor, he was the only one in that room, a single, solitary figure whose stained cloak and garments were almost anathema to the sterile opulence of that cold hallway.

As the doors closed with a resounding boom, Odo returned to his thoughts. Pine needles clung to the hem of his cloak and robe, a stray reminder of his long and harrowing journey. The road painted him with mud and debris, advertising to all who saw him just how far he had come. He longed for a bath and fresh clothes.

Now that he had arrived at his destination, the journey all seemed like a bad dream. He sat still, remembering the events of the road, transfixed by his own recollection. In his heart, he was anxious, mostly due to the stress of facing royalty. Kings and queens were never as noble as they portrayed themselves, as many stories and accounts warned.

The trek from the outpost to the city was perhaps the easiest stretch of road he had faced thus far. A detachment of twenty Elanni was sent to escort him the remainder of the distance, all but a day and a night on the road, moving at a slow clip. The comfort of a cot in the warm confines of a tent and a hot meal of porridge felt like a sinful extravagance after sleeping on the cold hard ground for days on end.

Stories of the grand walls of Horunass did not compare to seeing them firsthand. A city built on a hill overlooking the sea, it had stood as a major port for hundreds of years. Like a creature made of wood and stone, it grew with each successive generation that lived and died in the shadow of those walls. Back at the Crooked Tower, he often dreamed of such places. The images in his mind's eye conjured spires of shining perfection worthy of a young man's awe. In everything he had seen and encountered on the long, disastrous road from the wizard's abode, the city was the only thing that managed to rival his own imagination. It was a grand, sprawling metropolis where communities thrived sheltered by high walls and beyond. Sitting atop the crest of the highest hill, a magnificent palace stood like a sentinel garbed in white stone, surveying the timeless city, a palace where he now sat and waited, half-troubled, half-anxious.

Even then, he could not escape the horrors he had seen. Any thought passing through his head seemed to stir them up like biting midges in the tall weeds. He closed his eyes and shook his head, hoping that might disperse them, to virtually no effect. He sat up and straightened the strap of his satchel across his chest.

He took a moment to look to his left, leaning forward slightly and getting a better view of the guards that kept watch on the doorway. The light that streamed in from above yielded to shadows in the stone arch where they kept their watch. The shadows that gathered did little to diminish the gleam of their armor. Breastplates polished to a silvery hue, embossed with an eight-pointed star and the edges adorned with entangled vines. Greaves polished like silver protected their shins, and mail shirts their upper arms and waist. Great helms covered their heads, fashioned from a single piece of steel and adorned with a crest of long horsehair that was as white as snow. From the fringes of their headgear, long blonde locks hung down, spilling over their gorgets and breastplates. The long spears they carried were complimented by swords that hung at their sides. Little affected by the cold of the chamber, they had no need for cloaks. Yet, they stood at attention with military precision, looking ahead, seemingly disinterested in him or what might be transpiring beyond the door.

Once more the hinges groaned as the door swung open, with councilor Caryndyn standing in the growing gap. Stepping out into the hallway, he called out to Odo and motioned him to approach.

At once, Odo lifted to his feet, leaning on his staff as he did. Making his way to the doors, he had a chance to look over the guards, noting the finer details of their armor and garb, inwardly marveling over the craftsmanship and skill of their manufacture. He only allowed himself a cursory look before turning his attention to Caryndyn. Suddenly self-conscious, he set about straightening his cloak and his robe.

Caryndyn remarked in a low voice, "Do not be so anxious. Follow my steps and remember my earlier instruction." With a slight smile he added, "Do not fret so. Despite her reputation, the queen does not bite."

As instructed, Odo followed studiously behind, keeping his eyes fixed to the bottom hem of the councilor's robes, studying the way they moved. The throne room itself was bright, brighter than the hall. The floor and walls were made of the same white marble, save when they neared the dais upon which the throne was perched. There, a fresco of many-colored tiles ran like an avenue from the bottom stair to the arch of the main door of the chamber, the door where supplicants and petitioners were brought in. Assembled from stones or tiles of varying shades of blue, white, and green, it resembled the roiling waves of a fantastical sea. It was not as dark and drear as the depths of the Sorrowing Sea, whose waters could look black absent the sun. It was whimsical, filled with life, light, and color, making the sea seem like a watery gem whose facets mesmerized and awed.

His footfalls echoed in the space, for it was immense and the walls high. At times, he stole a glance out of the corner of his eye, seeing an upper tier—a balcony where others could view proceedings in silence. Turning in step with Caryndyn, they stopped at the base of a stair, his eyes seeing the green boots and bright metal greaves of the two soldiers stationed there.

"Come alongside," Caryndyn said to him in a whisper with the wave of his hand. Odo did as instructed, kneeling without prompting.

"Good. Good," Caryndyn said in a whisper.

"Who comes before my throne?" The voice was deceptively high-pitched and feminine—the queen. Each word was spoken with purpose, the tenor hinting of an iron resolve that wove its way through each syllable. Caryndyn was quick to answer.

"Odo, emissary of Master Remfrey, a wizard from the eastern moors, Your Highness."

"And what does he carry with him?"

"Items for the king."

"Approach," said the queen. Odo started to rise, halting as a gentle hand on his shoulder bid him stop. He slid back down to the cold stone of the ground.

"The letter," whispered Caryndyn. Odo held out his staff, looking up slightly at the counselor. Without need for explanation, the Elanni councilor took the rod from Odo's grasp. Hands free, Odo swiftly undid the flap of his satchel. Digging around into the contents of the bag, he retrieved the letter in question. Exchanging the parchment for the staff, Odo kept his eyes focused on the floor.

Listening intently, Odo heard the soft leather of Caryndyn's soles whisper as he ascended the dais to the top, seven steps in all. There was a pause followed by the soft rustle of parchment as the letter was unfolded.

"Why is the seal broken?" asked the queen.

"The commander of the garrison thought it wise to inspect the letter," answered Caryndyn.

"He knows the tongue of your kindred?"

"No, Your highness. A captain named Roendel. He assured me he did not read past the first line."

"Very well," said the queen before a long silence. Then, in a whisper she asked, "What is this word?"

Caryndyn's answer was too soft for Odo to understand, though it was understood by the queen. "Ah, yes," she said afterwards.

More quiet followed after and then the soft rustling of paper. Content with what she had read, the queen asked softly, "Odo, is it?"

"Yes, your Highness."

"Master Odo, look up," she commanded.

Slow to respond at first, Odo traced with his eyes the marble stair, step by step, until they reached the top. Upon the upper dais he saw two thrones carved from wood and padded with crimson and blue fabric, gilded with gold. One was empty, but on the one to the right sat a woman of exceeding beauty. She had hair of gold, its shimmer muted by strands of silver. Around her delicate form was an elegant robe of crimson and blue lined with fur, for the room itself was cold from the winter's chill. Two brass braziers flanked her, thin threads of smoke rising from the coals within. Around her neck was a golden chain studded with bright emeralds, and earrings of the same make dangled from her ears. Yet the item that most caught his attention was that of her crown. It was gold and fashioned in the manner of a wreath of brambles, golden thorns thrusting out and in from the woven stems, a fantastic and terrible thing that looked tortuous to wear, though she bore it without pain or marring on her skin. It was something that garnered his attention far more than her exquisite beauty or the prestige of her office. His brow furrowed briefly, a burning desire to ask after the crown gnawing at him.

Sitting on her throne, the only hint of her diminutive stature was the footstool upon which her feet rested, her soles and toes covered by richly appointed slippers. Still, she was a striking figure in an equally impressive room. The throne and the elevated platform upon which she sat was white marble from top to bottom, situated near the center of a rotunda. Spanning two-thirds of the circumference, a stone balcony ran supported by columns of contrasting black marble and streaked with veins of red, whereupon Elanni soldiers were stationed. Sconces were affixed to each column, the lights within extinguished due to the rays of the sun flooding in from above. Overhead, a dome capped the impressive chamber, gilded with gold. Thick panes of glass allowed light from outside to flood the interior, the iridescence of the stone doing the rest to scatter and diffuse the precious light. It had the same sterile feel of the hallway in which he waited and yet contained a grandiosity that instilled awe, plain but exquisite. A wonder of workmanship and design. An impressive room to compete with the beauty and stern contemplation of the woman who sat on high. A woman offering consolation and judgement from the treacherous authority of her crown.

The quiet of the moment was broken by the queen. "I see by the expression on the face of our guest that you did not inform him of my crown, yes?"

"Forgive me, Your Highness." Caryndyn's apologies were stalled with the subtle wave of her hand.

The letter in one hand, the other fell as she inspected Odo up and down, remarking, "He has not been properly bathed I see."

"Again, apologies, Your Highness," Caryndyn said. "The matter was deemed urgent."

It was then Odo noticed the only occupants of that room were the councilor, the queen, and numerous guards—Elanni by their look. He dared not look behind him at the balcony, but the stillness of the great chamber suggested no onlookers to the meeting. At least, none who were invited.

"Well then, cousin," she said after a time. "It seems only fitting that after meeting the king, someone will attend to finding him a proper suit of clothes. And perhaps a bath?"

"Yes, Your Highness," replied Caryndyn with a shallow bow.

Handing back the letter to the councilor, Queen Hertress leaned forward on her throne. "Master Odo, is it?"

"Yes maam," Odo answered at first before biting his lip. The scowl on his face forecast the words that followed. "I bid your pardon. I mean, 'Your Highness.'"

"Understandable, I think," said the queen. "You have never met nobility before."

"Yes, Your Highness."

"I have been told you have traveled quite a span of leagues to meet the king. Do you hunger?"

"Your Highness?"

"Do you hunger?" she inquired again, leaning forward. "Would you be willing to dine with the king and I this evening? We would be honored to have the emissary of a wizard dine with us this evening."

The question gave Odo a moment of pause. His answer stumbled past his lips. "Ye...yes, Your Highness."

"Very well then," answered the queen before reclining once more on her throne. Her head turned to face that of Councilor Caryndyn. "When the king has finished with him, make sure he is offered refreshment."

Turning her attention to Odo once more, she added, "After all, never let it be said that the court of King Merrith was discourteous or inhospitable to its allies and friends."

"Yes, Your Highness," answered Caryndyn.

"You are both dismissed."

Caryndyn descended the stair as Odo rose and bowed, suddenly remembering Caryndyn's instructions. One pace backwards, two, then three, he turned as the councilor approached, leading him away from whence they came.

"That went well," quipped Caryndyn. "Come, let us go swiftly to the king."

CHAPTER 27

It wasn't a long walk from the throne room. The halls they took were less impressive than those of the more formal areas. Clearly, the palace grounds had newer construction atop the much older dwellings. Councilor Caryndyn described them as the bones of the old city. "Much has been changed since then," he explained.

The councilor went on to detail how the Elanni came to involve themselves in the affairs of Horunass. "The king is the recognized son of Lord Elodel. Lord Elodel is my lord and a relation. I am his sister-son."

The name *Elodel* Odo knew from the scrolls and books. *King Merrith* he did not. He thought about asking more questions, but time did not permit. Once more, awe and wonder struck the young man as they entered the Solarium where King Merrith now waited.

Facing the direction of the rising sun, great triangular panes of glass were connected by a skeleton of metal, forming a semi-circular wall that thrust out from the main structure. Curving up and overhead, they formed part of a dome where light from on high could stream in. Vents overhead were connected to staves, allowing those that tended this place to regulate the temperature of the room from ground level. Odo's jaw fell as his head tilted back, his eyes beholding architectural wonders he could not have imagined. The connected panels of glass rose at least three stories high, if not higher. Almost immediately as they entered the room, thick air and an unseasonable heat struck Odo along with the earthy smell of late spring that spoke of growth and rejuvenation. It was then an elderly man approached them and addressed the pair.

"You must be Odo," said the tall man, who was dressed in robes of all green. He seemed an unusual sort, garbed in finery, though what moved beneath his garments had the face of a baker or a candle maker. Balding atop, he had a long, kind face with drooping jowls and baggy eyes in which blue irises flicked with a friendly fire. The last vestiges of hair atop his crown were combed over left to right, the ring of hair that surrounded it having turned a dull gray. A neat goatee hung from his chin. While Odo could not understand how he knew it, he immediately recognized the other man as a wizard, one whose name he did not know.

Caryndyn addressed Odo with a grin. "This is Master Gregor."

Odo offered a shallow bow, adjusting the strap of the satchel with his free hand. He wasn't sure how to address Gregor, belabored by the wonder and confusion he now felt. Remfrey had never spoken of him in the past, though it was now clear that he had spoken to Gregor of Odo in some manner.

"Come," Gregor said pointing to the interior of the solarium, "the king awaits."

It was a short walk to the center of the room. Passing by foliage that hung over the pathway, Odo could hear the chirps and songs of a handful of birds and even witnessed the scattered movement of tiny green lizards as they scurried along tree trunks. Below their feet, moss peeked through the cracks in pavers and gaps in the slate slabs. Bordering the pathway, stone walls rose just above their knees forming large, partitioned sections where plants grew. The soil was loose and well-tended, deep green flora growing thick and robust within. Select trees rose among the indoor garden, their green leaves wide and supple.

"The king is far less formal than the queen," mentioned Caryndyn as they made their way through the interior, shuffling along the stone path. "A simple, 'Your Highness,' will be sufficient when addressing him. The formality of bowing and such is less of a concern."

"Of course," replied Odo, his answer almost automatic in a way, the solarium having captured his rapt attention.

The path led the trio to a circular stone patio near the center of the room. An open space with marvelously cut pavers beneath their feet, it was surrounded by raised garden beds contained by cut stone. In the center, a wooden table was set, bare save for a sheet of parchment and two colorful sticks, each having an end shaved to a point. Three Elanni guards in their ceremonial armor were stationed there, one by each of the three paths that led into the circle. There was also an Elanni maid dressed in red, her long golden hair braided and curled into a bun. Opposite her on a stone bench sat a man addressing two children, all of them garbed in crimson and blue.

The children themselves were not much older than five years of age, looking enthusiastically at their father, his eyes scanning a parchment. They had brown eyes like their father and their hair was fair, gold tinged with brown. Both wore their hair long, making it difficult to determine whether each was a boy or a girl. The man himself wore his hair long, his chestnut mane spilling down his back and falling over the crest embroidered on his chest. A thick, neatly trimmed beard covered his jaws. A golden diadem was affixed to his brow, the ends of it tied behind his head. This, Odo deduced, was the king.

One of the guards noticed their approach and stepped aside to let the trio pass.

"Yes, it is very nice," said the king softly as he examined the paper. His attention fixed on the figure drawn on the page, he was unaware of Odo's approach. "What is it?"

"A soldier," one of the children answered.

As they entered the circle, the king looked up at their approach, taken unawares. His gaze turned serious for a moment then softened before he lifted his hand. With a brief wave, he motioned for the attendant to approach.

The maiden moved in, first grabbing the objects on the desk before nearing the king.

The lids of the king's eyes opened wide, and a grin graced his face as he answered the children. "Papa has matters to attend. Go with Rendesrae now, and I will find you later."

"Yes, Papa," said one of the children.

Rendesrae offered her hand to the children with the shorter of the two taking it immediately. As she departed the king and his newfound company, the other child followed dutifully, offering no protest despite the look of disappointment on his face.

Odo's mind began to wander back to his own childhood, or the absence thereof. Remfrey often used that same patriarchal tone, though the familial closeness between father and child was notably lacking. The moment between the king and his children, though commonplace, was a peek into the loving bonds between parent and child that Odo had rarely seen and often longed to have. Somewhere in the back of his head, he secretly wondered what life might have been like if he had known his own parents. Whether that craving for what might have been would have been sated in a manner like he had just witnessed. Something softer. Something warmer. Something familiar and welcome.

The voice of Gregor called him away from the stew of musings and regrets, returning him to reality in an instant.

"Your Highness. The emissary of Master Remfrey has arrived." Gregor announced Odo's presence in a far more official tone than before.

Odo stepped forward and offered a practiced bow, his satchel falling forward and threatening to unloose itself from his shoulder. Awkwardly, he pulled himself back up, a hand reaching out to steady the bag.

"Very good," answered the king. His manner of speaking remained soft.

Councilor Caryndyn stepped forward and handed him the note Odo had carried for so long. Answering the counselor with the flowing tongue of the Elanni, the king took the note and began to read. Odo was surprised how fluent he was in their speech. Leaning to his right, Odo asked of Gregor softly, "The king knows the speech of the Elanni?"

"Quite well," answered the king, his attention fixed on the note in his hands. The king's response caught Odo off guard, perplexity gracing his face, and his mouth hanging open. It was clear that in addition to being well studied in the culture of the Elanni, he had hearing beyond that of normal men.

A bird sang in the distance as the king read, high pitched and warbling. A welcome sound in the bleak quiet of the rising winter, Odo desired, once more, the warm embrace of spring. Gregor cleared his throat, disrupting the moment. It was followed by the unfamiliar clink and clack of metal whispering behind him as one of the guards shifted on their feet.

Few mortals knew the letters and script of the Ageless, Odo being one of them. Even his knowledge of their words was middling at its best, Remfrey having a far better grasp of the language. Yet, in a handful of seconds, the king folded the note once more and inspected the exterior of the parchment, wondering if there might be more.

The king stood. "Let me see what you carry."

Odo looked up to Gregor, who motioned to the table. Leaning his staff against the table's edge, he unbound the ties on the satchel. He pulled the individual items from within, setting them on the table one-by-one. Out first came the stone. The paper felt soft in his hands, and he was careful in setting it on the wood, eyeing the wax seals that held the wrapping firm. Then came the nails, Odo taking the time to unbind the knot that held the black cloth which covered them. Once they were exposed, he set each one gently on the polished wood top.

As the first nail was set down, a soft, shrill whistle came from Gregor. The very same sound made by a man repelled and repulsed. As the second was laid out, Odo's ears heard the name spill out from Gregor's lips. A name he loathed and still feared even now.

"Togoloshi." Gregor reacted with a distressed hiss.

Odo let the flap of his satchel fall, taking up his staff as the king reached out to the rock. "Your Highness," Odo exclaimed, wide-eyed and alarmed.

The hand of the king retracted as if on a spring.

Odo's tone changed abruptly, suddenly remembering he was addressing royalty. "I bid your pardon, Your Highness. The stone is warded, and I fear—"

"Warded?" Gregor's tone was dubious. All eyes were on Gregor as he reached down and lifted the stone. Pulling it closer, Gregor peered intently at the object, turning it in his hands, reading the markings thereon. At first, his expression denoted a deep curiosity. This changed quickly. A smile rose slowly on the wizard's lips.

Odo recoiled, and an arm went up to shield his face as Gregor peeled away the parchment surrounding the stone. As the paper tore and was pulled away, the wizard exposed more of the mystery that lay within. Palm up, a naked stone resting in the center of his hand, he held out the mysterious prize for all to see.

Odo could almost hear the questions brewing in the many sets of eyes leveled at the grayish-white rock, weathered and unexceptional. Even Odo wondered at the significance of the item.

"What is it?" Caryndyn asked, breaking the silence.

With a lingering hesitancy in his voice, Gregor answered, addressing the king. "A rock, Your Highness."

With a doubt that matched the reluctance of the wizard, the king spoke. "And what is the significance of this stone?"

Gregor scanned the surface of the stone, his eyes studious, his lips sporting a slight frown. "Flint, perhaps. Dolomite. It is hard to say without breaking the stone, Your Highness."

"Master Gregor, I ask not the composition of the stone. What is its meaning? For what purpose was it brought to me?" The king's gaze did not stray from the rock in Gregor's hand.

"I know not, Your Highness. Perhaps the note?" The wizard lowered the stone, setting it on the table once more. The object rumbled on the wood, rolling over once or twice before settling on a spot where it finally remained still. "Perhaps the note speaks more," he added, arching a brow.

The king unfolded the note again. Both Caryndyn and Gregor leaned in, looking over the shoulder of the monarch. They appeared puzzled by the total contents written within.

King Merrith was visibly puzzled as he reread the message. Gregor let slip a frustrated sigh as he read the last line, shaking his head dismissively.

"Lord Caryndyn?" Odo gazed quizzically to the councilor dressed in white. "Might I ask what is written within the note?" He had carried the thing halfway across the world, always wondering what message was inked within the folds, but never daring to look.

King Merrith began to read the note once more as Caryndyn stepped around the king and approached Odo. Leaning in, he spoke low so that others might not overhear. "There is very little contained within. A warning for the eyes of the king only. That a precious object had been delivered to him, and great care should be taken to preserve it until your master can retrieve it. This and the amount to be paid to those persons who delivered you here. Though, you have been delivered here alone."

King Merrith's expression was studious. His voice, however, was soft and sounded dubious. "All amounts given from my treasury to be repaid by your master at a later time. Quite a sum, I might add."

Odo looked up at the Elanni lord. "You did not know I was to arrive?"

"No," answered Caryndyn. "I was informed of your destination and of the importance of your mission by the captain who delivered you."

For a moment, they locked eyes, the gaze of each exhibiting the questions they both pondered. Then Caryndyn spoke. "Curious you should deliver the stone only for Master Remfrey to retrieve it later. Yes?"

Before Odo could respond, the voice of the king spoke, the pair giving him their full attention.

"Odo, is it?" said the king, his eyes fixed on a bare space on the table.

"Yes, Your Highness," answered Odo.

"Tell me the tale of your journey."

Odo subconsciously pulled at the strap of his satchel and gripped his staff tightly. Clearing his throat, he relayed a summarized series of events over the many days he spent on his fateful trek. Near the end, his voice began to quaver. Memories of the horrors, and those that fell, were all too new to be absent emotion. His chin began to shiver and his throat hurt near the end as he strained to keep his composure, but try as he might, his eye let slip a single tear. It ran from the corner of his eye, leaving a wet path along his reddish-brown cheek. Quickly, he wiped it away with his sleeve. Now was not the time for tears or remorse, he reasoned.

"None remain?" inquired the king.

"No, Your Highness," answered Odo, clearing his throat after.

The king let the note fall to the table. Thereafter, he leaned forward, hands on the table, fingers outstretched. Staring in silence at the whitish-gray rock, he pondered all he had heard and read.

"Is this some jest?" asked Caryndyn, his face stern despite the questioning tenor of his words. "Paying good coin for a common rock to the amusement of a wizard?"

"I have known Remfrey for some time," Gregor muttered in the ensuing silence. "While his ways are inscrutable, I have never known him to make mockery such as this."

The explanation offered by Gregor did little to convince the councilor. "Yet, here we stand, an emissary sent with a worthless rock."

"I assure you, Councilor Caryndyn, while Remfrey has a peculiar nature, I have never—" The wizard stopped abruptly as the king raised his hand to bid him to silence. Once more, the king took up the note and read, and for many minutes, the room grew silent as he scanned the words. Only the sweet warbling of a songbird in its perch cut the silence.

"Your Highness?" piped up Master Gregor.

"A ruse," muttered the king.

"Your Highness?"

The king looked up, eyeing the wizard briefly. "It is the only plausible explanation. The stone? The journey? A marvelous ruse, meant to distract from the true mission. All a fraud to lead the spies of the enemy away."

"To what end, Your Highness?" said Gregor.

The parchment still in his hand, the king pointed in Odo's direction. "That your Master

Remfrey could move without notice. To deliver something else to its true destination."

King Merrith's gaze fell once more to the table as he added, "A glorious gamble. One that seems to have paid well."

With an arched eyebrow, Gregor spoke. "That then explains the runes on the stone."

Odo cast a questioning gaze at Gregor. "Magus?"

Gregor turned to meet Odo's stare. "Those wards? On the paper? Naught but gibberish. Similar to runes we oft use, but not as exacting. Useless. Little more than decoration."

Stunned and with a touch of anger, Odo slowly turned away. Wistfully he spoke, "He told me they were to prevent scrying and to protect what was contained within."

"It seems Remfrey has taught you well," said Gregor, mildly amused.

"How so?" asked Odo.
The king answered for Gregor. "Wizards are a secretive lot. No doubt, your Master Remfrey relied on your own doubt and inexperience to make the ruse all the more real."

It took Odo some time to process the realization that Remfrey had sent him needlessly out into a dangerous world. At first, he tried to dismiss the notion from his thoughts. However, he thought carefully on the explanation of the king, and the logic of it was hard to deny. His cheeks turned hot as anger, birthed by a sense of humiliation and despair, filled his heart. All this time, he had looked to Remfrey as a father of sorts. Not the best father one might have, for he could be distant and lacking empathy at times, but Odo had trusted him. The notion of betrayal was not far from his thoughts.

The king grabbed the rock and examined it as he spoke. "I remember this Inoch. Tall man. Cunning. He had a woman among his soldiers."

"Maddie," muttered Odo almost automatically, his mind a virulent storm of befuddlement, doubt, and anger. "Your Highness," he added, realizing late his lack of formality.

Reaching into a pocket within the folds of his robe, Gregor produced a note of his own written on parchment. Like the letter Odo delivered, it was folded over and sealed with a glob of wax. Catching the glimpse of the seal, Odo recognized the rune as belonging to Remfrey.

Setting the stone and the note back down on the table, the king spoke. "My apologies, young Odo, for the many griefs you have suffered during this time of trial. I, like you, know the pain of loss and the tragedy of the conflict in which our fates are entwined."

Odo turned to face the king. Briefly, their eyes met. The king seemed cold, distant, and yet the embers of cunning and wisdom seemed present within, a person absent the depth of outward expression.

The king continued. "You have our gratitude, and my condolences, for what they are. I bid you, stay here in the palace. Rest. Recover from your journey. Perhaps you and I can speak more of deeper things when you feel the time is appropriate."

"What of the nails?" interjected Caryndyn.

"An ancient evil," replied Gregor. "Conjured up from the first war. A remnant of what once gave them life." His attention shifting briefly to Odo, he asked, "Yes?"

Snapped back to the moment, Odo answered with an uncertain nod, blinking as he did.

The king spoke woefully, his voice having a distant quality to it. "So it is that evil thought long extinguished has resurfaced once more. The Watchers are but a new face on an old villain." He halted for a moment, his head tilting in the general direction of Caryndyn. "We should convene a council on this matter soon."

"Yes, Your Highness," answered Caryndyn with a nod.

"Until then, let our guest rest and refresh himself."

With a sidelong look at Odo, the king asked, "No doubt the queen has bid you dine with us this evening, yes?"

"Yes, Your Highness," answered Odo with a nod.

"Very well," replied the king with a forced smile. "I will leave you to the care of Master Gregor."

Turning and approaching Odo, the king drew near before halting. Awkward, as if fearing to touch the young man, he laid his hand on Odo's shoulder. "Until then."

As the king lifted his hand from Odo, Odo offered a shallow bow that went unanswered.

With a nod from the monarch, there was a shuffling of feet. The wizard reached out and laid a hand gently on Odo. "Stay with me here, brother. You and I must speak." The voice of the wizard was soft, barely audible above the commotion being made.

Eyes filled with wonder, Odo watched as the guards formed around the king and his councilor. Speaking to one another in the sing-song tongue of the Ageless, the king and the councilor conversed with a fluent rapidity that made it hard for Odo to understand what they were saying. Before long, they were gone, the rustle of mail, leather soles, and cloth amidst the tramp of martial feet. Feathers ruffled, a sparrow roused from its perch as the king and his entourage departed. And before long, Odo found himself alone with Gregor.

A sealed note still held firm in his fingers, Gregor pivoted to face the young man. The note flapped against the silken cloth of his robe as his hand seemingly moved on its own accord. A nervous gesture, perhaps, or one of those unconscious ticks took place as the wizard's mind formed the words he was about to speak. Curling up in a smile, Gregor's lips seemed half glad and half filled with consternation.

"Let me see the stone." Gregor spoke after a time.

"Magus?"

"Brother Gregor, please," the wizard corrected. "A stone that Remfrey gave you? Containing a dull light within?"

In the many distractions of the hour, Odo had almost forgotten about the talisman. At once, he shoved his hand past the flap of the satchel and dug within. Wrapped around the fingers of his hand came the necklace, the dull, lifeless stone dangling from his fingers. He lifted it high for Gregor to see.

For a moment, Gregor inspected the object. The dim light within was gone, the stone translucent and gray. The wizard let loose a troubled sigh. "When did you draw the power into yourself?"

Odo's eyes fell, shamefaced. "Early in my journey." Reluctant, he expounded on his answer. "I lied to Captain Inoch. I told him I needed to be alone for prayer. I used the sage, and the—"

"Well, this explains much. How both you and I had the sense of one another."

Odo immediately knew the inference. The odd sense of familiarity he felt when meeting Gregor for the first time.

"Were you aware of the consequences of such an act?"

Slow to answer, Odo spoke low, looking ashamed. "The Magus instructed me on the ritual. He was very specific that I was not to perform it lest I feared myself in grave danger. He also informed me there were lasting consequences of doing so, but—"

As Odo's voice trailed away into silence, Gregor looked on expectantly. "But what?"

"I was afraid. We were being hunted. I did not trust the captain, a fear I know now was unfounded. Still, with Watchers at our backs, I contemplated what might befall me and that which I carry. I did not know the significance of the stone set with wards but did know for certain what it was I wore about my neck. The stone they could take from me and perhaps discover a way to use the power within. I could not take that chance."

"What if they were cunning enough to discover what you had done?"

"I would not yield it." Odo's words were uncertain but spoken with a frankness that surprised Gregor.

"Even under the threat of death?"

"Even as my life slip away," Odo said, his voice more resolute. "They would not get the power in the stone. What consequences might come, they were secondary to that which was entrusted to me. The stone I carried in my pouch was already warded and sealed. At need, I could bury it and protect it with wards. But for that, I needed the power granted to me from the Magus. Or so I reasoned."

Head up and looking down his nose at Odo suspiciously, Gregor asked, "The same ward you laid to slay one who pursued you."

At this, Odo's head fell. With a sheepish voice he answered, "Yes, Brother Gregor."

"And what do you think Brother Remfrey would say, knowing you used the power granted to you to take human life?"

"I think he might be ashamed," answered Odo, his head sinking lower. "He has always told me of the value the Allfather places upon life and the consequences when life is taken. I fear I have failed him in this regard."

Inhaling deep, Gregor let out a long, frustrated sigh. Yet, when he spoke, they were not words of judgement and condemnation. Instead, his voice was soft, conciliatory even. "It is a grave matter indeed, brother."

"I would beg forgiveness for my actions. Yet, I cannot see how it is I find forgiveness from myself."

With a quizzical look, Gregor's brow creased at the remark. "How so?"

"Is not life precious?"

"It is," answered Gregor with a confused nod.

"Are we not instructed to lay down our lives for others?"

Eyes fixed on the young man, the gaze Gregor offered back was both awed and confused. "Brother," he said before pausing a moment, "your life is precious as well. It, too, is a gift given to you from the Allfather. And one that should not be so mindlessly disregarded. True, yes, it is considered the height of love and wisdom to sacrifice what life you have for the benefit of others. Yet, I cannot see how the taking of your life by evil men furthers such ends."

Odo stood silent, letting the wizard talk. He had not the heart to look Gregor in the eye. Gregor continued unabated. "The man you slew was a Watcher—one who has bartered his service and his soul for a cause he believes will reap great rewards. And in these lands, we know all too well the evil perpetrated by their kind.

Imagine, now, if the man did not die. Imagine if those who pursued finally overtook you in your flight. No doubt, they would have taken what you carried at the very least. And there is little doubt in my mind your life would have been forfeit in such an encounter given the events as you described them. How then would your sacrifice benefit anyone, save those engaged in the cause of evil?"

After a time, Odo shook his head, the movement appearing little more than an exaggerated twitch. With a sigh, he answered, "I do not know." A moment of silence followed. "Yet, what I carried was of no significance. It was merely a rock. A stone...found in a field, by your account."

"You did not know this," Gregor answered quickly.

In the midst of continuing his thoughts, Odo found himself speechless given the wizard's answer. His mouth opened, silence followed, and then his lips shut.

Gregor continued in the absence of a counter. "And it is clear Brother Remfrey knew well in advance that such a thing might come to be."

"How so, Magus?" Odo looked at Gregor with a measure of surprise.

"Brother Gregor, if you please."

"Apologies," Odo said, flustered. He quickly corrected his error. "Brother."

"Remfrey knew the letter would be unsealed by an Elanni, did he not?"

Odo nodded, still perplexed.

"Even naming the rank, I believe."

Odo's head tilted and the lids of his eyes narrowed. "You mean to say Brother Remfrey knew in advance I would survive the journey?"

His eyes dashing this way and that, his head bobbing to acknowledge the question, Gregor answered with a certain measure of uncertainty in his voice. "Well, yes. One cannot ignore the evidence."

"He knew I would take the power of the stone into me?"

"So it seems." Gregor's answer came with a slight smile. "Why else would he teach you the ritual? After all, such things are simply not done."

"That he would know to what ends I might use the power given to me?"

It took Gregor a moment or two to answer. "How long have you known Brother Remfrey?"

"Most of my life," answered Odo. "He is very much like a father to me."

"And in that time, have you ever known him to be reckless? Foolish in his actions? To not weigh and consider matters of great importance?"

Odo thought long and hard on this question, summoning many years of memories, trying his best to recall something to counter the question. "No," he answered after a time.

"Then, given the evidence at hand, it is only reasonable to conclude that he gave serious and profound thought to all he has done for you prior to sending you down the road you have taken. That and the gifts given to you for such a task."

Stunned, Odo looked away. His mind was a blank, the revelation offered by the wizard striking him like a thunderbolt. The germ of a thought sprang into his addled mind, growing swiftly into a question. He spoke in a near whisper. "What of the others?"

"What say you?"

"The others. Rojo. Inoch. Maddie. Those he paid gold to protect me."

Gregor considered Odo's words thoughtfully. A solitary bird sang in the profound silence which grew between the pair. "There could be many reasons for this. Perhaps the use of freelancers added a certain credibility to the ruse. What is clear, however, is that Brother Remfrey chose wisely, this Captain Inoch risking his life for you in the end."

Noticing the note in his hand, Gregor extended his arm and offered the letter to Odo. "Perhaps this will explain more. I received it only a day ago. It is addressed to you."

Odo gazed at the note, dumbly at first. His eyes inspected the seal of Remfrey pressed into the wax along the seam. Cradling his staff in his other arm, he took the folded parchment from the fingers of the wizard. Holding it before his eyes, Odo scanned it closely, indecisively.

Gregor began to slowly pace as Odo moved swiftly to break the wax seal. Separating the folded wings of the parchment, he exposed the fine, delicate script he had seen hundreds of times before. His fingers trembled as he held the folds open. Fear and wonder filled his heart as he read the words of the only father of flesh and blood he had ever truly known in this world.

"Dearest Odo," the letter said, *"I praise the Allfather for your safe delivery. I fear you know now what has transpired, and the deception you have toiled and suffered beneath. I have no apology, save for the urgency of the moment and the terrible peril you and I had to face. Whatever words of excuse I write will no doubt seem feeble in the wake of the trials you have faced.*

Were it possible a wizard to have a son, you were and are mine. So it is that no loving father desires to send their son into the maw of death and peril as I have done. Yet, as I have taught you many a time, we do not live in this world solely for our own sakes. The Allfather desires us to live for the sake of others. So, whether you be a wizard hiding in his tower, a husband, or a father, others come to need and rely on you to do what is right and just.

I know King Merrith will take you under his care and keep you safe. I will arrive in a few days. When we meet, we will further discuss your future, though I fear we both know the path you will take. Regardless of your choice, I will respect your wishes on the matter.

I have no doubt you have taken the right path in the trials that were set before you. If I had any such doubt, I would not have taught you that which I did, gave to you that which I have, and sent you so readily to where you have gone. Yet, we must be mindful that, in the end, the life within you is your own.

Lovingly Yours,

Remfrey.

His attention immediately drawn to the wizard once more, Odo looked Brother Gregor in the eye. "You spoke of consequences?"

"Yes."

"What are they?"

For a moment, Gregor stared at Odo, one brow arched. When he spoke, it was slow at first, his tone bordering on uncertain. "We wizards are not mortals. What pleasures or terrors this world might offer have no hold on our hearts. We have seen glories far beyond those seen or felt by mortal eyes. We do not feel the pull of age and time as do you. So, it is that we do not share in those gifts given to mortals. Rest. Dreams. Love. Matrimony. Children. Memories both pleasant and unpleasant. Ours is one of continual servitude, ever furthering the Will of the Allfather on these shores."

"And by taking in the power of the wizard—" said Odo, only to be interrupted quickly.

"You have taken unto yourself the burdens of Brother Remfrey. Even the smallest portion."

"I am now a wizard?" The note fell from Odo's hands as he whispered the words to himself, his brows downturned in consternation, his lips turned into a frown.

"Very much so, I fear," Gregor answered. "This is why such things are not done. All power comes with a price." While Odo let that knowledge sink in, Gregor continued. "In time, I suspect your need to sleep will lessen. Time will no longer ravage you with age—"

"Is there a way to return it to the stone?" Odo looked up to Gregor, his face riddled with concern.

"I believe so, yes," answered Gregor.

"Can you do it?"

"Me?" Gregor pressed his hand against his chest, his brows lifting with surprise and taking a few of the wrinkles on his face with them. "No, I fear. This is a matter best discussed with Brother Remfrey."

Odo looked away for a moment, the concern on his face not having diminished in the slightest. Gregor let out a sigh before he began to speak. "I certainly understand your concern. There are those who envy our craft and our ageless existence. They do not fully understand the weight of the burden we carry."

"That is not the reason."

"Oh?" His head tilted to one side, Gregor's eyes grew wide at Odo's answer. "Might I ask the reason why?"

Odo stewed as Gregor watched, his interest being piqued by the young man's silence. "You can tell me what it is that troubles your heart, Brother. I will listen."

Reluctant at first, Odo was not quick to answer. When he did, his eyes fixed on the ground, his voice sullen and low. "I was a poor wizard. I could not heal Rojo. I could barely make fire."

"You are a mortal, and young," answered Gregor. "Magic is a complicated craft. In time, you will learn and practice and become more capable"

As Gregor looked at Odo, his eyes probed something deeper than the young man's expression. "Yet, I suspect that is not the only thing that troubles you."

"You spoke of a price?" Odo's eyes locked on those of Gregor. "Was blood the price for what I carry with me?"

"You speak of the Watcher you slew?"

"I speak of the Watcher I slew. And of Inoch and Rojo. Maddie and Snickers. They died for what I now carry."

"They died for gold," answered Gregor. "And as for the Watcher you slew with a ward—

we have already spoken of this. You cannot carry blame for the death of those who intended harm upon you. When one wanders the path of evil and destruction, one cannot escape the blame and consequences when the path leads them to ruin."

Passion and sorrow filled Odo's voice as he answered, his face warm as his cheeks flushed. "All I have ever desired is to know the family I have never known. Mother and Father. Sisters and brothers. To live a life that so many have. And yet, mine has been filled with loneliness and questioning. Now I find myself burdened with guilt and doubt. This is not the life I would have desired."

"On this I can offer council," answered Gregor, confidence heavy in his voice and gleaming in his eyes. "Even those whom you consider fortunate long for those things they cannot have. This is as constant and assured as the sunrise. A lonely miser lamenting his solitary state, all the gold in the world bringing him no love and affection. The smith who envies the farmer. The farmer who envies the merchant. Each of them desiring the benefits of the other and blind to their burdens.

You seek a family, yet you speak of Brother Remfrey as if he were your father."

"In many ways, he is," answered Odo, though he spoke with reluctance.

"A father who has given over a portion of himself that his progeny might be protected. Someone who has not only fed and clothed you but sheltered you and offered instruction. Who helped mold you into the proper young man you are."

After a moment of silence, Gregor continued. "Brother Odo, there is one thing that is assured for one who follows the Allfather—we may not get what it is we most desire. We do, however, receive those things we most need."

Hearing this, Odo looked around, seeking a place to sit. Crouching, he picked up Remfrey's note from the ground. After that, with a despairing sigh, he settled into a nearby chair, his eyes seeking the ground.

Gregor stood there, patiently looking at the young man. Odo cradled his staff in his shoulder and inspected Remfrey's note once more. Two birds sang now in the silence that hung between Odo and Gregor as Odo scanned the note—one calling, the other responding.

For a long time, Odo read and reread the words written in the neat hand of the wizard. All those many years harbored beneath the stone of the Crooked Tower came back to him as he feigned his interest in the note. His mind grappled desperately with a question he had yet to answer. His loneliness and anger at his predicament were tempered by Remfrey's concern and a newfound understanding of what he had all along. While it was not the family he desired, it was the family he needed. One that looked after him with as much love and concern as those who shared the same blood.

His mind turned to the freelancers. Despite being crude and avaricious, each still gave their life to shield him. And Odo knew that, despite his cold and unfeeling nature, Inoch remained until the end for something other than gold. The man he called Captain paid a price whose debt no amount of gold could cover.

"It is a grave decision you must make. Whether to keep the power bestowed upon you and remain one of our sacred brethren, or to return it and reclaim the mortal life ahead of you. I am sure whatever decision you do make—"

"I will keep the power," Odo said looking up. The words of the young man caught Gregor by surprise. His head went back as if struck and his brows lifted once more.

"You should not feel obligated to bear our burden," said Gregor. His voice hinted of concern.

"I am obligated," answered Odo. "For Inoch, who saved me. For Rojo, who showed me kindness when few others did."

"Soldiers for pay."

"For Brother Remfrey, who is my father."

Gregor's head shook slightly, his eyes filled with deepening concern. "Brother Odo, your life is your own to live."

"That it is," Odo said with an assured nod. "And I choose to live it in a manner befitting my father's son."

Heavily influenced by pulp fiction, epic fantasy, the Bible, Dungeons and Dragons, and even the occasional scary movie, Herman P. Hunter seeks to blend these influences into every story he writes.

IF YOU ENJOYED *THE WIZARD'S STONE*, CHECK OUT *THE REVENANT AND THE TOMB*, AVAILABLE AT THE FOLLOWING OUTLETS:

amazonkindle

BARNES & NOBLE

Google Play
Books

...AND MANY MORE.

THE REVENANT AND THE TOMB

HERMAN P. HUNTER

www.ingramcontent.com/pod-product-compliance
Lightning Source LLC
Chambersburg PA
CBHW050314160726
48002CB00001B/32